Through His Eyes

NIKKI ASH

Through His Eyes
Copyright © 2019
Nikki Ash
All rights reserved

Cover design: Jersey Girl Designs
Cover photograph: Taylor Alexander Photography
Formatting: AB Formatting

Dedication

To all of the women who have never been told…you are enough.

One

QUINN

Sitting on my terrace, in a comfy lounge chair I purchased when Rick first bought us this place, I hold a glass of red wine in my hand—one that I have yet to take a sip of. I want to. I look forward to my nightly glass of wine. I buy my favorite brand in bulk and have it delivered to the condo. But for the last several weeks, I haven't been able to drink it. I still pour it and bring it out here like I've been doing every night for the last four years. Only, once I go back inside, I pour the crimson liquid down the sink and rinse the glass out. I think, somewhere deep in my subconscious, I believe that if I continue to pour it every night, eventually I'll be able to drink it. I've put it in my head that if I pretend like my life isn't about to change—well, technically, *already* has changed—then it won't. As if I can will my life to go back to what it was only a few short months ago. And that says a lot since I hated my life the way it was.

Drinking my nightly wine isn't just about drinking, though. It's about finding comfort in my nightly routine. It makes me feel like I have the tiniest semblance of control in a situation that, in reality, is completely out of my control. I can handle my current life. I know what to expect. It's routine and dependable. Rinse. Wash. Repeat. Now, though, not being able to drink wine means my routine is about to be shaken up, and I'm scared of what the future holds. It's easier to fight the monster you know than to take on the one you've never seen.

As I stare down at the hustle and bustle of the city, from the forty-seventh floor, I try to focus on what's in front of me and not what's inside of me. The problem is, from this high up, and this late at night, there's not really much of a view to focus on. Down below, I spot several flashes of lights from the cabs and bikes that make their way to their destinations. Tiny dots of people litter the sidewalks, but they're too small for me to see their features. I wonder how many of them are couples, holding hands and kissing, in love. My heart knots at the thought, and without thinking, I bring the wine to my lips. The liquid has only barely wet my tongue before I'm spitting it back into the glass and setting it down.

My eyes glide upward. The sky is clear tonight, so it should be filled with beautiful stars twinkling above. But with the bright lights that make up New York City, it's difficult to spot a single star. What I would give to be back in Piermont, in my old apartment in North Carolina that I shared with my brothers, staring up at the sky and counting the hundreds of stars that wink down at me.

My cell phone vibrates on the table. When I see it's my

sister-in-law, Celeste, I hit ignore. I've been pushing everyone away for years. I know I have. But I don't know what to do, how to handle the situation I've found myself in. Once upon a time, I dreamt of being right here, in this moment: married to the love of my life, living in the most beautiful city in the world, in a gorgeous home. Pregnant with my husband's baby. Looking toward our future. How ironic is it that when my dreams finally come true, nothing is the way it's supposed to be.

I'm married, but my husband doesn't love me—and if I'm honest, I don't love him either. How do you love a man who hates every part of you? It's hard, trust me, I've tried. Over and over again. And through trying, I've lost a large piece of myself that I'm not sure I'll ever be able to find. When I look into the mirror, I'm not even sure who I see anymore, and that scares the crap out of me, because I wasn't always this way. I was strong and determined and full of life, and now…I'm not. I'm weak, and I hate that I know it, yet choose not to do anything about it. It makes me feel even weaker.

I might live in a beautiful city, but it's one I no longer get to experience because I'm stuck in this suffocating ivory tower, going through the motions but not actually living. Where I live is beautiful. The furniture, the paintings, everything expensive and top of the line, but it's not a home. It's simply a dwelling. A place to eat and sleep. And I can't imagine what it will feel like to raise a baby here.

Rick and I tried for years to get pregnant. He wanted a baby with his last name, and I wanted someone to love. After four years of trying, at thirty-four years old, I didn't think it would happen. I brought up the idea of using in vitro fertilization a couple years back, but my husband scoffed at me and told me he's not defective, and only defective people need to use IVF. Then, he proceeded to tell me I was probably the defective one, and if that were the case, he didn't want a baby with me anyway. I swallow thickly at the memory of crying myself to sleep that night. My eyes burn, and I close them tight, willing the tears to vaporize. Rick doesn't deserve any more of my tears. I know that. But, still, they come. Because I'm weak.

Glancing at the time on my cell phone, I see it's almost ten o'clock. Rick should be home soon. I'm planning to tell him about the baby tonight. I'm not naïve enough to believe that a baby will repair our marriage, but I don't know what else to do. It's not as if things can get worse. My thoughts go back to when I was a little girl. Of my father and mother yelling and screaming at each other. Of my mother hitting him and calling him names. Of the way she turned her hatred onto me when he died from a heart attack, and she found out the extent of his cheating. I was only eight years old, but I can still remember the way my brothers tried to protect me. I know they would protect me now, if they knew, if I let them in.

I pick up my glass of wine, and once again, have to stop myself from downing the entire glass. Closing my lids, I try to imagine how my baby's life will look. I refuse to let him, or her, grow up like I did. Scared to talk out of turn, frightened of what mood my mother would be in when I got home from school. Terrified, that the nasty words she spoke about me were true.

It wasn't until my eldest brother, Jax, turned eighteen and gained guardianship of me, that I was finally able to breathe. At the same time, my other older brother Jase became emancipated. From the time I was eleven years old, I grew up in a loving home. I was given everything I could want or need. They treated me like a princess, and when I grew up, all I wanted was to meet a man who would treat me like his queen. Boy, was I naïve. Fairytales are overrated if you ask me. Maybe the problem was that every girl wants a Prince Charming, and I got a king. One who rules with an iron fist to keep his castle in order. He's well-respected by everyone and answers to no one. Maybe what I should've looked for, instead, was a sweet prince, one who would find my glass slipper, or show me a beautiful library. He would kiss me awake to save me from the evil witch, or take me away from the horrendous stepmother. Maybe the problem was that, because my brothers told me I deserved the world, when I wished upon those shooting stars, I aimed too high. You know what they say: *be careful what you wish for because you just might get it.* Well, I wished and wished and wished, and I got it…and now I have no damn clue what to do with it.

Glancing over at my phone, I notice five more minutes have passed. It's time to go inside. I need to clean the kitchen and put Rick's dinner out for him. He texted me earlier that he would be home at ten. After rinsing out my wine glass, I take his dinner out of the warmer and place it on the table for him along with some silverware and the scotch he always has with his dinner. Then I head into the bathroom to freshen up. Using a makeup wipe, I swipe under my eyes so the black is no longer smeared, and I no longer look like a racoon. When I reach into my drawer to grab a night shirt, I spot the lingerie I bought while out shopping with Celeste a while back. I was hoping to spice up my marriage, only when I put it on, Rick told me I looked like a trashy hooker and demanded I take it off. I'm not even sure why I kept it.

Instead of grabbing my cotton shirt, I pull out the silk, beige negligée that Rick bought me for our honeymoon, from out of the bottom of the drawer. It's on the shorter side, touching just above the top of my knees, and is thin, showing all of my curves that Rick used to love but now despises. Taking a deep breath, I throw it on. It's probably a stupid idea, but I'm desperate—for affection, for attention, for any sign that my marriage isn't completely over. Maybe the sight of this negligée will remind him of a time when he actually found me attractive, and he'll go back to being the man I first met. The man I gave my heart to. The man I wanted so desperately to have a family with.

When I hear the door alarm chime, indicating Rick is home, I rush out to greet him. He's toeing off his expensive loafers and shrugging out of his suit jacket, when I make my presence known. He looks up, and I hold my breath, praying his reaction will be receptive. That he'll once again look at me like I'm his entire world. He'll take me into his arms and lay me down on the bed and make love to me. I'll tell him about the baby, and he'll spend the rest of the night worshipping my body.

I'll be the respected queen to my king.

For a brief moment, he stares at me. His gaze rakes down my body, and I think maybe today will be different. But then his face contorts into his usual look of disgust, and

I know whatever he's about to say won't be good. So I do what I have learned to do over the years—put up my broken and fragile wall and pray his harsh words aren't strong enough this time to completely demolish it.

"You would think with all the time on your hands, you would make an effort to lose weight," he quips. "What else do you do all day?" He shoots me an accusatory look that makes me want to tell him to go fuck himself. And that makes me a bit proud that I still have even a single ounce of strength left in me to consider saying it. Even though it does no good when I don't actually have any intention of acting on it. Been there, done that. Not stupid enough to ever do it again.

Instead, I stay stuck in my place as if my feet are glued to the ground beneath me—my voice refusing to speak the words I so badly want to say. I'm well aware I don't do shit all day because he gives me a hard time every time I leave— always pointing out a woman's place is in the home.

After the first few times of Rick putting me down, I started to go to the gym in our building, only he showed up and caused a scene when he saw me talking to one of the men who worked out there. It didn't matter that he was only showing me how to properly use one of the machines. He forbade me to ever return, telling me I could workout at home. Months went by, and he kept pointing out I was putting on weight. He then began to put me down during sex, making comments about everything I ate, and pointing out the type of woman he *does* find attractive. At that point, I met with a nutritionist, who mentioned that stress can cause weight gain. It doesn't help that I'm an emotional eater, and dealing with my husband can be emotionally stressful. I try to eat healthy, but it doesn't matter because I'm not what he wants, and I never will be.

Whenever I would go to Forbidden Ink, my brothers' tattoo shop, to hang out, he would give me a hard time, saying it's not appropriate. When I would try to hang out with my sister-in-law, Celeste, and my niece Skyla, he would come up with a list of items that needed to be done. I still make it a point to see them when Rick goes away, but the more unhappy I become, the more my family notices, and the less I bring myself around them, not wanting to have to explain that my entire life is a lie and in shambles.

Setting his jacket on the table, Rick steps closer and takes the silky fabric of the negligée between his fingers. "Delicate items like these are meant for women who take care of their bodies, not for women who let their bodies go to shit. Take it off. *Now.* You don't deserve to wear something so exquisite when you clearly don't appreciate it."

Knowing better than to respond, I nod once and turn on my heel. I knew this was going to happen, so why would I willingly put myself in this situation? Maybe I just needed to hear it one last time. For him to confirm where we stand.

"Wait," he says, and I turn around, my heart filling with false hope. "Put my shoes and jacket away," he commands, his voice devoid of all emotion.

I nod again, walking over to grab his jacket, and then reaching down to grab his shoes. When I stand upright, I feel his hand on my wrist. I look up into his cold, blue eyes. The same eyes I once found warmth in. "How do you think it makes me feel as your husband, to have to see the way you've let yourself go? I'm the one who has to see you naked…touch you… How can you expect me to want you when you don't care about your own body?"

"I'm sorry," I murmur softly, unsure of what else to say. The truth of the matter is, I've only gained about twenty-five pounds since we've gotten together, but it's enough that my husband no longer views me as attractive. I've always been on the thicker side: wide hips, thick thighs, big breasts. I was never the most popular or the prettiest, but I was okay with who I was. Until Rick made sure to point out every flaw. Every imperfection. Day after day he broke me piece by piece. I don't know how I even let it go on this long.

But, I finally did reach my breaking point and made the decision to leave—to go to my brothers and tell them everything. I formulated a plan to move out and file for divorce. I knew Rick would give me shit, but it couldn't be any worse than living under his roof. But fate is a fickle bitch and the day I was going to meet with my brothers, I realized I missed my period. I waited and waited, but it never came. Now, three months later and I still haven't gotten it. I've yet to take a test, but I know what the results will say. I'm pregnant by a man who hates me.

Rick's brows dip together at my apology—in confusion or frustration, I'm not sure—and I wonder, maybe, if I'd worked out harder, dieted more seriously, my husband would want and love me. It's too late now, though. Pregnant women only get fatter. I've already started to put weight on, and my body is already changing. My clothes are becoming tighter. What will he think of me once I'm fully showing? Will he despise our baby for doing this to my body, like he despises me for letting myself go? No, he's wanted an *heir* for too long. I refuse to believe he won't love our child. *But does he even know how to love?*

My thoughts and feelings are scattered all over the place. I'm a mess of hormones. Getting pregnant was what I wanted for so long, but now that it's happened, I can't help but wish it wouldn't have. I feel a tremendous amount of guilt for even thinking that, but the last thing I want is to bring a baby into this unloving home. I was raised in one for years before Jax saved me, and I wouldn't wish that on anyone, especially my own child. Even if Rick, by some crazy chance, loves our child the way a father should love his baby, he, or she, will still grow up watching him treat me like shit— the same way I watched my parents treat each other. Will my child resent me for being weak, or will he, or she, view me the same way Rick does? The thought has me wanting to throw up.

As I scurry back to the room, I try to recall when Rick changed. You hear about it in books and movies. They talk about it on those shows like Dr. Phil or Oprah. The woman who lives in the abusive household. How does she not notice? Why doesn't she leave? She must be blind, deaf, and dumb not to see the signs. All I can say is, until you are standing where I am, you won't understand. Words can hit as hard as fists. Without even realizing I was standing in the ring, being thrown into a fight I wasn't ready for, I had already been knocked to the ground. Did I get up? Of course. But when you get knocked down so many times, eventually you realize it's better to just tap out. I'm aware it makes me sound weak. But in my defense, the fight isn't even close to being fair. I never really stood a chance.

I can still remember the days when Rick would kiss me lovingly. The way he would hold me in his arms and tell me how much I meant to him. I can't pinpoint the moment when things changed. When we went from having sex every day, to a few days a week, down to once a week, and eventually it turned into once a month. When our weekly date nights turned into me leaving dinner out for him. And our weekend getaways turned into Rick going away by himself while I stayed home alone.

I kept telling myself we were just in a rut. His job is stressful. His father puts a lot of pressure on his shoulders. But at some point, I realized it was me. In my husband's eyes, I was no longer beautiful. No longer attractive. I didn't make him smile or laugh anymore. I didn't turn him on. He saw me as a burden, a nuisance. I was no longer his queen who was meant to stand by his side. Instead, I became a prisoner he kept holed up in this condo, waiting in the background to be at his disposal. I once was building a successful photography company, but he demanded I stay home. He said it would be an embarrassment for his wife to be working. We were trying to have a baby, and he told me he wanted me to be a stay-at-home mom just like his mother was. If I were working, people would think he couldn't take care of what was his. He cared more about the outward appearance than what was actually happening in our home.

I place Rick's shoes neatly on his shoe rack, then grab a hanger to hang up his jacket. As I'm shaking out the material to ensure there are no wrinkles, I catch a whiff of perfume. Bringing my nostrils to the lapels, I inhale deeply and confirm it. His jacket smells like a woman. My stomach roils in disgust. My hands begin to tremble in fury. My husband is having an affair. I am now *officially* the cliché.

The thought of him cheating on me sparks something inside me. I've given up everything for this man. Meanwhile, he's out screwing another woman. I don't doubt she's gorgeous. She's probably a size one with perky breasts, silky blond hair, and has flawless skin with zero tattoos—pretty much the exact opposite of my black, lifeless hair, dull black eyes, and tattoo-covered overweight body.

Peering out of the room, I see he's sitting at the dining room table, eating his dinner and texting on his phone. And a plan surfaces. Changing into a pair of sweats and a tee, I go pee and then lay down in bed, closing my eyes and pretending to fall asleep. As I wait for Rick to finish eating, I think about the woman's scent on his jacket. This isn't the first time I've spelled woman's perfume on his clothes, but I chose to remain in denial, making excuses—he was probably standing too close to his secretary, or he had lunch with his mom. I didn't want to admit that my husband was having an affair. But deep down I always knew. It's only now, that I'm pregnant and carrying an innocent precious baby in me, that I'm finally opening my eyes and looking around me.

A little while later, Rick enters our room without saying a word. I hear the bathroom door shut, and I jump out of bed. He takes a shower every night when he gets home, after dinner, and he always brings his cell phone into the bathroom with him. Because of the bathroom being so big, he can't see me enter, but the door creaks, and he calls out, "Quinn?"

"Sorry," I say, "I need to go pee. I'll be right out." When I don't hear him respond, I peek around the corner and see him standing in the shower under the water.

Cheater. Asshole. Homewrecker.

Snatching his phone out of his pants that he has folded on the vanity, I type in his passcode and pull up his messages. I click on the first one: Sylvia. The name sounds familiar. I think she's his secretary. Just as I'm about to click out and go to the next one, I spot their most recent thread.

> Sylvia: I miss you already.

> Rick: I'll take you out tomorrow night. Send me a picture.

> Sylvia: <insert topless image>

Of course, he's cheating on me with his damn secretary. Because my entire story wasn't cliché enough, it had to add the young, hot blond with huge, fake breasts. I skim through a couple more texts before I get nervous of being caught. I'm not sure why I even care. Our marriage is obviously over, but something in me screams that I need to tread lightly. It's no longer just me. I now have my baby that I need to protect. Screenshotting the messages, I text them to my phone and then send Sylvia's contact information to myself as well. I quickly scroll through Rick's other messages and find several other women he's been messaging with. I send all of their info to myself, then delete all the evidence that I was ever on his phone. Exiting out of his apps, I lock his screen and put his phone back where he left it, tiptoeing out of the bathroom and climbing back into bed. Putting my phone on silent, I store it in my nightstand drawer, so he won't see it, just in case.

When he gets out of the shower, he walks over to the dresser with a towel wrapped around his waist. I take a second to check him out. He's not fat like I am...he's skinny. Not toned or muscular, but thin and lanky. His skin is tanned, not a tattoo in sight. His brown hair is wet and combed over, and his face is clean-shaven. He's a good-looking guy, but he isn't like *Wow*. His looks aren't what attracted me to him, though. It was his charm and self-confidence. He was so sure of himself, sure of his place in the world, and even though I came across like I was just as strong and confident, I felt lost. I thought when he found me, I would feel like I finally belonged, and I did...until he decided I was no longer what he wanted, and he left me alone once again. Now I'm more lost than I was before, and my only hope is that I somehow find my way on my own.

"What are your plans this weekend?" he asks, not looking at me as he drops his towel and pulls his boxers up his legs.

"Celeste is throwing Sky a birthday party at their place. She's turning eighteen." Skyla is my niece—Jase and Celeste's daughter. When she was younger, before Jase and Celeste got together, we were close. Helping Jase to raise her is what made me realize I wanted my own family. I wanted someone to love and to love me back. I wanted to feel wanted and needed. Once Jase and Celeste got together, Skyla and Celeste hit it off straight away. They're like two peas in a pod. I'm glad Skyla has a fulltime mother-figure in her life, but I can't help but wish that I had the bond they share. Maybe one day I'll have the kind of relationship they have, with my son or daughter.

"I have to work, so I won't be able to go." I don't know why he's letting me know this. He never comes to any of my family functions anymore.

"Okay, will I see you at home afterward?"

He stills in his place for a split-second, and if I wasn't looking for it, I wouldn't have noticed. But now my eyes are wide open, and I'm definitely looking. "Probably not," he says. "I have a late meeting." He clears his throat then continues. "I might not make it home. I'll probably just stay at the office."

Liar. Cheater. Asshole.

"But tomorrow is the weekend," I push. I never push. I never question. I just accept. And I hate that I've become that woman who just accepts. "Why would you spend the night when it will be Sunday? You don't work on Sunday…I was thinking we could go to the farmer's market like we used to. Pick up some fresh fruits and vegetables." When we first got together, we used to go to the farmer's market every Sunday. We would check out each booth, hand in hand, laughing and talking about our week. Even when he was busy, he would make sure he left Sundays open for us.

"Maybe next weekend," he says, his eyes meeting mine through his reflection in the mirror. "This meeting is too important." And it's in this moment that I know without a doubt my husband cheating on me isn't something new. His flat tone and blank expression are identical to the ones he's been giving me for too long. Of course, I couldn't have dug my head out of the sand before I got pregnant by my lying, cheating husband. And of course, after years of trying, and failing, we were successful the one time he came home sloppy drunk and actually wanted me—only to wake up the next morning and not even remember it.

He pulls his shirt over his head and says, "I have work to do. Goodnight," then leaves the room as quickly as he came.

Two

QUINN

I'm sitting in the backyard of my brother and Celeste's home, at Skyla's birthday party, watching everyone's kids run around and play. The laughter that fills the air should have my heart swelling with love, but instead, it fills me with dread. I was going to tell Rick this morning that I'm pregnant, but when I woke up, he was already gone. No note, no kiss goodbye, not even a text message. Some would say I'm crazy for telling him I'm pregnant. I should run as far away from him as possible, but I know better. This isn't some romance novel. I'm not going to escape and find myself some perfect single guy next door to fall in love with while I attempt to rebuild my shell of a life. This is real life, and in my reality, I have to deal with the cards I've been dealt. If I don't play nice, I know Rick will have no problem taking our baby away from me. He has more money than God, and I've seen the cruel and ruthless way he does business. There's a reason the companies he and his father run are so successful. My husband is a smart, conniving, businessman who never holds back. The last thing I need is for him to do what my father did to Jase and Jax's mom—prove me to be an unfit mom and take my baby from me.

I'm going to have to play nice. Let Rick take the lead. He's apparently busy screwing his way through New York, and as long as I continue to turn a blind eye, he will continue to do so while I raise our baby. His money will pay for everything materialistic our child needs, while my love will provide everything he, or she, emotionally needs. *That is if I can somehow keep him from putting me down in front of our child...* I will not allow my baby to suffer like I did. I won't argue with Rick. I won't fight against him. I won't let my baby become a pawn in this horrible game I'm being forced to play. I'll do my best to be the wife he wants me to be, so I can give my baby a stable and loving home.

I listen as Celeste and Jase's friends laugh and joke with one another. At one point, their friend Killian announces that he and his wife, Giselle, are expecting their second baby. Everyone congratulates them, and then Olivia, another friend of Celeste's, announces that she and her husband, Nick, are also expecting. It will be their third, and they are beyond ecstatic. Not able to take another second of being surrounded by all of these happy couples—knowing my husband is somewhere most likely fucking his secretary—I duck out quietly and head inside. I'm not ready to go home yet, but I also don't want to be around people, so I slip into Celeste and Jase's bedroom, so I can use their bathroom without running into anyone.

I go pee, wash my hands, and then find myself sitting on the edge of the tub, unsure of where to go from here. What if I did run? What if I took whatever cash I could find and bought an old, used car to drive away from here? Would he search for me? Hell, he doesn't even like me. I don't understand why he even wants to keep me. He doesn't know I'm pregnant. If I ran away now, would he even think twice about me? I could send him divorce papers from wherever I end up and hope he signs them. I could raise my baby in a loving home by myself. But what if he comes after me? What if one day while I'm walking down the street, taking the baby for a walk, he finds me? He would take my baby. I know he would. He would make me regret leaving, every single day for the rest of my life.

I'm not even aware that I'm crying, until a soft voice interrupts my thoughts. "You okay?" I look up and see Celeste standing in front of me.

"I think I'm pregnant," I admit nervously.

"And that's a bad thing…" she says carefully. I hate that she treats me like I'm fragile, but it's my fault. Both my brothers are happy and in love, and I want what they have. I want to be in love, and being around them every day has become harder and harder. So I've just stopped coming around. It's easier this way.

Not knowing what to say to Celeste, I just shrug.

"Well, there's only one way to find out." She pulls a box of pregnancy tests out from under the counter.

"You keep tests on hand?" I ask, shocked.

"We've been trying for the last year," she admits. As she rips the test open, she tells me how difficult it's been for them. The first time they got pregnant, it happened rather quickly, and they had twin daughters, Mariah and Melina, who are now two years old.

She hands me a disposable cup to pee in, and I blurt out, "I'm sorry, Celeste. Here I am, unsure if I'm happy or sad that I'm most likely pregnant, and you're wishing for a baby."

"Everyone has their own stories," she says with a soft smile. "Take it, and I'll be right here with you."

A few minutes later, the test confirms what I already knew. I'm pregnant. Celeste, as if she knows exactly what I need in this moment, pulls me into a hug. "Jase and I will be here for you no matter what." Not wanting to lose it right here in her bathroom, I thank her and tell her I'm going to head home.

"Okay. If you need anything, call me."

When I get to my car—a Porsche Cayenne Rick bought me for my birthday a couple years ago—I lay my head against the steering wheel and let every emotion out that I've been holding in. As my chest racks with gut-wrenching sobs, I allow myself to mourn over the loss of myself, my future, the loving family I long for. With every tear that falls, I'm one step closer to accepting my fate. And when all my tears have released, and I'm incapable of shedding another drop of salty liquid, I turn my car on and drive home.

The sound of my phone continuously vibrating against the top of my nightstand wakes me from a restless sleep. I contemplated leaving Rick more than a hundred times last night. Packing up my stuff and taking off. But in order to do that, I need to plan, and by the time I figure it all out, I'll already be showing and he'll know I'm pregnant.

Reaching over, I grab the phone and press answer without even looking at who's calling. "Good evening, I'm calling from New York General Hospital. May I please speak to Quinn Thompson?" *New York General?*

"This is she," I say, sitting up slightly. Pulling the phone from my ear, I quickly check the time: two a.m.

"For security purposes, can you please confirm your current physical address and date of birth?" she asks.

After I raddle off my home address and date of birth, she thanks me and says, "You are listed as Richard Thompson's next of kin. We need you to come in, please."

My heart pounds against my ribcage and my breathing becomes labored—out of fear or hope, I haven't determined. "Did something happen to my husband?"

"Unfortunately, we can't give any information over the phone. We're going to need you to come in."

"Okay," I say, robotically standing and finding clothes to put on. I'm about to head to the hospital when Celeste's earlier words come back to me: *"Jase and I will be here for you, no matter what…If you need anything, call me."* I don't know how, but something tells me I'm going to need my family.

Not wanting to wake up Celeste and Jase since they have two little ones, I dial my brother Jax's number. He answers on the first ring, his voice groggy from sleep.

"I need you," I whisper.

Twenty minutes later, he picks me up and we head over

to the hospital. When I get to the front desk, I give the receptionist my husband's name, and she gives me directions on where to go. As we step around the corner, I spot her. Blond hair, petite body, perky, young breasts. Sylvia, my husband's secretary-slash-mistress is sitting on the couch of the waiting room, bawling her eyes out. I've seen her a few times when I visit Rick at work, but he's never formally introduced us. I only knew she was his secretary by her name because she always answers the phone when I call.

Averting my gaze, I walk straight over to the desk I was told to go to and give them Rick's name. The woman types on the keyboard for several seconds before her eyes meet mine and she gives me a look of sympathy mixed with sadness. "The police have requested to speak with you." She stands and walks me over to the two men in uniform. Both are standing in the corner, near the coffee machine, but only one is drinking a cup of coffee.

"This is Richard Thompson's wife," she says, and both men's eyes widen.

When neither of them say anything, Jax loses his patience. "Can someone please tell us what the hell is going on?"

"Yes, sir," the cop, who was just drinking the coffee, says. "We received a call tonight about a man who was held at gunpoint." My body begins to tremble as I take in the words he's saying.

Pulling me into his side, Jax asks, "What happened?"

"A homeless man, under the influence and armed with a stolen weapon, approached your husband when he was getting into his vehicle. According to the witness—"

"What witness?" I ask, already knowing the answer, but needing to hear him say it.

The cop without the coffee, frowns. "The woman who was walking with your husband to his vehicle."

"Who?" I push. My hands fist at my sides in frustration.

"We're not at liberty to say, as the case is still under investigation," the cop with the coffee says, but his eyes dart over to where Sylvia is sitting. I nod once to thank him, and he grants me a sad smile.

"I'm sorry, ma'am," the cop without the coffee says. "According to the witness, your husband was asked for his wallet when they were coming out of the restaurant. Unaware the man had a gun, he told him no, and when he turned his back to get into his vehicle, he was shot from behind. The man took off, and the woman called nine-one-one. He was brought in, but didn't make it through surgery."

Jax's arm around me tightens, and when I look over, his gaze is flitting from the officers to Sylvia. He's putting the pieces together.

Liar. Cheater. Asshole.

"Did you catch the man who shot him?" I ask.

"We did. We found him shooting up on the corner. He wasn't even trying to hide. He's been arrested, and is being held, while we complete the investigation, but we wanted to be here to tell you what happened ourselves."

"Thank you," I tell the cops, fully aware that my voice isn't even cracking. This is the part where I'm supposed to cry. Even though my marriage was in shambles, and my husband hated me and was cheating on me, I should still feel something. Anything. I was with him for just over four years—married for almost three of them. Surely, that has to amount to at least a tear. But standing here, in the hallway of the hospital, I can't conjure up a single damn drop of moisture. Maybe it really is possible to run out of tears...

And then I hear sobs coming from behind me. I look back over at Sylvia. Her tiny body is shaking uncontrollably. *That should be me*, I tell myself. I should be the one crying like my life is over. I'm pregnant, and my husband is dead.

Before I can think about what I'm doing, I'm standing in front of Sylvia. She looks up, her perfect, flawless face, streaked with her makeup.

"You realize you're crying over a married man who you were having an affair with, right?" I say, my voice flat, devoid of all emotion. I hear several gasps, but I don't look anywhere but at Sylvia.

She wipes the snot from her nose and takes several deep breaths before she finally speaks. "You might've trapped him in a loveless marriage, but Rick loved me. He was trying to find a way to divorce you because he didn't love you. He didn't want you," she says, her voice getting louder with each word she speaks.

"Is that what he told you?" I ask, stifling the manic laugh I feel bubbling up inside of me. "That's a lie. He could've divorced me at any time he wanted. *Nothing* was keeping us together."

"He was afraid you would take all his money," she hisses. "He worked so hard and he knew you would try to take it all...because you're trash!"

"We have a prenup," I inform her, and her eyes go wide in shock. Yep, looks like he's been lying to you, too. "Did he mention that he was sleeping with several other women besides you?"

Sylvia glares and stands. "You're lying. You are a lying, fat, needy bitch," she spits.

"Hey!" Jax booms, ready to defend his littler sister's honor, but I hold my hand up to stop him. I should be mad at this woman, but I'm not. Every time a man cheats on a woman, the mistress gets blamed. She's called a homewrecker, told she's destroyed their marriage. But the thing is, if a marriage is solid, there's no wrecking a home. There's no destroying a marriage. This woman was lied to, just like I was. Just like all the other women I'm sure were lied to. Sure, she knew Rick was married, but he's the one who made the vows, not her. And I can see it in her eyes, she loves my husband.

The only thing I feel is pity towards her.

Pulling out my phone, I select the screenshots I saved and send them to her. "Rick Thompson was a lying, cheating, selfish bastard," I tell her. "I've sent you the proof that he was sleeping with at least three other women aside from us that I know of. I wish you the best."

As I turn to walk away, Sylvia says, "Aside from us? That's how I know you're lying. Your husband wasn't sleeping with you. He could barely stand to look at you, let along fuck you." I consider pointing out that I'm pregnant just to spite her, but decide against it. It's none of her business.

"That's enough!" Jax roars. "Let's go, Quinn." Wrapping his arm around my shoulders, he walks me out of the hospital. When I ask him to please take me home, he refuses and brings me back to the townhouse in Cobble Hill, the one I was living in with him and Jase before I fell for Rick's charm and agreed to move in with him. Since then, Jase and Skyla have moved out and in with Celeste, and Willow, my brother's girlfriend, has moved in. When we get back to his place, Willow makes me a hot cup of tea, while Jax holds me until I fall asleep. I have no idea what I would do without my family.

Three

QUINN

I considered going to the funeral, if for no other reason than to gain some closure. Jax insisted he and Willow would go with me so I wouldn't be forced to face Rick's parents on my own. The morning of, he came out of his room dressed in a suit, with his hair gelled neatly, and Willow came out looking gorgeous in a tight yet modest black dress. Jax drove over to the condo, and I picked out a black dress and heels, then showered and got dressed. But on the way, I told them I couldn't do it. I couldn't walk into that church and put on a fake front, playing the part of the heartbroken, mourning widow.

Especially after calling Rick's parents to tell them what happened, only to learn Sylvia was over and had already told them. Jacquelyn, Rick's mom, went on to say that she and Sylvia would handle the funeral. That she knows what her son would want, and Sylvia, the amazing secretary she is, would help organize everything. While I should've been offended my husband's mistress was helping to plan his funeral, instead, I felt relief.

Kenneth, Rick's father, called me to let me know when and where the funeral would be held, and also to let me know the following day would be the reading of the will. While the thought of taking a single penny from my cheating husband made me sick, I now have a baby on the way, and I'll be damned if he, or she, will go without because of my stubbornness.

So, here I sit, in a chair in my father-in-law's office across from my mother-in-law, waiting for their attorney to begin the reading of the will. Jax, of course, offered to go with me, but I told him this was something I needed to do on my own. It's time I start standing on my own two feet again.

"Does anybody need anything? Water? Coffee?" I glance over and see Sylvia standing in the doorway. She's wearing a loose, almost see-through flowy blouse matched with a conservative pencil skirt. Her blond hair is neatly pulled back into a harsh bun, and her makeup is done to perfection. As she strides across the room, her tiny ass sways, and I briefly wonder, if I completely starve myself, could I ever be as small as she is? I can't even picture it.

When I don't answer her, Jacquelyn says, "Quinn, don't be rude. Sylvia is asking you a question."

"Excuse me?" I snap, wishing now that I would've let Jax accompany me.

"She asked you if you wanted something to drink. The polite response would be yes, please or no, thank you." A very unladylike snort comes from me, and Jacquelyn's eyes widen. In all the years I've been with Rick, I've never shown any kind of disrespect to his parents. Without having any of my own, I was hoping to develop a relationship with Rick's. Unfortunately, I learned fairly quickly that the only people more cruel and cold than Rick, are his parents.

"Let me get this straight," I say. "You want me to be polite to the woman who was fucking my husband for the last several months, maybe even years. The woman, who was with him the night he died because instead of being with his wife at a family get together, he was taking his mistress out to dinner with the plan to fuck her afterward." Jaquelyn gasps, Sylvia sniffles, and Kenneth glares. And I take a deep, cleansing breath because holy shit, it felt good to speak my mind and stand up for myself.

"Oh, you didn't know? That your son was a lying, cheating, piece of shit? And spoiler alert." I take a moment to look at each of them before I continue. "She wasn't the only one. There were several."

"How dare you!" Jacquelyn yells. "My son is dead! Don't you dare spread lies about him. You will not tarnish his reputation." Of course her only concern is his reputation.

Before I can respond, the family attorney walks in. Needing to keep up their appearances, Jacquelyn and Kenneth both compose themselves and greet Mr. Levine. Sylvia asks if he would like anything, and when he says no, she scurries out.

The will is read. Due to the prenuptial agreement I signed, and the fact that we were only married for three years, everything that is related to the company goes to his father since they are partners. Rick left me the condo, since he paid it off and put my name on the deed as a wedding gift. The Porsche is also mine, as well as whatever is in our joint checking account where he used to deposit my "allowance" as he liked to call it. His sole bank accounts apparently go to his father, as it states in the will, to be used for the business. I am the sole beneficiary of the life insurance policy he took out on himself after we were married, though, so there's that. Mr. Levine hands me all of the paperwork, and when I look at it, I see the policy is worth a million dollars. Outwardly, I don't show any emotion, but inwardly, I'm breathing a sigh of relief that I'll have the means to take care of my baby.

After thanking him, and without saying goodbye to my in-laws, because good fucking riddance, I walk out of the door and out of the building for the last time. Of course, Jax is waiting outside for me.

"You okay?" he asks, walking with me.

"I will be," I tell him truthfully. When we get to my car, he takes my keys from me so he can drive.

"What's next?"

"I was thinking I would put the condo up for sale. I don't want to live there anymore," I admit, instinctually placing a hand over my belly. I can't imagine raising my baby in the same home where Rick would tear me down and belittle me on a daily basis. I need a fresh start. I can't change the past, nor would I want to, since it gave me the precious baby in my belly, but I can sure as hell control my future.

Jax notices my hand and asks, "Is it true?" He nods toward my belly. "Are you pregnant?"

"Did Celeste tell you?"

"No, she wouldn't say anything, but Jase hinted at it."

"Yeah, I am, which is why I want to move. I need a fresh start."

"You know, there's a perfectly decent-size townhouse with two out of the three rooms available." He smiles softly at me, and for the first time in a long time, my heart feels content. "And I heard it's a great place to raise a baby until you're ready to get back on your feet again." He's referring to Jase raising Skyla there until she was thirteen and they moved out to start their life with Celeste.

"Are you sure?" I ask. "I don't want to impose on you and Willow." Jax and Willow have been together for almost as long as Rick and me, but I've never once heard them discuss having babies or getting married. I can't imagine a couple with no kids would want their home to be overtaken by a single mom and her baby.

Jax grins. "I'm more than sure. It was actually Willow's idea."

"Can I ask you a question?" I don't want to get in their business, but I've always wondered… He nods once. "Is there a reason Willow and you haven't gotten married or had any kids?"

Jax's smile drops, and I worry I've overstepped. I've always had a close relationship with my brothers—sharing a home with them for the first thirty years of my life will do that. But over the last four years, since I got together with Rick and my life slowly began to spiral out of control, our relationship has deteriorated. Now, I fear, I may never be able to repair the damage that's been done.

"I don't usually like to share someone else's story, but

Willow already told me that if the time ever came when I was in a situation where I needed to explain, I could." He scrubs his hands over his face before he looks back at me. "Willow was diagnosed with endometrial cancer at a young age. It required a full hysterectomy."

I gasp at his words. Poor Willow. I was over here feeling sorry for myself for getting pregnant by my asshole, cheating husband, meanwhile, she can never have a baby of her own. "I'm so sorry, Jax." I lay my hand on his arm. "Are you…" I feel bad even asking this, but I have to. He's my brother. "Are you okay with not having kids?"

Jax smiles and nods. "I am. I love Willow. I offered to adopt with her a few times, but she's said no every time. I think by getting cancer so young, it made her realize how short life can be. So instead of dwelling on what she can't have, she focuses on what she does have. And we're blessed with all our nieces from Jase and Celeste, and soon we'll have one from you. Who knows? Maybe you'll be the one to finally give everyone a damn nephew." We both laugh, and it feels good. It feels right.

"Seriously, though," he says with hearts in his eyes, "Willow is my other half. She's all I need to spend the rest of my life a happy man." I swoon over his admittance. Why couldn't I have found a guy more like my brothers?

"Well, if you guys are sure, then I'm there. But if, at any time, you guys want your privacy back, please just tell me. I'm not broke," I tell him. "I received money in Rick's will that will take care of my baby and me."

"Good," Jax says, "it's the least the asshole could do after what he put you through."

After we pack up a suitcase of my clothes, Jax tells me he'll have a moving company handle the rest. I let him know I don't want any of the furniture and it can be sold with the place. Anything that's Rick's, his parents can have, and whatever they don't take, can be donated to charity. He says he'll handle it all.

When we pull up to the townhouse, I spot Celeste's SUV in the driveway, and Jax says, "Celeste thought it was a nice day for a family barbeque. If you're not up for it…"

"No." I shake my head. "That actually sounds pretty damn perfect."

We walk inside, and I'm immediately greeted by Celeste, Jase, Willow, and Skyla. Everyone takes turns hugging me, and Willow even welcomes me home. Then, my two adorable nieces, in their little black pigtails and frilly matching dresses, come running over.

"Card for Auntie Quinn," Melina says, handing me a scribbled on, folded piece of paper.

"Love you," Mariah adds.

Bending down to their level, I scoop them both up into a hug, taking a moment to breathe them in and get lost in their innocence. In a few months I'm going to have one of my own. My own baby to love and spoil. The thought brings me to tears.

"Skyla, would you mind taking the girls out back to play for a few minutes?" Jase suggests, confusing my happy tears for sad ones.

"It's okay," I tell him. "I'm okay." I wait until the three girls are out of the room before I continue. "I was just thinking that in a few months I'm going to be a mom." My sobs get harder as I admit the truth to my family for the first time. "He was so mean, and I was so weak." I shake my head. "He would call me names and tell me I'm fat and should lose weight. And instead of leaving, I joined the gym. But then he accused me of cheating and forced me to quit." Tears fly down my face as I rush to get everything out.

"And he wouldn't let me work. I told you guys I didn't want to continue my photography business, but I was lying. He wouldn't let me. He gave me an allowance. A fucking allowance." I choke on my sobs. It feels almost cathartic to finally tell my family everything. "He would only have sex with me when he was drunk. He was cheating on me with God knows how many women." I bury my face in my hands, completely embarrassed, but Willow pulls them away.

"Don't do that," she demands. "Don't you hide. You have nothing to be embarrassed of."

"I'm okay," I repeat my earlier words. "Even though my husband was a horrible, despicable person, before he died he gave me the most precious gift." I cover my belly with my hands. "I was scared to admit I was pregnant. Terrified what my life would look like raising a baby with him. I thought about running away and never looking back. But he's dead." I smile because I'm finally free. "And I'm going to love my baby with everything in me. I'm going to be the best damn mother I can be."

Celeste and Willow both smile back, Jase looks like if Rick were still alive, he would find him and murder him, and Jax looks at me with brotherly love.

"So, where do you go from here?" Celeste asks. "What can we do?"

"First things first, I'm changing my last name back to Crawford, and then I'm going to take it one day at a time. It's time I finally find myself."

"And we'll be here for you every step of the way," Jase says, "just like you were there for me while I was trying to figure out how to raise Sky, how to navigate being a single dad." Jase pulls me into his arms for a hug. "We're family, Quinn. Let us be there for you, please."

Four

QUINN

Five Years Later

"But Mom," Kinsley whines, "I don't want to go to the tattoo shop. It's not fair." I look in the rearview mirror at my frowning five year old daughter. She still has leftover tears in her eyes, and a red nose from all of the crying that ensued about twenty minutes ago in the front office of her school as she threw herself onto the ground in a breakdown of epic proportions. During which time, I was forced to pick her up and carry her to the car, all while she screamed and cried and told me I was the worst mom ever.

As I drive to Forbidden Ink, the tattoo shop my brothers own, I remember that my daughter isn't always like this. She's generally a very sweet and adaptable child. But today, she's mad at me. Because in the chaos and insanity of dealing with two engagement parties, a wedding, and a pregnancy photoshoot, all this week, I forgot that Kinsley needed to be at school early for a field trip. The entire kindergarten class was going to the science museum and my little girl was counting down the days. Literally. With a red pen on our calendar that's pinned to the wall in our kitchen. She lives for the science museum, is obsessed with everything science related.

When we got to the school, late, we were told she would have to remain in the office all day because her teacher isn't there. I suggested taking her to the science museum and dropping her off, but was told, legally they can't allow that. Which left me no choice but to take my very pissed off and disappointed child to the tattoo shop, so Willow and my brothers can keep an eye on her while I drive across the city to the pregnancy shoot I'm already late for.

"I'm sorry, Kinsley," I say, for what feels like the millionth time. There's no worse feeling than that of a mother who's let her child down. "I'll make it up to you. This weekend, you and me, science museum all day. We'll get there before it opens and stay until they kick us out."

She lets out a frustrated huff, crossing her tiny little arms over her chest, and glares my way. It's during moments like these, when her features are put on display, I'm reminded of how much she looks like her father. I'm not about to blame the genetic card for her attitude. She doesn't have an ounce of malice or cruelty in her body. But with her shockingly bright azure eyes, light brown hair, and willowy body, Kinsley Crawford might've resided in my belly for nine months, and share the same last name as me, but she, one hundred percent, looks like her father—well, aside for our skin type. My poor girl inherited my pale complexion, that alerts everyone, whether we want it to or not, of every emotion we're feeling.

"It's not the same," she murmurs softly, and my heart breaks at her letdown, defeated tone, which is a thousand times worse than the pissed off tone.

"I know," I tell her, turning off the car. I get out and open her door while she unclicks her seatbelt and jumps down out of my new SUV. After having the Cayenne for eight years, it finally was ready for retirement, so I traded it in and got the same model, only newer. My brothers laughed at me, saying I'm so predictable. It's not my fault, though. I'm not good with change. I know the SUV is good and reliable, so why chance buying something else? I'll be forty years old in less than six months. It's a little too late to take a walk on the wild side now.

We walk into the shop, and since it's only nine in the morning, they're not open yet. I haven't been here in quite a few months, but it still looks the same as it has since they opened the place over fifteen years ago. Graffitied walls, black leather comfy couches, a pool table on one side, and a front counter on the other. In the middle is the hallway that leads to each of the six rooms. When Jax and Jase first opened this place, it was just them. Now, every room is filled with a tattooist.

Forbidden Ink is one of the most well-known places to get tattooed. It probably has something to do with their best friends being retired NFL players, and Jase's wife, Celeste, being an international supermodel, who owns her own clothing line. But the truth is, even with all of that publicity, a business will only flourish if it provides quality service and product, and my brothers, along with their employees, are the best of the best when it comes to tattooing. People drive from all over just to get inked by them. Hell, I have several tattoos, and I would never let anyone but them ink me.

"Who are you?" Kinsley asks, grabbing my attention. When I look to see who she's talking to, I spot a guy standing at the front counter, who I've never seen before. He must be the new guy Jax mentioned he hired. The first thing I notice is his silver barbell brow ring. Moving my eyes downward, they land on his neatly trimmed mustache and thick, bristly beard. It's well-groomed, but still long enough that if he were to go down on me, he would leave rug burn behind on the inside of my thighs.

With a grey beanie on his head, I can't see the color of his hair, but I imagine it's the same golden copper color of his facial hair. He's wearing a white T-shirt that stretches across his chest, showing off all of his ink that covers his arms. I spot the Forbidden Ink signature logo in the corner. When I take a closer look, I notice he has sea-foam green eyes, and under all that facial hair is a baby face. He can't be any older than mid-twenties. And with that thought, my cheeks heat up, remembering that I was just imagining his face between my legs. Which is kind of crazy in itself because I can't even remember the last time I thought about a man in that way, let alone him doing those types of things to me.

Without meaning to, my eyes lock with his, and I know without looking in a mirror, my entire face and neck is now flushed pink—thanks to my pale complexion I was just talking about. He smirks knowingly, and if it's even possible, I'm positive my flesh is now scorching hot. Jesus, he's fucking gorgeous…and young, I tell myself. Too damn young.

"I'm Lachlan," he says with a tinge of an accent that sounds like it might be Irish. He smiles warmly at my daughter before he looks back over at me—his smile turning from warm to arrogant. He totally knows I was checking him out. "We're not open yet," he tells me, "but I would be more than happy to help you in any way I can." His gaze trails down my body, and even dressed in a modest pair of dress pants, a loose blouse, and professional pumps, I feel completely exposed. I stare at him for a long second, waiting for the look of disgust to come now that he's gotten a closer look at me. And then I mentally slap myself for thinking like that.

Every time I think the wounds Rick caused have finally healed, these self-conscious, self-deprecating thoughts resurface. I should push them away, bury them right next to Rick, six feet under. I know I should. I've spent the last five years finding myself. Finding my strength, my voice, my sass—as my brothers call it. But one look from a good-looking guy and I shrink back into my old self. Worried I won't be enough. Scared he's not going to like what he sees. That he'll take a good look at me and be disappointed or let down or repulsed.

So, even though it makes me sick to feel like this—weak and insecure—I wait with bated breath for him to realize he's checking out an overweight, almost forty, single mom. But it doesn't happen. Instead, he cocks his head to the side and licks his lips like he wants to make me his next meal. His muscular arms flex slightly as he crosses them over his chest, and the side of his mouth pulls into a cocky grin. "Please tell me you're inked under all those clothes and my day will be made," he says.

My body ignites at his words, making me feel things I haven't allowed myself to feel in years. I haven't wanted anyone to see what's under my clothes since Rick, but with the way he's looking at me, and talking to me, my hormones are taking over and telling me to strip down right here and show him what he wants to see.

"My mommy has lots of tattoos," Kinsley says, reminding me that there's a five year old in the room who's listening to every word he's saying.

And with that realization, I'm able to regain my voice. "What's underneath my clothes in none of your business," I state matter-of-factly, cringing on the inside because if he did, in fact, actually see what's under my clothes, he'd probably stop looking at me like he wants to devour me. "I'm here to see Jax," I say, grabbing Kinsley's hand and pulling her behind me down the hallway.

"Whoa! Wait!" he yells after me. "We're really not open yet, and Jax is appointment-only." I see him in my peripheral vision rushing to catch up to me, but I don't stop. I don't have time for this. I don't have time to play whatever games he's trying to play.

"I don't need an appointment."

"We have a no kids in the back rule," he informs me, chasing after me. When we get to the back office, I swing the door open to find Willow in Jax's lap, and the two of them making out like horny teenagers. Jesus! It's not even noon yet.

Kinsley giggles, and I quickly shut the door.

"I'm going to have to ask you to come back up to the front," Lachlan says with a scowl. I roll my eyes—a childish habit I've been unable to break over the years—as the office door opens and out walks Jax and Willow. Both dressed similarly in a black Forbidden Ink shirt and jeans—only Willow's shirt is lower, showing off her tattooed cleavage, and her jeans are a lot tighter.

"Uncle Jax," Kinsley yells, throwing herself into her uncle's arms, while a fresh set of tears fill her eyes. While I know my daughter is genuinely upset over missing her field trip, I'm also way too aware at how well she's learned to play her aunt and uncle over the years.

Jax, of course, buys her tears and picks her up. "What's the matter, K?" he asks, even though he already knows. I explained it all to him on my way here when I asked if they could please watch Kinsley for a couple hours. Speaking of which…I pull my phone out of my pocket to check the time. Shit! I am so late.

"Mommy made me late, and I missed going to the science museum," she cries, like it's literally the end of the world. Willow's brows furrow in sympathy as she rubs Kinsley's back. My heart swells as I watch my brother and his girlfriend love on my daughter. One of my biggest fears was that she wouldn't grow up in a loving household, so it makes my world feel complete to know that my daughter is surrounded by so many people who love her and would do anything to make sure she's taken care of and happy. Even if it means buying into her dramatics.

"I'm sorry, K," Jax says. "I know it's not the same, but

Willow and I are looking forward to hanging out with you today."

"It's not the same," my way too honest daughter says with a pout, causing Willow and Lachlan to laugh under their breath.

And then Lachlan glances my way. "Sorry. I didn't know you were Jax's sister." He shrugs unapologetically, then extends his hand. "It's nice to meet you, Quinn."

"No worries," I tell him, quickly shaking his hand, while trying like hell not to stare at his sexy mouth. "Kinsley, I'll be back in a couple hours," I tell my daughter, who's now refusing to acknowledge me. Apparently, we've left Upset Avenue and have ventured back onto Pissed Off Avenue. At least she's no longer yelling at me and saying I'm the bane of her existence.

"I love you," I tell her, giving her a kiss on her cheek. As I walk away, I try not to look back. For one, my heart is breaking over how upset my daughter is, and from the fact that I caused it. And two, I have a strange feeling Lachlan is staring at my ass. I make it halfway down the hallway before I give in and steal a glance back over my shoulder. And sure enough, my daughter is back to crying on her uncle's shoulder, and Lachlan is, in fact, staring at my ass.

Five

LACHLAN

Holy mother of MILFs. As I watch Quinn breeze by me out the door, with her shiny black hair and matching onyx eyes, I only have two questions: Who the hell is that woman? And how do I make her mine? When Jax and Jase mentioned they had a younger sister, my brain created one of those filters—you know, the ones that take the animal body and place a human head on it, and everyone posts it on their social media like it's not at all fucking creepy. Only in my filter, it took Jax's body, and put Jase's head on it. Okay, maybe I'm not making much sense right now. But bear with me. My world has just been rocked by a sassy woman in high heels.

My point, that I'm doing a piss-poor job at making, is that I never imagined the Crawford brothers' sister would be so goddamn beautiful. In my twenty-seven years of existence, I've never been so turned on and thrown off by a woman. She's a walking fucking contradiction. Even in that uppity professional attire she was wearing, I could still make out the perfect swells of her tits and those luscious fucking curves. And Jesus, those thick hips…and that ass. I could imagine taking her from behind and leaving fingerprint marks from gripping her flesh. And what I'd do to that ass…spank it…fuck it…both at the same time.

When she pursed those fuckable lips in a shitty attempt at glaring at me, the first thought that came to my mind was how I wanted to bite them and then lick them. I wanted to kiss her fleshy lips until they were red and puffy. Which led me to my second thought. The visual of her on her knees, with me watching as she wraps those same plump lips around my dick. I wonder if she's ever been with a man who has a Prince Albert piercing. I sure as hell would love to show her the benefits of fucking a guy with one.

And *that* visual has me imagining what she looks like naked…again. Although her clothes covered most of her skin, I still managed to catch a glimpse of a tattoo peeking out along her collarbone, and fuck if it didn't have me wanting to beg her to strip down so I could see all of the other tattoos she has inked on her body. And for a brief second, the way she looked at me looking at her, I think she might've agreed.

Her brothers are covered in tats, so if I had to guess, I would say she probably has quite a few. And as a man who spends his days inking people, I'm now wondering who Quinn has let ink her. Was it just her brothers and Willow? Or has she let Evan and Gage permanently mark her? And that thought has me feeling a ridiculous amount of unjustifiable jealousy toward them—that they were allowed to touch her when I haven't yet. Holy shit! What's wrong with me? I'm standing in the hallway of my workplace working myself up over a woman I literally met less than ten minutes ago. Pissed off at two guys I work with because they *might've* inked her.

When I hear a throat clear, I snap out of my craziness. I look over and see Willow and Jax both staring at me. Willow is smiling, and Jax is glaring. "I'm going to go get my station ready," I mumble, needing to get the fuck away from the both of them, and also needing to adjust the semi in my pants I'm now sporting.

The next couple hours fly by, with only a minimal amount of fantasizing about Quinn. I tattoo some dates on a retired Navy officer and a butterfly on a girl who is getting a tattoo for her eighteenth birthday. Because I'm new to this shop and haven't been here long enough to establish a clientele yet like the others, I generally get the walk-ins and piercings.

At ten thirty, Willow knocks on my door. When I turn in my chair, my eyes go to the cute little girl peeking out from behind Willow's leg. "Hey, Lach," Willow says, "my client got here early, and Quinn is running late. Would it be okay if Kinsley hangs out in here with you for a little while? Everyone else has someone in their room."

"Sure," I tell her. Even though I'm an only child, I come from a huge family with tons of cousins who have all had no problem adding to the world's population. I love spending time with my nieces and nephews. I look at it like practice for one day when I meet the woman I'll want to spend my life with and we start a family.

"Thanks," she says to me. Then to Kinsley, she says, "I'll be right next door. If you need anything, just ask Lachlan and he'll get it for you. Okay?" Kinsley nods once then enters my room. I've seen her laughing and talking to everyone else, so I'm assuming that she's only shy around me because she doesn't know me.

"You having fun with your aunt and uncle?" I ask in an attempt to break the ice. Kinsley climbs up into my tattoo chair and shrugs, and that's when I remember she's here because her mom was late to drop her off for her field trip. I think she said it was the science museum. "Sucks you missed your field trip."

"That's a swear word," she says. "I'll give you a warning, but next time I get a dollar." She's dead serious, not even a hint of a smile on her face. It takes me a second to put together what she said, but once I do, I bark out a laugh.

"All right... So, what's your favorite part of the science museum?"

This gets me a small smile. "All of it," she says softly. "The bodies and dinosaurs and space and music and…and…water and animals and all of it." Her smile grows with each word she speaks, and by the time she stops to take a breather, her face is lit up like a Christmas tree, reminding me of the way her mother's skin flushed pink in embarrassment earlier. They don't have the same hair or eye color, but both of their skin is that shade you see on dolls, almost a translucent porcelain, and their smiles are identical, just a tiny bit crooked with a hint of mischief.

"I'm sorry you missed it," I tell her. We're both quiet for a long beat, and I'm not sure what to do with her. Being in a tattoo shop kind of limits what I can do to entertain a small child.

I glance around my room, trying to find something that might interest her. When I spot my markers, an idea forms. "Want me to give you a tattoo?" I flash her a playful grin, holding up my markers so she knows I don't mean a real one. And just like her damn mother, her eyes roll to the top of her head.

"My mom told me never to get a tattoo by anyone except my uncles and Aunt Willow because they know what they're doing." She shakes her head to emphasize her point. "Just because you can pick up a pen, doesn't mean you can draw."

"What?" I ask. I mean I heard her, but how old is this little girl? Twenty? "I work at the same shop as your uncles and Aunt Willow," I say, unsure why I'm trying to convince this mini version of Quinn that I'm not just another guy with a pen in his hand.

"Yeah… but how do I know you can draw? They're my family, and I can't really draw that great, and my mom can't draw at all." Her eyes go wide, and I laugh.

"Check these out," I say, grabbing my portfolio and placing it in her lap. She spends the next few minutes flipping through the pages before she finally reaches the end and closes the book.

"So?" I prompt.

"I guess you're good." She eyes me with cautious eyes…just like her fucking mother.

"You *guess* I'm good?" I scoff. "Listen here Mini-Q, I'm damn good."

"What's a Mini-Q? Wait! You owe me a dollar." She puts her hand out, and it takes me a second before I catch on that I just said the word damn. Pulling out my wallet, I flip through my bills until I find a dollar, then hand it to her. I can't even imagine how much she's made over the years from her uncles and Willow. Those three curse like drunken sailors.

"Where does the money go?" I question. "Into a swear jar or something?" My cousin Milstead uses one with her kids because her husband has a horrible habit of cursing in front of the kids, and when it gets filled to the top, they use the money to do something fun.

"Nope, right into my pocket," she says, folding the bill and shoving it into her pocket as she answers me. "We tried a jar once, but I caught Uncle Jax 'borrowing' from it." I laugh at the way she actually uses air quotes when she says the word borrowing. She's obviously been hanging out with too many adults.

"So what happens when you curse?"

"I don't," she says, deadpan.

"What if you did?" I press.

She thinks about this for a moment. "I guess whoever catches me gets to keep the money."

"Nice. So am I good enough to tattoo you or not?"

"I suppose so." She shrugs a shoulder.

"Great!" I smile at the thought at having won her over. Hopefully it will be just as easy to win her mother over. "So, what do you want? A butterfly? A pretty heart? How about a unicorn?"

Her nose scrunches up in disgust, and she gags.

"Mommy says a unicorn dies every time one is tattooed above a woman's ass."

I laugh hard, loving that Quinn would say something like that. I seriously need to get to know this woman. Then it hits me that she just cursed. "Hey Mini-Q, you owe me a dollar."

"I wasn't cursing," she says, her tiny brows furrowed. "I was telling you what Mommy says."

"You still cursed." I tsk. "Dollar."

"Fine." She huffs, pulling the dollar out of her pocket and dropping it into my hand.

"Thank you," I say with an overzealous grin.

"Why do you keep calling me Mini-Q?" she asks, one of her brows raised. "My name is Kinsley Elizabeth Crawford, but Uncle Jax is lazy and calls me K."

"Because you look like and act like a mini version of your mom…Quinn," I say, emphasizing the Q. "Get it? Mini-Q?"

She tilts her head to the side and glares, proving my point.

"Now, what tattoo do you want?"

"Mommy read me a book about the planets last night. Can you tattoo them on me?"

"Sure!" I pull my phone out and google planets. It only takes me a second to find a cool image. "What colors?"

"The colors that the planets are," she says, dragging her sleeve up. "Are you sure you know what you're doing?"

"Yes," I say with laugh. "Alright, colors matching the planets. Got it."

When I take her tiny arm in my hand, she says, "Wait,

you have to prep me first."

Stifling my laugh, I nod. "You're right. Sorry." This little girl is too fucking much.

She lets out a loud sigh. "I really hope you're good. My uncles and Willow never forget to prep me."

Twenty minutes later, I finish Kinsley's tattoo, pretend to rub ointment on it, and cover it with plastic.

"Thank you." She jumps down to check it out in the mirror, even though it's on her arm so she could just look down. "It's really pretty," she says. "You should take a picture and add it to your book."

"You're welcome." Pulling out my phone, I snap a picture of her arm. "There, I'll get it printed and added today."

Just as I'm finishing capping up my markers, Quinn enters the room. Her eyes go straight to her daughter, as if I'm not even in the room. "Wow, Kinsley! What a cool tattoo." She takes her daughter's arm in her hands and admires it.

"It's all the planets," Kinsley states matter-of-factly.

"I can see that. Who tattooed it?" she asks.

"Lachlan," Kinsley tells her. Quinn's gaze bounces over to me, finally acknowledging I'm in the room.

"Really?" Quinn asks. "I thought only your uncles and Willow were allowed to give you tattoos."

Feeling the need to gloat that I've won her mini-version over, I say, "She trusts me."

Quinn lets out a loud snort, then quickly covers her nose like she can't believe she just did that.

"I'm going to go show Auntie Willow my tattoo,"

Kinsley says, running out of the room. "Bye, Lachlan!"

Quinn looks from me to the door like she's either willing her daughter to come back, or scared to be in the same room as me. Both leave me grinning. I make her nervous.

"Snort all you want, but it's the truth." I step toward her, encroaching on her space. "I'm a trustworthy guy."

"I bet you are," she says with a bit of a laugh. "I better go…" She waves her hand in the air, not even bothering to finish her sentence.

"Wait," I say, sliding in front of her to block her only way out. "Since I'm such a trustworthy guy, how about you let me take you out sometime?"

"No," she says flatly, not even taking a second to consider it.

"No? Just like that? Why not?"

"Umm…" She places her purple-painted fingertip to her chin and pretends to think for a second before she says, "For starters, I'm old enough to be your mother."

I laugh at that. Sure, she's a few years older than me, but she's definitely not old enough to be my mom.

"What are you, like…" I'm about to say a number and then remember women hate when people guess their age. What if I guess too old and offend her? She obviously thinks she's way older than me.

"Go ahead," she presses. "Say the number."

"Thirty…one." I was thinking thirty-three, so I went two years lower to be on the safe side.

She stares at me for a brief moment and then throws her head back in laughter. "Wow, thank you. I don't know if you're just bullshitting me to make me feel better, but thank you. You seriously made my day."

"How close was I?" I'm assuming I went too low since she's happy I thought she's younger.

"You were off by eight years." I quickly do the math in my head. She's thirty-nine years old. Well, damn, I never would've guessed that. But that's not going to deter me. Age is just a number and all that jazz.

"And you?" she asks with a knowing smirk.

"Thirty-seven," I tell her, lying out my ass.

She laughs, knowing I'm full of shit. "Try again."

"Fine…minus ten."

I wait for her to do her own math, and once she does, her eyes bug out. "You're twenty-seven? Jesus." Her cheeks tint a light shade of pink, an indication that I've already learned means she's embarrassed.

"What's going through your head?" I ask, taking another step forward.

"Nothing." She shakes her head.

"Yes, you were definitely thinking something." I run the backs of my fingers along the side of her neck. "You're all flushed. It happened earlier too. Whatever you're thinking has got you embarrassed."

"No," she squeaks.

"Yes," I argue. "Tell me, Q, what were you thinking?"

"One, my name is Quinn, not Q, and I was thinking, you're so young, I could probably get arrested just for talking to you." Her cheeks flush darker.

"What you mean is, you could probably get arrested for thinking about all the things you want to do to me." When her cheeks and neck get even warmer, I know I'm right.

"Doesn't matter," she states. "I was right. I *am* old enough to be your mother."

"My mom is forty-seven, so, no."

"Where are you from?" she asks, changing the subject and giving me whiplash.

"Here."

"You have a small accent. Are you Irish?"

"Ya," I say, putting emphasis on my half-ass accent. "But I was born and raised here. The accent only comes out because my family all have it and I visit Ireland often."

"Thought so," she says, a smile tugging on the corners of her lips. "I watch Sons of Anarchy and you sound like the Irish dude. Anyway, your mom is only eight years older than me, and I'm twelve years older than you. I'm closer in age to your mom than you."

"I don't care," I tell her honestly. "My mom always told me when I met the woman I want to spend my life with, I'll just know. I'm not saying it's you, but at the same time, I'm not saying it isn't. I want to get to know you. You intrigue me, and I'm not about to let something as stupid as an age difference deter me."

Her jaw drops open, and for a second I think I've stunned her silent. Probably for the best so she won't argue. She blinks once, twice, shakes her head slightly, and then speaks. "Well, you should. Besides, I imagine a good-looking guy like yourself has plenty of young, gorgeous women to choose from." The way she inadvertently puts herself down by referring to other women as gorgeous, as if she's not in that category, rubs me the wrong way. I don't care how fucking old she is, she's sexy as hell.

"That's neither here nor there," I tell her, trying to keep the annoyance out of my tone. "I'm staring at a gorgeous woman right now who I want to get to know."

"My answer is no," she says, pushing my shoulder slightly so I'll move out of her way. I consider not moving, but know it will only piss her off if I don't.

Following her to the back, I say bye to Kinsley, who thanks me again for her tattoo. Quinn says hi to Jase, who wasn't in yet when she dropped her daughter off earlier, and tells Willow and Jax she'll see them at home later.

When Quinn and Kinsley are both out the door, Jax and Willow step on either side of me. I can feel both of them staring at me and know they're going to say something. So, rather than prolong the inevitable by walking away, I wait.

"My sister is not someone you mess with," Jax finally says. "She's been through a lot, and if you fuck with her, I *will* choose her, regardless of our friendship, or the fact that you work here. She's family."

Meeting his gaze, I look him in the eye so he knows I understand what he's just said. "I would hope you would always choose your sister over me," I tell him, "but all I want is to get to know her. I'm not trying to mess with her in any way." He nods once, then walks away back to the office, leaving just Willow.

"Your turn," I tell her, and she grins.

"Good luck," is all she says. And with a pat on my shoulder, she joins her boyfriend in the office.

"Thanks!" I call out after her, knowing damn well I'm

going to need all the luck I can get on my side. Something tells me Quinn isn't your average woman, and getting her to agree to go out with me won't be as easy as it usually is for me. But that's okay because something else tells me that she's worth the challenge.

QUINN

My mind is a whirlwind of mixed emotions the rest of the week, which thankfully goes more smoothly than Monday. Every time I recall the way Lachlan looked at me like he wanted to devour me right there in his workplace, I'm at a loss. Or the way he point blank told me he thinks I'm gorgeous and wants to get to know me. Surely, a guy as young and hot as he is, has a line of equally young and hot women at his disposal. Even after I told him my age, it didn't seem to discourage him in the slightest.

Maybe it's because I was dressed professionally, covering the majority of my skin. I make it a point to buy work clothes that hide the rolls and imperfections as much as possible, but even the most expensive, flattering outfits can only do so much. He couldn't see the cellulite on my thighs that turned Rick off, or the newly formed stretchmarks on my stomach that came with being pregnant.

I cringe, thinking about how Rick would've reacted to my stretchmarks. He would've blamed me for gaining too much weight during my pregnancy. Damn it! I hate that even after five years, I still allow that asshole to make an appearance in my thoughts. He doesn't deserve any place in my life, alive or dead.

The last few years I've made a conscious effort to eat healthy, and I work out at the gym a few times a week—when time permits. I'm proud to say I've lost the majority of the baby weight I put on. I'd like to say that my hard work has nothing to do with my dead husband's last words to me, but I would be lying if I didn't admit that more often than not I hear him telling me how I've let my body go, and use it as motivation to workout harder. That being said, I'm still not skinny. My hips are still too wide, and my ass is too big. I hope one day to be at a size I can be proud of, but today is not that day…and tomorrow isn't looking good either.

Which is why I'm so confused as to why Lachlan was so insistent about taking me out. Maybe he saw it as a challenge. I told him no, and most men hate that word. Hell, most people do. But then I think about the way Kinsley droned on about him the entire way home and for several days afterward. How nice and funny he was. When he cursed, he paid her a dollar, she said. When I asked her where the dollar was, her cheeks flushed and she admitted she cursed, and then blamed me because she was only repeating what I always said. My daughter is a lot like me…well, the me before Rick. She's sassy and smart and takes nobody's shit, while at the same time, she wears her heart on her sleeve and trusts too easily. The last two are both a blessing and a curse.

It's now Sunday morning and I have nothing booked for today. Kinsley and I are on our way to the park to practice soccer and then we're planning to go to the science museum afterward. It's her first time playing a recreational sport and she's nervous, so she asked to practice first instead of getting to the museum for opening. She loves kicking the ball around at school, but it's different once you're playing an actual game—at least I imagine it is. I wasn't exactly one to play sports. I was more of a sit-in-the-stands-and-photograph-the-people-playing kind of girl.

"Can we invite Uncle Jax to play?" Kinsley asks as we walk down the sidewalk toward the neighborhood park. "No offense, but you're not very good, Mom." I stifle my laugh, shooting her a mock glare, and she shrugs. Damn kid is too honest. "Sorry, but it's true."

"I texted him and Aunt Willow earlier." They had already left for the shop before we were up. "Uncle Jax said if they get done with inventory and ordering early enough, they'll meet us."

When we get to the park, we head straight to the soccer field. There are a few other families playing as well, so we find an empty spot in the corner to kick the ball back and forth.

"Go stand at that end!" Kinsley exclaims. "I'll kick it to you, and you kick it back, okay?"

"Sure!" I yell with as much fake enthusiasm as I can muster.

About thirty minutes later, as I'm chasing down the soccer ball for what feels like the millionth time, I hear Kinsley yell, "They're here!" I breathe out a sigh of relief. Jax being here means I get to sit down on a blanket in the grass and watch, and take some pictures.

"Hey, Lachlan!" Kinsley squeals excitedly, and I find myself spinning around in shock to confirm he's here. And sure enough, dressed in another white T-shirt—this time with some band logo across the front, black jeans that are molded to his thighs perfectly, and a pair of Vans that match the color of the logo on his shirt, is Lachlan freaking Bryson (I may have stalked him on social media and learned his last name). He's sporting a beanie similar to the one he was wearing the other day, but this one is black.

As I watch him approach us, with his clear as the sky cocky smirk splayed across his perfect lips, and all of his various tattoos on display, my breath hitches. I felt it the other day, the unexplainable attraction to him, but I chalked it up to it all being in my head. I'm a single mom who hasn't gotten laid in over five years. My vibrator gets more action than Bruce Willis...you know, because he does action movies. Okay, maybe that was a bad analogy. But my point is, I'm having to charge that thing quite often. But now, standing here staring at the way Lachlan is looking at me once again, I can't deny it. The sparks are there, threatening to turn into an all-out fire.

Someone call 911 because I need a firefighter to put out these flames. There's only one outcome when you're dealing with a fire—someone's going to get burned. And I don't doubt for a second, that someone will be me.

What the heck is he even doing here?

When I finally peel my eyes off of him, I notice my brother and Willow are also heading toward us. He must've been at the shop and decided to join them. But why? I'm sure he has better things to do on his day off than hang out with a single mom and her daughter.

"Hey, Mini-Q," he calls out, and my eyes, of their own accord, roll upward into my head. Kinsley told me all about his nickname for her. Apparently because she's a little me. I would love to know if he considers that a good or bad thing. *Well, he did say he's intrigued by me and wants to get to know me…*

When the three of them reach us, Kinsley grabs the soccer ball and drags Jax down the field. Of course, Willow follows. Lachlan, though, remains standing in front of me. "Hey," he says, giving me a nonchalant chin lift.

"Hey," I parrot. Reaching down, I grab a bottle of water from the small cooler I brought with me and down half the bottle. When I lower the bottle from my lips, I see Lachlan is once again staring at me.

"What?" I ask, glancing down at myself. Today, I'm dressed for the occasion in a pair of grey Victoria's Secret boyfriend style sweatpants and a matching hoodie.

"I'm just wondering when I'll get to see you without all that clothing covering your body." He nods toward my outfit with a glare, as if it's personally offending him.

"Sorry." I scoff. "But I'm not exactly in the habit of leaving my house in my birthday suit, so I'm pretty sure any time you see me, I'll be in clothes."

"I get that," he says with a hint of a smile, "but right now, all I have to go by is my imagination…and it's been running fucking wild." Jesus! This man sure has a way with words.

"Well, I can assure you," I volley back, "whatever

images your *wild* imagination has conjured up is probably better than the real thing. Trust me when I tell you, you do *not* want to see all that is hidden under here. Stick to your imagination." I meant it as a joke, kind of. Okay, more like a warning, but Lachlan doesn't laugh, nor does he heed my warning. Instead, he frowns and steps closer to me.

"I highly doubt that," he says, his tone serious, "but I wasn't referring to your *body*. I was referring to your tattoos. Both times I've seen you, you've had them covered up." Oh...well, shit. He is a tattoo artist, so it makes sense he would be curious about what my tattoos look like. "But, I will admit," he continues, "I have *also* fantasized on more than one occasion since we've met, what you would look like splayed out across my bed, naked, and spread open for me." The way he grins, tells me he's being crass on purpose to get a rise out of me.

"Well, like I said," I say, trying, and failing, not to get flustered, "stick to the fantasy. The reality will be a severe let down." I laugh humorlessly, and Lachlan's frown deepens.

"Why do you do that?"

"What?"

"Talk about yourself in such a self-deprecating manner. Both times we've spoken, you've put yourself down." When my eyes fall to the ground, embarrassed, Lachlan lifts my chin so I'm forced to look at him. "You're an extremely beautiful woman, Quinn."

"Whatever," I mutter, unsure how else to respond. "What are you doing here?" I take a step back so he's no longer touching me.

Lachlan gives me a look I can't decipher because I don't

know him well enough. If I had to guess, I would say he's considering arguing with me, but he must think better of it because he says, "Jax mentioned coming here to play soccer with Kinsley, so I asked if I could join."

"Why?"

"Why not?" He gives me a perplexed look. "She's a cool kid, and I grew up playing soccer."

"Okay, well, I just hope you're not doing it as a way to get me to change my mind about going out with you…because…"

Lachlan chuckles. "Yeah, I know, it's not going to happen." Then he mutters something that sounds like "such a contradiction" under his breath. But before I can ask him what he means by that, he's already running over to join Jax, Kinsley, and Willow.

Despite the rocky start, the morning spent with Lachlan—and my family—is enjoyable. I watch while Lachlan shows Kinsley tons of moves, and join in so we can play a game of two-on-two—Willow offers to referee. Kinsley is on cloud nine with all of the attention Lachlan gives her. She laughs and talks animatedly with him. She even insists on being on the same team as him. At one point, Jax jokes that he should've just sent Lachlan here.

"He's just someone new," I explain, not wanting him to feel bad.

"I know." He grins, not the least bit upset. "Lachlan is a good guy, and Kinsley is a good judge of character." I allow his statement to swirl around in my head for a few seconds before I push it to the side.

When Kinsley is finally worn out, we say bye to Jax and Willow. I always feel bad with how much time they spend with Kinsley and me. They never complain, but I know they love their time alone as well. On Sundays, which is their only sure day off, I try to keep Kinsley out of the house so they can have time to themselves. Now that Kinsley is in school fulltime, I've been thinking more and more about the two of us getting our own place. I've looked at a few places online, but it kind of scares me. I've never lived on my own before. It's something I know I need to do, though. For me and my daughter.

"Mommy and I always get a hot dog at the park for lunch," Kinsley tells Lachlan, who is sitting on the blanket, drinking a bottle of water. "Wanna go?"

"Oh, Kins," I say, "I'm sure Lachlan has other plans." Like my brother and Willow, I think Sunday is his only day off as well.

"Actually, I don't," he says. "A hot dog sounds perfect."

"Yay!" Kinsley yells. "Oh! Can you go to the science museum with us too? I can show you all the planets you drew on me. Please." I stifle my laugh at the way she flutters her eyelashes and exaggerates every letter in the word please, just like she always does to her uncles to get her way.

"That sounds like fun," Lachlan says, not even bothering to speak to me first.

"Lachlan, can I talk to you over here for a moment?" I

drag him off the blanket and away from where Kinsley can hear us.

"What's up?" he asks, knowing full well what the hell is *up*.

"What's up is that you just agreed to pretty much spend the rest of the day with us."

"Yeah…I know," he says, the corners of his mouth turning up into a lazy smile.

"I know you don't have kids, but when you're approached by a child, you don't just say yes without speaking to the parent first."

Lachlan chuckles. "I may not have my own, but I have several nieces and nephews."

"Okay, then you should know this."

"I know it…" He nods. "But I also know if I were to ask, you would say no." He grins, and damn it, if it doesn't do something to my insides. Why can't he have an ugly smile?

"So, you're using my daughter to get to me?" My voice comes out harsher than intended, and Lachlan's playful grin instantly diminishes.

"Now you're twisting shit," he says. "I asked you out, and you said no, despite the fact that I *know* you felt something between us." He raises his pierced brow, daring me to argue. "I wanted to get to know you, and the last time I checked, your daughter is a part of you, which means I want to get to know her as well. And at this moment, out of the two of you, she's the only one willing to give me a chance." His shoulders sag in defeat, and I suddenly feel like a mega bitch. He's right. I did feel something—I do—but I'm too damn scared to act on it. "I wouldn't use anyone," he continues, "especially a child, but you don't know that because you don't know me."

He walks away, leaving me standing here in shock, confused as to how we went from playing soccer to arguing. But I know how we got here. Through my insecurities and hang-ups. Instead of giving Lachlan a clean slate like everyone deserves, I've already placed him in the same category as Rick, simply because he's a man—and that isn't fair to him. I'd like to think I've come a long way in the last several years, but at the same time, I still have a lot further to go.

I watch him bend down to my daughter's level and talk to her. I'm not sure what he's saying until I see her tiny brows furrow and her head shake.

Speed walking over to them, I catch the end of whatever he's saying. "...can't wait to see what you want me to draw the next time you visit the shop."

"Okay," she says, her voice soft.

"See ya later, Mini-Q," he tells her before he turns to me. Without meeting my eyes, he says, "Have a good day, Quinn," then takes off toward the park's exit. Lachlan using my full name shouldn't bother me. It's what I told him to use. But for some reason, it does. It makes me want to drag him back and tell him to call me Q.

"I really wanted him to go," Kinsley says, and although, I don't admit it out loud, I feel the same way.

I watch as his body gets smaller and smaller, the farther away he gets, and then something in me snaps. As if the thought of him disappearing altogether is unfathomable. "Wait!" I yell, grabbing Kinsley's hand and running to catch up with him. When he doesn't slow down, I repeat myself. "Wait! Lachlan!" I shout. This time, his steps falter, and he turns around. Out of breath, and mentally telling myself that I really should get serious about going to the gym more often, I finally reach him.

"We would…um…" I take a deep breath, nervous to actually speak the words I want to say. *It's just a hot dog and a museum*, I tell myself, but somehow I know it's more than that. And while I'm not sure exactly what more means, it scares the hell out of me. "We would really like it if you would join us." I let out a loud exhale, waiting for Lachlan to respond. Afraid he's going to dismiss me.

"You sure?" he asks, his face showing no emotion.

"Yeah, I'm sure."

"All right," he says, a small grin teasing his lips. "Let's go."

"Yay!" Kinsley squeals.

Seven

LACHLAN

I can't help the grin I'm sporting as I pay for the hot dogs and drinks. When Quinn pulled me aside, I knew I overstepped. I gambled and lost. So, I said my peace and then walked away. It sucked, but I wasn't about to force myself on the woman, no matter how much I want her. I know firsthand you can't make someone want you. You might feel the sparks, but if the other person doesn't, you have no leg to stand on. I knew she felt the sparks between us, but for whatever reason, she was trying with everything in her not to acknowledge them. Until I walked away and heard her calling after me.

I barely know the woman, but I could see it in the way she nervously spoke, the unsureness in her tone, it took a lot for her to chase me down and ask me to join her and her daughter. For a second, I considered giving her a hard time, but then I looked into her eyes and saw fear. Afraid of being vulnerable, afraid of putting herself out there and open to rejection. So instead, I asked if she was sure, offering her an out, and when she said she was, I considered that a huge step in the right direction.

"You don't have to get me one," Quinn says. "I'm not really hungry." I tilt my head slightly, not liking what she's saying. It shouldn't surprise me, though, since she's made quite a few comments pertaining to her figure.

"Yeah, you are," I say, holding up three fingers to the guy and handing him a twenty dollar bill. When he hands me the food and drinks, I hand them out. Both girls say thank you and open their wrappers to take a bite.

"Eww, Lachlan," Kinsley says, watching me add every condiment available to the top of my dog.

"Have you ever tried all these together?" I ask her. She shakes her head no. "Then you don't get to judge." She rolls her eyes as she takes a bite of her plain hot dog.

We walk down the sidewalk, eating and listening to Kinsley talk. She keeps the conversation flowing, telling us all about the mean boy in her class who bugs her, how she's excited for her first soccer game next Saturday, and all of the exhibits she wants to visit once we get to the museum. When we stop by their house so they can quickly change, I look up the museum to find the easiest subway route. But when I mention it to Quinn, she says, "That's okay. We can just take my car. It'll be quicker."

Not many people drive in New York. I own a vehicle because I lived in Boston for a few years, but I keep it parked at my parents' place since I don't drive it often here. Not only does Quinn have a vehicle, she has a fucking Porsche SUV.

From what I've heard, she has a photography business she's building. I'm not trying to get up in her business, but I'm definitely curious to know how much photographers make. Clearly, I'm in the wrong profession. But you know what they say: you don't become a tattoo artist for the money; you become one because of your love of the art.

The ride there doesn't take too long. When Kinsley falls asleep on the way, Quinn says, "She's reenergizing her batteries," with a laugh that makes the corners of her eyes crinkle. It's the first playful thing I've heard from her, and it has me wanting to make her laugh more often.

We spend the afternoon at the science museum, being dragged by Kinsley from exhibit to exhibit. Quinn was right. Her batteries are fully charged, and she's on a mission to see every single thing available. The only reason we leave is because the museum announces that it's closing. Kinsley pouts, and Quinn tells her they'll return again soon.

I offer to take the subway home so she doesn't have to cross back over the bridge, but she insists on dropping me off. I live in a decent apartment, walking distance to the shop. It has two bedrooms and two baths, and I share it with my best friend and cousin, Declan, who is currently over in Ireland visiting his sister who just had a baby. He'll be back in a couple weeks.

"That's me," I say, pointing to the brick building. "Thank you for letting me crash your day."

Quinn smiles softly. It's not much, but I can tell I'm wearing her down slowly. "You live here?" she asks. I can tell she's curious how I can afford such a nice place when I ink people for a living.

"Yeah, I share the place with my cousin." I shrug, not bothering to mention that I own it outright and he barely pays rent.

"Oh, well, thank you for joining us."

"I have a soccer game Saturday!" Kinsley says. "You have to come."

Quinn closes her eyes and shakes her head. "I would tell you that you don't have to come, but at this point, I feel like a broken record." She laughs. "It's at the same park we practiced at today. Nine o'clock. If you can't make it...or have to work..."

"You'll understand," I say, finishing her sentence for her.

"Yeah."

"Can you step outside for a second?" Quinn gives me a confused look, but opens her door and steps out anyway.

"Bye, Mini-Q," I say to Kinsley. "I'll try to make it Saturday." I don't want to say I'll be there and not show up. It's still six days away, so anything can happen. She waves goodbye, and I get out of the SUV and walk around to Quinn's side.

"What's up?"

"I didn't want to ask you in front of Kinsley..."

"Oh, wow, a man who listens." She grins playfully. "Thank you."

"Yeah." I chuckle softly. "Anyway, I was wondering if I could take you out one day this week." Quinn's smile drops, telling me I'm about to be rejected once again. "Or not," I add to lighten the mood.

"I really enjoyed hanging out with you," she says, "but

I'm a single mom to a five-year-old."

Running my hand over my beard, I tug on the end, something I tend to do when I'm nervous or frustrated—right now I'm the latter. "I'm aware of all of that," I tell her. "I just spent the last nine hours with you and her."

"No, I know." She groans. "What I meant was…my life is crazy and chaotic on a good day. Take the day you met me for example. I was late, forgot my daughter had a field trip, my sitter was out of town and my back up was sick with the flu. I needed to leave my daughter with my brother and his girlfriend at their tattoo shop, so I could go to the photoshoot, which I was late to. And after I picked up Kinsley, I found out it was the last day to sign her up for soccer." Her eyes go wide dramatically, reminding me of Kinsley. These two are clearly two peas in a pod. "Can you imagine if I would've missed *that* deadline?" I laugh, but don't say anything, letting her finish what she needs to say.

"I raced all over town, signing her up and taking her to get shin guards and a soccer ball."

"You're a good mom," I tell her. I'm not sure why, but I just felt like she needed to know that.

"Thank you," she says warmly. "But part of being a good mom is putting my daughter first."

"That excuse sucks," I say honestly.

"Maybe, but it's only part of it."

"What's the other part?"

"I'm almost forty, and you're twenty-seven. You're a single guy with no kids, no strings. I'm a single mom with a child who has an eight o'clock bedtime."

"So what?" This woman has every excuse in the book, and if I thought they were being slung at me because she really doesn't like me, I would give up. But my gut is telling me they're being used as a shield because she's scared.

"What did you do last Saturday night?" she asks.

"Played poker at Gage's place."

"Exactly. You know what I did? I watched The Little Mermaid for the hundredth time, baked cookies, then after putting my daughter to bed, spent the rest of the evening cleaning up, taking a bath, and working on some edits before falling asleep only two pages into the book I'm reading."

"Jax and Willow were there too," I point out.

"They're kid-less," she says, "just like you."

I look at her, at a loss of what to say. I feel her slipping through my fingers before I've even gotten her. Figuring this is my last chance, I say what's on my mind. "Look, Q, I like you. I want to take you out. I get you have all these reasons why you don't think it would work between us, and in your head they very well may be relevant. But I don't see why any of those reasons you mentioned should prevent me from taking a beautiful, hard-working, woman out—kid or no kid."

When her eyes drop to the ground, I lift her chin. I hate when she feels like she can't look at me. "I think you like me too," I tell her. "But I also think you're scared." When she nibbles on her lower lip, I know I've hit the nail on the head. "So, here's what I'm going to do." I reach around her and pull her phone out of her back pocket. When I swipe up, it opens, indicating she doesn't have a passcode on her phone. "I'm going to put my number in your   phone. If, or hopefully when, you want to get to know me, text or call me. We can take things slow, I promise. I just want to get to know you."

I type my number into her contacts list then hand her back her phone. "I hope to hear from you." Leaning over, I give her a chaste kiss on her cheek before I wave to Kinsley one last time and then head up to my place. The ball is in her court now. I just have to hope she thinks I'm worth stepping out of her comfort zone for.

Eight

QUINN

It's Friday night, and for the first time in I don't know how long, not only do I not have any shoots booked, but I'm completely caught up on all my edits, and I'm off all weekend. And for the first time in what feels like forever, I'm kid-less. As I sit on the couch, with my Phish Food ice cream in one hand, I flip through the channels on the TV, hoping to find something to watch that doesn't involve princesses or talking dogs. On the coffee table is my phone, taunting me, the same way it's been taunting me the last five days since Lachlan input his number into my contacts list. I've typed out enough messages to have an entire one-sided conversation, but I haven't built up the courage to actually hit send on a single one.

The truth is, I don't have a lot of dating experience. Growing up, my two older, tattoo-covered, football playing brothers were several years ahead of me, yet made sure everyone knew who they were, so the boys tended to stay away. We lived in a small town. It wasn't until my senior year of high school I convinced Tommy Pines to take my virginity the night of prom. I know, how cliché. He was boring, to say the least. A book nerd of sorts, and because of that, he didn't know who my brothers were. A month later, he left to some crazy, smart college, and I started at the Art Institute. I dated on and off over the years, slept with a few guys, but never felt that spark you read about in those super mushy romance novels.

And if I'm honest, I'm not sure I ever *really* felt them with Rick. I think I was lost and felt lonely. I know I shouldn't have felt that way when I have two brothers who love me like crazy. But it's not the same thing. They were so career oriented. They knew what they wanted and were making it happen, while I was floundering around. First, I thought I wanted to work in a museum, so they picked up their entire life and moved to New York with me. Only a few months later, I realized I hated it, so I quit.

I did learn, though, that my true passion was photography, and that's how I came to start my own photography business. The problem was I had no idea what I was doing or how difficult it would be to try to build a business in New York. Every day I felt like I was failing while my brothers were succeeding. So when I met Rick, and he promised me the world, I took the easy way out by latching onto him.

At first, he was charming and said all the right things. He made me feel like an equal. But all too soon, his attitude changed, and I learned too late that my husband was a snake.

He had me in a trance, mesmerized, and before I knew what was coming, he bit his poisonous fangs deep into my flesh, and I was fucked.

I never want to be in that situation again. The problem is, how do I ever move forward if I'm too afraid to give another man a chance? In theory, the solution is easy. Open myself up and let Lachlan in. The reality, isn't so black and white. I can't afford to make those mistakes again. Especially now that I have Kinsley. If I'm wrong about Lachlan, I won't be the only one hurt. It's clear my daughter already cares about him.

So that leaves me at a crossroad. Do I text him or not? The sexually deprived woman in me wants to text him and beg him to fuck me. I can just imagine the stamina that man has. When he was sweating on the soccer field, he lifted his shirt up, and I caught a glimpse of his six-pack of abs. He works out for sure.

But the responsible, single mother, whose heart has been shattered into a million pieces by my husband is yelling at me to run, and run fast. No good can come from this— well, aside from some potentially mind-blowing sex. But then he'd need to see me naked…which is why, while I won't admit it out loud, I've worked out at the gym every day this week. After seeing how fit Lachlan is, I can't imagine what he would think if he saw me naked.

Sighing heavily, I stare at my ice cream-covered spoon, recognizing that I'm stress eating again. I haven't felt this out of out of sorts in a long time. Putting the lid back on, I take it back into the kitchen. Damn Ben and Jerry and their delicious ice cream. Throwing the container back into the freezer, I slam the door shut. Sulking like…well, my five year old, I'm walking back to the living room, when the front door swings open and in walks Willow and Jax…and Lachlan.

Willow and Jax don't notice me standing here as they yell something about going out while running upstairs to change, but Lachlan does. With the front door still partially open, his gaze is glued on me. He's dressed in his usual T-shirt, jeans, and Vans, but added to the mix is a black leather jacket. Of course he's wearing a damn leather jacket. Because he wasn't already hot enough without it. I also notice he's not wearing a beanie, and I was right—his hair, messy and all over the place, is the same ginger color as his facial hair. It makes me want to run my fingers through it to see if it's as soft as it looks.

While imagining running my fingers through his hair, my gaze lands on his bright green eyes which are widened almost comically, and I snap out of whatever lust-induced coma I'm currently in, looking around to see what has him in such shock. But when I follow his line of vision, it takes me to…well, me. And it's then I wish the floor would crack open and swallow me whole. Because as I was standing here checking out Lachlan, I forgot that I'm dressed in the shortest, tightest, pair of boy shorts, and a tiny cotton camisole. Yep, you heard me right. I'm standing here in my goddamn underwear! In my defense, I ran out of clothes, and they're currently in the washer and dryer. Not that it will do me any good right this second.

As if this moment couldn't get any worse, I hear my brother and Willow descending the stairs, talking and laughing. My own brother is about to see me in my freaking underwear. Great! As if Lachlan can read my mind, his eyes briefly go to the stairs and then he's pulling me by the curve of my hip behind him and against the wall to shield me from embarrassment. His hand stays holding onto my flesh as Willow and Jax enter the living room.

"What the hell is going on?" Jax asks, confused as to why his friend is hiding his sister behind him. Lachlan's so tall, that when I try to look over him, I fail, and instead have to look around him. He backs up slightly, and I'm sandwiched between his body and the wall. Without realizing what I'm doing, I slide my hands up his strong, muscular back to keep my balance, so I can peek around him. In response, his fingers tighten on my hip, and a soft moan escapes my lips before I can stop it.

"I'm…uh…not dressed," I say with a bit of an awkward laugh, fully aware that I also sound slightly turned on and breathless. Remember those sparks I mentioned that I've never felt? Well, holy fucking hell, I feel them with Lachlan, right now, between my legs. Willow cackles, and Jax fake-gags. Lachlan groans, and the way his body vibrates, sends heat flooding through mine. "Can one of you please grab me the throw blanket from the couch?"

Thankfully, Willow snaps into action and hands me the blanket, which I wrap around my shoulders to cover my body up. Lachlan moves forward and turns to face me. I'm so embarrassed, I can't even look him in the eyes. Nobody since Rick has seen me in such a vulnerable position.

"Where's Kinsley?" Jax asks, breaking the awkward silence.

"Sleepover at Celeste's with Olivia's and Giselle's daughters." Olivia and Giselle are two of my sister-in-law's best friends. Between the three of them, they have eight girls. It's a running joke how Olivia and her husband, Nick, are the only ones with a son, Reed. When I got pregnant with Kinsley, the three of them were all pregnant at the same time. We took bets on who would be the one to have the second boy, but all four of us ending up having daughters. When Celeste mentioned having Kinsley over, she asked me to join, but there was no way I was passing up a night to myself.

"You should join us," Willow suggests, but I'm already shaking my head no.

"Oh, no. I'm too old and tired to keep up with you party animals," I joke.

"Yeah, yeah." Willow laughs. "Well, don't wait up." She winks dramatically and pulls Jax behind her.

"Night, sis!" Jax yells, following his girlfriend out the door, and leaving Lachlan and me alone.

"You better get going before they leave you behind." I nod toward the door with a small laugh.

"You never texted me," Lachlan says, changing the subject.

"I thought about it," I admit, which has him smiling, and in turn, has me smiling.

"And what did you think about texting me?"

"I don't know." I shrug a shoulder, refusing to tell him about the fifty different texts I thought about sending.

"I was thinking I could stay here…keep you company," he says, his eyes wandering down my blanket-covered body. Worried that at any moment I might drop said blanket, I tighten the corners around me. The blanket knocks my loose bun out and several stands of hair fall into my eyes. With my hands full of the fabric, and not wanting to chance dropping the blanket, I attempt to blow the hair out of my face. Lachlan laughs and, stepping forward, tucks the wayward strands of hair behind my ear. The simple touch of his fingers brushing my flesh shouldn't affect me the way it does.

"So, what do you say?" he asks. "You up for company?"

I shoot him an incredulous look. "Trust me, you don't want to miss going out with your friends and possibly getting laid, just to lounge on the couch and watch a cheesy romcom with me."

"Don't tell me what I want," he says, his tone serious. "I wouldn't have suggested us hanging out if I didn't want to."

"Hey Lach!" Jax yells from outside. "Quit hitting on my sister and let's go!"

I roll my eyes, and Lachlan coughs out a laugh. As I look at him, I already know I'm going to give in. I've been fighting it since the first day I met him, but my resolve has been slowly weakening each time I'm around him and he says and does all the right things—then again, so did Rick in the beginning. I push that thought from my mind. Rick doesn't belong here with Lachlan and me. I'm so tired of allowing him, even dead, to rule my thoughts and decisions. It's my life!

Lachlan must mistake my silence for no because his smile drops, and he says in a defeated, very unlike Lachlan, tone, "All right, well, have a good night." He shoots me a half-smile and is walking away before I even know what's happening.

"Wait!" I say, running to stop him. This seems to be becoming our thing—he asks, I say no, and then I chase him. Only this time I wasn't going to say no. "Sorry, I was in my own head. If you want to stay and hang out, that's fine." Lachlan raises a single brow, and I cringe at how rude that sounded. "That came out wrong. I just meant if you really would rather hang out here instead of going out, you're more than welcome to join me."

The corner of his mouth quirks up into a sexy smirk, and he nods once. "I'll let Jax know I'm staying here while you go get dressed." His eyes light up mischievously, then he adds, "Or you can stay just how you are." He bites down on his bottom lip before turning to go outside. *What I would give to have him biting down on my bottom lip.*

When he's out the door, my body sags in relief. Holy hell, he is so freaking intense. Running up the stairs, I scour my room for a single clean article of clothing, but can't find anything. Damn it! I really shouldn't let my laundry pile up until I have nothing left. Uncertain of what the hell to do, I stand in my closet willing for something to appear. I have a couple dresses, but how stupid would I look walking down there dressed like I'm ready to go to church or work?

Hearing the door shut, I know Lachlan is downstairs waiting for me. I open each of my drawers again, knowing I won't find anything. *My goodness, I seriously have a lot of laundry to do.*

Just then, I hear the dryer buzz, and thank the laundry gods above. Now I just need to get to the dryer, which is downstairs in the laundry room. Tiptoeing down the stairs, I pray Lachlan is in the kitchen, the only room you can't see the stairs from. Of course, he's sitting on the couch and looks over at me as I descend.

"Decided to keep what you have on?" he says with a smirk. "I approve."

"No." I roll my eyes—I really need to break this habit. "I'm out of clothes, but I heard the dryer go off."

"Well, don't feel like you have to get dressed on my account."

"I'll be right back," I mumble, running off to the laundry room. Thankfully, there's a dry pair of sweats and a hoodie in there. I throw them on then head back into the living room with the blanket in my hands.

"So, what are we watching?" Lachlan asks as I sit down on the other side of the couch. When he notices, he shakes his head but doesn't say anything.

I flip through the channels but can't find anything to watch. "How can we have like two hundred channels and not a single movie is on?" I pout. "I told you, you should've went out."

Lachlan edges across the couch toward me, and I stand. If I let him get too close, there'll be no turning back. "I need to rotate my laundry," I blurt out awkwardly.

Once I'm in the laundry room, I open the dryer and start folding and hanging up Kinsley's and my clothes. If I thought doing laundry would be an excuse to give Lachlan and me some distance, I was wrong. He, of course, joins me, and catching on quickly, starts handing me the pants and shirts hangers whenever I need one.

"I'm going to run these upstairs," I say, having no idea

how to handle having this guy in my home, being sweet and helpful. I'm so completely out of my element with him, it's embarrassing. I haven't the slightest clue why he's even still here, when he could be out with his friends, getting his party on.

"I'll help you," he offers, grabbing the clothes that are hung up, while I grab the ones that are folded. All three bedrooms are upstairs. We stop by my room first, and I'm surprised when Lachlan doesn't comment on how girly my room is. It's Skyla's old room, and she was all about the pink. When I moved in I was too lazy to change the wall color.

When we get to Kinsley's room, though, he laughs. Her walls are half-black, made of chalkboard paint, and half bright green, with science posters covering them. "This is awesome." He sets her clothes down on the bed and walks around, checking out her room while I put her clothes into their proper drawers. When I open her closet to hang up her clothes, Lachlan is right behind me.

"Oh, man, she has all the classics," he says, referring to her large stack of board games. He reaches over me and pulls one out. "Wanna play?" When I turn to look at him, I can see the evil glint in his eye. He's up to something.

"You want to play Candyland?" I'm not buying it for a second.

"My cousin Declan and I are the only boys in the family, and we're also the oldest. When we were younger, and our parents would make us play these boring games with his sisters and our other cousins, we would change up the rules to make it more fun." He grins wickedly. "Because they were younger, they didn't know we were making them up." He cackles, and I can't help the smile I'm currently sporting. Lachlan is so damn adorable and playful.

"Like how?" I ask, wanting to know more.

"Well, take this game for instance." He holds up the board game. "We would tell them if they landed on red, they had to give us a piece of their candy." He's smiling so hard, even his eyes are twinkling. "If they landed on blue, they would have to do one of our chores." He laughs, and the sound hits straight between the apex of my legs. Everything about Lachlan is sexy, even his laugh.

"That's so mean!" I say, but find myself laughing along with him.

"Yeah." He shrugs. "But that's part of growing up, right? I bet your brothers used to do shit like that to you."

"Nope," I tell him honestly. "They're a good six and seven years older than me and they treated me like a princess. They never would have done anything like that."

"Well, then you missed an important rite of passage," Lachlan says, his tone serious, which has me laughing harder.

"What a shame," I reply, sarcasm dripping from every word.

He looks down at the box that's holding the game, then up at me. "Let's play."

"I'm not falling for your chores rule," I joke.

"New rules."

"No way!" I can't remember the last time I laughed so hard. "I can just imagine the shit you'd have me doing."

"C'mon, it will be fun! Live a little," he taunts, and even though I don't doubt that whatever rules he's about to make up will be dirty and leave me embarrassed, I suddenly want to play. He's right, it's time to live a little, have some fun. And then an idea forms. If I'm going to play his games, I need to even the playing field.

"I get to make up the rules."

"We both do," he volleys.

"Fine."

Nine

LACHLAN

When Jax mentioned going out tonight, I checked my phone, hoping maybe Quinn would finally send me a text since it's the weekend, but when nothing was there, I agreed. After shutting down our stations for the night, he mentioned he and Willow needed to go home to change first, and that's when I formed my plan. All I needed for it to work was for Quinn to be home. Granted, I assumed her daughter would be there. I figured I would convince her to let me hang out with them, maybe watch a movie or play a game. I'm not picky. Getting Quinn to open up hasn't been easy, so I'll take whatever I can get. If it wasn't for the way I've caught her looking at me on several occasions, I wouldn't believe I even stand a chance at this point. Most people would wonder why the hell I'm even bothering. Quinn was right. It would be easy for me to find a woman to hook up with, but that's not the kind of guy I am. People assume because of the tattoos and piercings and the job description, I'm some bad boy looking for my next fuck. But that couldn't be any further from the truth. And if it was, my mom would tan my ass.

When we arrived at their place, Quinn's car was in the driveaway, so I knew she was home. I walked through the front door, expecting to see her and Kinsley hanging out, so imagine my surprise when instead, I saw Quinn in nothing more than a tiny pair of black and white polka dotted underwear and a white tank top, so thin, I could see her perky nipples poking straight through the material. I couldn't take my eyes off her. I knew she was hot, but damn! My imagination didn't even begin to do her justice. I've been with a few women over the years, but compared to Quinn, they all look like little girls. Her thick hips, heavy tits, and shapely thighs are all damn woman, and I've never been so turned on in my life. And if that wasn't enough, I was finally able to get a glimpse of her tattoos. And I was right...fuck, was I right. They cover parts of her upper arms, a little bit of her chest and collarbone, and span across her legs. I was too in shock at seeing her half-naked, I didn't get a chance to really check them out, but I'm going to. I could see it in her eyes when I mentioned making up the rules—she knows what's coming, and if she didn't want it to, she would've refused to play.

I set the game on the dining room table and open the lid. Pulling out the gameboard, I open it up and place it in the middle of us while Quinn organizes the cards into a neat stack and places them on the board. We pick out our colored gingerbread pawns—she picks purple, and I pick yellow—and then she excuses herself for a moment.

When she comes back, she's holding a skinny blue bottle that has blue and pink puffs on the front. "Is that cotton candy flavored vodka?" I ask, giving it a closer look.

"I figured it was fitting." She glances down at the board game with a small smirk, and I'm grinning on the inside because she's finally letting loose. "I was thinking for the candy spots, we have to take a shot."

"I like it." Maybe if she gets some alcohol in her, I can get her to open up more. "Okay, so the rules," I say, sitting down in the chair. "We each pick two colors."

"I go first." She sits at the square dining room table, diagonal from me. "I want pink and purple."

"Such a girl," I joke. "I'll take blue and red."

"Such a boy," she mocks.

"Yeah, yeah. Name your rules."

"If someone lands on pink, they have to answer a truth."

"So, I can ask you any question I want, and you have to be honest?" I clarify.

"You too," she says.

"Got it."

"The purple spot..." She thinks for a minute, her perfectly manicured finger tapping on her chin. "You have to explain one of your tattoos."

"And you have to show it to me," I add.

"Fine." She rolls her eyes as she twists the cap off the bottle and pours us each a shot.

"My turn," I tell her. "If you land on blue, you have to let the other person kiss you."

Her eyes widen even though she knew this was coming. "Where?"

"Anywhere the kisser decides."

"Fine." She huffs, giving in a lot easier than I expected. "And the red?"

I lick my lips and smirk, looking her dead in the eyes. "You have to take off an article of clothing." I doubt she's going to agree to this rule, but I have to try. I have a backup rule in mind just in case.

She chokes out a cough mixed with a shocked laugh, then grabs her shot glass, throwing back the liquid and slamming it down onto the table. "Okay."

"Okay?" I ask, just to be sure.

"Yep." She fills her shot glass back up. "I need to use the bathroom before we start."

While she's gone, I check my phone for any texts or calls. My mom is in Ireland with my dad for an extended vacation until my cousin's wedding, which is in December. With me being their only child, she usually calls or texts me on a daily basis. I'm looking down at my phone when I hear Quinn coming back down the stairs. When I glance up, something about her looks different, but I can't put my finger on it. And that's when I notice she's wearing socks. *Why is she wearing socks?*

And then it hits me. "You fucking cheater!" I bark out a laugh, and she cracks up. "How many articles of clothing did you put on? Ten shirts and twenty pairs of underwear?"

"No!" She cackles, sitting back down. "My toes were cold." She's so fucking adorable, I can't even be mad. She totally played me at my own game.

"You go first," I tell her. She picks up a card and it's pink.

"A truth," she says, moving her gingerbread to pink.

I consider starting off easy—asking her a simple question like what her favorite color is, but with my truths limited, and knowing how guarded Quinn is, I decide not to waste them. There's one question I've been wondering since I met her…

"Where's Kinsley's dad?"

Quinn's eyes widen slightly, and she frowns. "Starting off with a bang, huh?" She laughs softly.

"Go big or go home," I say to lighten the mood, and it works because the corners of her lips curl into a smile.

"Richard Thompson, Kinsley's father, is dead." Fuck… I wasn't expecting that. She grabs her freshly filled shot and gulps it down.

"Shit, Q, I'm so sorry." I bring my hand up to her arm and squeeze lightly. "I didn't know," I add, feeling like an ass. "How long has he been gone?"

"Since before Kinsley was born. He never even knew I was pregnant," she says with a shake of her head. "We were married for three years, together for a little over four. He was shot in the back by a druggie who wanted his wallet, when he refused to give it to him." Jesus, I can't even fathom how Quinn handled all that, especially while pregnant.

Being as she doesn't have to tell me anything more, I'm shocked when she continues. "He was getting into his car from dinner."

A thought hits me that has my stomach roiling. "Were you…were you with him?"

She laughs, but it sounds off. *Why the hell is she laughing?* "Oh no," she says with a sad smile. "One of his many mistresses was. I was at home trying to figure out how to tell the man who despised me that I was *finally* pregnant with our child."

It takes me a second to string all of her words together. Her husband, the man who was supposed to love and protect and be there for her, was out fucking around on her while she was home alone and pregnant. If he weren't already dead, I would kill him my fucking self. Then another part of what she said hits me.

"What do you mean he despised you?"

She exhales a deep breath. "I can't believe I just said all that. I've never told anyone...not really. Only my family knows the basics. It must be the liquid courage," she muses, taking another shot. This time I join her.

"Quinn, if you don't want to talk about it, you don't have to," I say, giving her an out.

"I do," she says slowly. "For some reason, you make it really easy to talk to. But not now… If it's okay, I'd really like to play some more Candyland." She smiles softly at me, and my heart speeds up. I'm so fucked when it comes to this woman.

"Okay, it's my turn." I pick up a card, and it's red, so I move to the first red square.

Quinn laughs. "Your rule, and you're the first to strip! Take it off, Lach, now!" She laughs harder, waggling her eyebrows playfully. I know it's the alcohol helping her break out of her shell, but I'm loving this version of Quinn. I imagine that at one time, before her dickhead husband, she was like this all the time.

Reaching back, I lift and pull my shirt off my body.

When she yells, "Yeah, take it off," I playfully throw it at her, and it smacks her in the face. She giggles loudly, and I want to bottle that shit up for later.

"Wow." Her eyes light up as she assesses my half-naked body. "You work out a lot, huh?" Her gaze drags down my chest and over my abs. I've never really cared what a female thought of my body. I work out because I enjoy it, and I want the art on my body to have a decent canvas. But right now, with the way she's eyeing me, makes me damn glad I do work out.

"A few times a week. I have a gym in my building."

She groans. "I have a gym membership, but I rarely go. I really need to change that."

"You're perfect the way you are," I tell her. She rolls her eyes as if what I'm saying is bullshit. We're going to have to work on that. If I have to tell her every day she's fucking perfect, until she finally believes me, I will.

"What does that tattoo mean?" She leans over, and the tip of her fingernail hits the top of my ribcage. Goose bumps dot my flesh at her touch. When I glance down, I see the tattoo she's pointing at is the one I had done after my grandfather passed away.

"When my grandfather was alive, we would go fishing every weekend on the dock behind his house." I point at the wooden dock with the fishing pole hanging off the edge. "We would sit and talk for hours. Rarely ever caught a fish, but they were some of my best memories with him."

"That's really sweet. I don't have any grandparents," she admits sadly. "My dad's family disowned him when they found out he was cheating on his wife, and my mom's parents passed away when I was little." Damn, so not only did her husband cheat, but so did her father. It's no wonder she has a hard time opening up.

"I'm sorry," I tell her. Then to lighten the mood, I say, "You asked about my tattoo…" When she gives me a confused look, I add, "I didn't pick up a purple card. Now I get to ask you about one."

"Gah! Fine!" She holds out her left arm, which is covered completely by her hoodie, and lifts up her sleeve, exposing a small tattoo on her wrist. "This was my very first tattoo. Jase tattooed it on me when I was sixteen." At a closer glance, I see it's a small anchor with a rope wrapped around it. "Jase, Jax, and I all have the same one."

"You guys are close, huh?"

"Yeah, until they met their significant others, we were all each other had. They're my best friends."

Quinn picks up a card. It's yellow, so nothing happens except her moving. I pick up orange, so I move. Quinn goes again, picking up a blue card. The second she flips the color over, her teeth bite down on her bottom lip. She's nervous. And suddenly I'm regretting my rule. Because while I want to kiss Quinn, I want her to want me to kiss her.

"You know what? I was just kidding about that rule." I force out a laugh to emphasize my point.

When she looks at me, her brows are drawn together. "You don't want to kiss me?" she asks softly, hurt evident in her tone. She continues to nibble on her bottom lip, and my heart drops into my stomach. Was it her husband who made her this insecure? She said he despised her, cheated on her with several woman. Is he the reason she's so self-deprecating when she refers to herself? Why she thinks it's crazy that I would want her?

Standing, I step the two feet to where she's sitting, then crouch down so I'm eye level with her. She looks down at me as I cup her soft cheek with my callused hand and bring her face down to mine. My lips first land on the corner of her mouth, and I can feel it, she's not breathing. She's waiting anxiously to see what's going to happen. I wonder if I'm the first guy to kiss her since her husband.

"Breathe," I whisper against her lips, just before I claim her mouth. Our lips crash against each other, then part. Our tongues stroking and teasing. Our mouths moving in perfect rhythm. I can taste the sweet vodka on her tongue. I suck on it, needing more.

More of her taste.

More of her touch.

More of her body.

Just. Fucking. More.

Oh, sweet, Quinn. I'm going to make you mine.

Quinn moans into my mouth, and her hands find their way to my chest. I think she's going to push me away, but instead, I'm shocked when her nails dig lightly into my chest. Not wanting to take it too far, and knowing I very well will if we keep going, I pull back gently. Needing her to know how much I want her, though, I go back in for one last chaste kiss.

When I sit back down, I give Quinn a look that I hope conveys how much I want her. Her cheeks and neck are flushed, and her breathing is labored. She's turned the hell on. And the thought has me wanting to thump my fist against my chest like a fucking caveman. I did that to her.

"Your turn," she squeaks out.

I pick up a card. It's an image of gumdrops or some shit, so I down the sweet as hell shot. When I set it back down, Quinn fills it back up. She goes next, and it's red. She laughs, then slowly unzips her hoodie. When a white shirt appears, I laugh along with her.

"You're killing me." I groan. "I'm sitting here, shirtless, meanwhile you have God knows how many layers on you."

"Trust me. Seeing what's under here"—she waves a hand over her front—"*would* kill you."

I can't help rolling my eyes, and she giggles. "Are Kinsley and I rubbing off on you? I think you roll your eyes as much as we do."

"Why do you always put yourself down?" I ask, even though it's not her turn to answer a truth.

She looks stunned at my question, but doesn't deny it. "I-I don't know," she says with a frown.

"Yes, you do. You said your husband despised you. Did he call you names, Quinn?"

She considers my question for a moment before she nods once. "Yes," she answers softly.

"Did he think you were fat?" Another nod. This guy is so fucking lucky he's already buried six feet underground.

I stand abruptly, and the chair knocks back slightly, making a loud scraping sound against the wood floor. Quinn's eyes widen curiously, and if I'm not wrong, maybe a little in fear, which only makes me that much more pissed. Fear of a man doesn't happen on its own. A violent man causes a woman to fear.

Lifting Quinn into my arms, I carry her over to the couch. Her legs tighten around my waist, and I do everything in my power to ignore the warmth I feel between her legs.

"What are you doing?" she asks, breathlessly.

"Showing you something." I need her to see what I see. I need to wipe away every negative and nasty thought her disgusting fucking prick of a husband put into her head. Fuck him for thinking it's okay to make a woman feel like she isn't beautiful, isn't worthy of affection and attention. That because her hips are wide and her ass is plump, she's any less perfect than anyone else.

Setting her gently onto the couch, I kneel between her open thighs and press my mouth to hers, needing to feel her soft lips against mine once again. Her lips part slightly, and I dart my tongue out and into her mouth, tasting the sweetness mixed with Quinn.

"Your lips are perfect," I murmur. Even with my mouth so close to hers, I keep my eyes open, and she does as well. I need her to not only hear my words, but see the truth in them. "They're soft and full, and if I could, I would spend hours kissing them."

She averts her gaze, embarrassed. "Don't do that," I say. "Look at me, please." When she does, I smile. With one hand holding myself over her, I use the other one to trail a finger down her neck to her throbbing pulse point. My lips move from her mouth to that spot. I place a soft kiss to her flesh, my lips lingering for a second as I suckle gently on her skin.

"I love the feel of your skin." I run my nose along her flesh, breathing in her sweet scent.

"I'm pale and translucent."

"It's flawless and shows every emotion," I argue, reluctantly lifting my head, when what I really want to do is bury my face into the crook of her neck. "Take your shirt off for me?" I request. I don't doubt that right now, with her thighs clenching around mine, she wouldn't let me take her clothes off, but I need *her* to do it. It has to be her. Her decision. Her facing her own fears of letting a man see her body.

Her mouth twists into a nervous frown, but then she nods and lifts her shirt off, leaving her in only a black cotton bra and sweatpants—and those socks she put on for the game. I trail kisses down her neck and over to her collarbone. There's a small quote: *this too shall pass.* When I lick my way slowly across the words, she inhales sharply.

"I don't like this quote," I tell her honestly. It means something bad happened. I can imagine her sitting in the tattoo chair, getting it inked onto her body to remind herself that one day things will get better. "Did you get this after your husband died or while you were married to him?"

She swallows thickly and her eyes gloss over. "While," she says, and I nod once in understanding.

"Your collarbone is so fucking sexy," I tell her, leaning down to give it a kiss. "So delicate." I trail my fingers across her chest, to the other side that doesn't have any ink on it. "One day you're going to let me ink you right here, and it's going to be something good. Something that makes you smile."

Quinn bites down on her bottom lip and sniffles once. "Don't cry," I tell her softly. Her eyes flutter shut, so I lift up and give each of her lids a soft kiss.

"I really love your eyes," I tell her when she opens them back up.

"They're just black," she says dismissively with a small laugh.

"No." I shake my head in disagreement. "They remind me of the night sky…dark and mysterious…the possibilities are endless. They're just waiting for the bright stars to shine and reflect in them."

"Lachlan…" Quinn whimpers, but I ignore her. She needs to hear my truths.

Moving downward, I place an open-mouthed kiss to each of the swells of her perfect breasts. "I really, really like your tits," I tell her with a wolfish grin. She laughs, shaking her head.

I slide my body down the couch until my face is parallel with her stomach. Her hands fly downward to cover her flesh, so I take her hands in mine and pin them to her sides.

"Lachlan, I don't want to do this anymore," she pleads, tears suddenly racing down the sides of her face. My heart constricts at the thought of her being so insecure and self-conscious, the idea of me looking at her naked body brings her to fucking tears.

Lifting back up onto my knees, I kiss where the tears are landing. "Because you're uncomfortable with me seeing you, or because you think you're fat?"

"I'm uncomfortable with you seeing me *because* I'm fat," she admits.

Cupping her face in my hand, I kiss her softly before I pull back and say, "I'm not going to push you tonight because I think just you taking your shirt off and letting me see you like this was a lot for you, but this isn't over, Q. I don't think you're fat. I think your fucking gorgeous, and one day, you're going to be comfortable enough to let me see all of you. And when that day comes, I'm going to worship every single inch of your body until you're screaming my name. Got it?"

With a sniffle, she nods, but I need to hear the words.

"Say the words, baby."

"Got it."

Ten

QUINN

When Lachlan climbs off of me, I stay lying on the couch, watching as he bends and grabs my shirt. His words are on replay in my head. The way he described my eyes and lips and breasts. Nobody has ever described me in that way. And when I freaked out over him seeing my stomach, he responded with such patience. I looked closely to see if he was mad or frustrated, but all I could find was compassion and want and understanding.

Sitting up, I reach out to take the shirt from him, but instead he takes my hand in his and pulls me into a standing position, then puts the shirt on me himself. Once I'm back to being covered, I grab the bottle of vodka and pour myself a much-needed shot.

"Bring the bottle and glasses over here," Lachlan says, so I do. Once I set them down on the end table, he picks me up and sits back down on the couch, situating me across his lap, bridal style, with my legs stretched out in front of me. I lay my head back against the arm of the couch and he leans over and kisses me, starting with my neck, then moving to my cheek, the corner of my mouth, and finally my lips, his beard scratching my chin briefly before he pulls back.

"No more Candyland?" I ask.

Lachlan's eyes shine with laughter, but he shakes his head. "No," he murmurs. "I think we're past needing a card to tell us what to do." He tucks a wayward hair behind my ear. "It's your turn. Pick a color."

"No way. I just went. You pick a color."

"Fine. Pink. Ask me anything."

"Hmm…" I think about what I want to know about Lachlan. "When was the last time you were in a relationship, and how long did it last?"

His smile dampens, and his hands encircle my waist. I can feel his fingers clasp together, holding me to him. "That's two questions," he says, kissing the tip of my nose. "Her name is Shea. We dated for about three years on and off, finally ended things about six months ago."

"Is that why you moved here?"

"Kind of," he says. "I grew up in New York. My dad is Irish-American and was on vacation in Ireland when he met my mom. They fell in love and she moved to New York to be with him. They run his family business here. That's why I don't really have the accent. Growing up, we would visit often, but New York is our home. While I was on vacation in Ireland, I was hanging out with everyone, my friends and cousins, and Shea and I ended up hooking up. She's been around for years, but I never really noticed her before." He shrugs. "We did the long distance thing for a couple years, and then one day she showed up. I was living and working in Boston at the time. I had gone to college there and ended up staying, even though it drove my mom nuts for me to be so far. It was at the same time my dad had a minor stroke and needed my help running his business."

"Oh no." I frame the sides of his bristly-haired face in my hands. "I'm so sorry. Is he okay now?"

"He is," he says with a smile. "But at the time, he needed to take a break, so I moved down here so I could help out. I still tattooed part-time, but I mostly focused on running the family business. I have a degree in business management, so that came in handy, I guess."

"That's really selfless of you," I tell him. "My brothers moved here for me too. I still feel bad about it because I didn't end up liking the job, so the move was kind of pointless."

"Hardly," Lachlan says. "Have you not seen their shop? It's one of the top tattoo shops on the east coast."

"Yeah, I guess you're right." Maybe moving here happened for a reason. Jase did get back in touch with Celeste because of the move, and Jax wouldn't have ever met Willow had we not moved here. And both couples are hopelessly in love...

"So, you moved back and what happened?"

"Shea moved with me to New York, but she wasn't really happy here."

"Was she happy in Boston?"

"No." He shakes his head. "She missed Ireland but wanted to be with me and knew my life was here. Once our relationship went from long distance to every day, I realized she wasn't who I wanted to spend my life with. We had different wants... different dreams. Eventually we broke up and she moved back to Ireland."

"Are you still working for your dad?"

"No, Dad is back to work now. That's why I took the job at your brothers' shop. I met Jax at an inkers convention and we hit it off. By the end of the weekend he had offered me a job."

"You must be really good," I say, remembering how Kinsley let him draw on her.

"Well, Kinsley did let me ink her," he says, voicing my thoughts. "Plus, my best friend and cousin, Declan, lives here, and so do my parents, so I decided to stay. Declan and I share the place you dropped me off at, but he's in Ireland right now. One of his sisters just had a baby, so he's visiting, but should be back in a few weeks."

"I've seen Ireland on Sons of Anarchy. It's really pretty."

Lachlan laughs. "I doubt the show does it any justice, but yes, it is beautiful. I think I got off track." He scratches the side of his beard, which reminds me of the first time I saw him and thought about that same beard between my legs. My neck and cheeks heat up, and Lachlan smirks. Thankfully, he doesn't ask what I'm thinking about.

"Your turn," he says.

"I pick the picture card," I say with a giggle that tells me the alcohol has worked its way through my body. Lachlan chuckles, pouring me a shot and handing it to me. Once I throw it back, I say, "Okay, your turn."

"I pick red," he says mischievously. Without waiting for him to prompt me, I sit up and press my lips to the tattoo of the Irish flag on his chest. It's one of my favorites of his that I've seen so far. It's 4D and looks like the flag is in his skin with his flesh being ripped open. When I let my lips linger, Lachlan groans. Blaming it on the alcohol flowing through me, I move my lips to his other pectoral muscle and kiss the tattoo there. This one is of a four-leaf clover with the leaves in the shape of hearts.

"Quinn," Lachlan rasps. "I'm trying to be good here, but you putting your mouth on me isn't making it easy."

"I can't help it," I murmur, trailing my lips up his chest, to his collarbone, and ending at his neck. "You taste so good."

Lachlan tilts his head to the side to give me access, and I kiss along his pulse point and up to his ear, sucking on the bottom of his earlobe. Then I trail more kisses over his scratchy beard and to his cheek. "I pick blue," I murmur, my mouth only a hairbreadth from his. His lips brush against mine teasingly, and when mine part on a sigh, his tongue delves into my mouth. I suck on it, craving the taste of Lachlan. As our kiss deepens, I find myself turning in his lap so I'm straddling him. My arms wrap around his neck, and my fingers thread through his soft, messy hair. We kiss for several minutes, and not once does Lachlan attempt to touch me in any way. His hands stay situated behind my back, holding me to him. I don't doubt for a second he's doing this so I'm in control. So I feel comfortable. And ironically, the idea of him allowing me to go at my own pace has me wanting him that much more.

Just as I break our kiss and trail my lips down his bearded jaw and back over to his neck, a cell phone rings out loudly. Remembering Kinsley was supposed to call me before going to bed, I reach over to the end table and grab it, fully aware I'm still on Lachlan's lap.

"One second," I tell him, then answer the phone. "Hey Kins, how's it going?"

"I'm having so much fun, Mommy! We played the Wii and I'm a really good fake dancer! And then Uncle Jase made a big fire and cooked us all s'mores. They were so yummy! I asked Auntie Celeste if I can bring one home for you, but she said they would be bad tomorrow." As I laugh at my daughter's enthusiasm, I glance at Lachlan and see he's also listening with a big smile splayed across his face.

"I'm so glad you're having fun, sweetie. I'll be there in the morning to get you so you can go to soccer."

"Okay! And can you please ask Lachlan if he's going to come? He said he'll try." When she mentions Lachlan's name, his grin widens, and he winks at me. When I roll my eyes dramatically, his hands go to my sides, and he tickles me.

"Ahh!" I squeal before I can stop myself. Kinsley asks if I'm okay. "Yes, I...stepped on something by mistake. I love you, and I'll see you tomorrow."

"Okay, love you too. See you tomorrow. Don't forget to call Lachlan, okay?"

"Okay, Kins. Night."

"Night."

We hang up, and I drop my phone onto the table and then smack Lachlan in the chest. "Not cool! You can't tickle me when I'm on the phone."

"How was I supposed to know you would be that ticklish?" He laughs, then attempts to tickle me again. This time I see it coming and try to climb off his lap to get away, but Lachlan is stronger and holds me to him, not allowing me to get up. "I think your daughter likes me almost as much as her mom does," he says with a wink.

Gripping the back of my hair, he pulls my face into his for a quick kiss. "So?" he asks.

"So, what?"

"Aren't you going to ask me to go to her game tomorrow?"

"That's not what she asked me to do," I point out. "She asked me to ask if you're going."

"Okay, so ask." His hands move from my hair down to my waist, gripping the curves of my hips, and distracting me.

"Q," he prompts.

"Are you going to Kinsley's game?"

"That depends."

"On?"

"If her mom wants me there." His hands move down to my ass, and he gives my butt checks a squeeze that has me jumping in shock and laughing at the same time.

Wrapping my arms back around his neck, I lay my head down on his shoulder. His beard tickles my face as I kiss the side of his neck. "It feels like everything is happening so fast," I murmur, closing my eyes and relaxing further into his lap. The amount of alcohol I've drank is definitely catching up to me. I feel warm and tingly all over.

"Maybe so," he says, running his fingers through my

hair and pushing it to the side so it's out of my face. "But maybe when it's right, it doesn't matter how fast things move."

I nod into his shoulder in agreement, but not entirely sure if I really do agree. Things moved fast with Rick, but it definitely wasn't right. I think for a moment, trying to decide if I should voice my thoughts or just let it go. I'm so comfortable in Lachlan's arms, I don't want to say anything that will ruin the moment. His fingers move from my hair to my back, trailing lines up and down, forcing my body to become even more relaxed by his touch.

"When I was with Rick, it all happened so fast, but it wasn't right," I admit softly. "How will I know if it's right this time?"

Lachlan's fingers still momentarily and then start up again. "I wish I could say you will just know," he says, placing a kiss to my temple. "But the truth is, you never know. I was with someone for three years before I finally admitted to myself that she wasn't the one for me. There are no guarantees, Quinn, but I've only hung out with you a few times and I can feel the difference. The way my heart beats when you look at me and touch me. The way I missed you all week while I was waiting to hear from you. I could go days without hearing from Shea, and I wouldn't feel half of what I felt while checking my phone every twenty minutes, all week long, hoping to see a text from you."

Releasing a content sigh at his words, my eyes flutter closed. "I'm scared," I confess. "I think I'm falling for you."

"You don't have to be scared. I'll be right here waiting to catch you."

"I really like you holding me," I admit through a yawn, snuggling my body closer to his.

"I really like holding you," he says back. My eyes try to fight sleep, but the moment he nuzzles his face against mine, I'm a goner.

When I open my eyes, it takes me a second to recall the details of last night. Folding the laundry, which led to playing Candyland with Lachlan and me drinking for the first time in years. The last thing I remember was sitting in his lap on the couch, so when I look around and see I'm lying in my bed, I'm a bit confused. Twisting my head to the side, I notice Lachlan is here and in bed with me. While I'm on one side of the bed under my blankets, he's on the other side with only a thin sheet covering his bottom half. He's asleep and shirtless, and I use the moment to admire how beautiful he is. He could've taken advantage of my inebriated state last night—and I would've let him—but he didn't.

As I watch his chest rise and fall, I think about everything we talked about last night. I learned a lot about him, and I'm surprised by how much I shared. Even during all the years I spent with Rick, I never felt this comfortable with him. We never just…talked. I really like talking to Lachlan…and kissing him. I *really* liked kissing him. The way he used his tongue…I can just imagine what that tongue is capable of.

"What are you thinking about that has your flesh heating

up like you're standing close to a fire?" Lachlan rasps, his voice scratchy from sleep. He turns over to his side, and his lips curl into a sleepy smile.

"N-nothing," I stammer, taken aback by how much Lachlan's presence affects me. His voice. His smile. Separately, they have the ability to take my breath away. But together...holy hell, together, I feel like I've just jumped off a plane and am soaring through the sky without a parachute. "I'm going to make coffee. Do you want any?"

Lachlan, grabs the curve of my hip before I can get away, and pulls me into him until our bodies are flush against each other. "What were you thinking about, Quinn?" he asks again.

I consider lying to him but go for the truth. "I was thinking about how much I enjoyed last night."

"Oh yeah?" He grants me the most adorable yet sexy grin. "What about it?" He kisses the tip of my nose.

"Playing Candyland."

"What else?" He kisses my cheek.

"Kissing you," I whisper, and he glances back to me. "I was thinking about how skilled you are with your tongue," I admit, shocking myself. What the hell is this man doing to me? "And how I wonder what else your tongue is capable of." I can feel my skin heating up like a freshly lit stove, but Lachlan doesn't comment on it. Instead, he flips me onto my back and climbs up my body, placing kisses along my jaw and down my collarbone.

Without him having to ask, I pull my shirt over my head to give him better access. *Who is this woman?* As he kisses the swells of my breasts, I hold my breath, waiting for him to move downward to my stomach. With one kiss to the center of my belly button, he keeps heading down until he's lying on his stomach between my legs. He stills for a second and looks up at me, silently asking for permission to remove my pants. Alarm bells go off in my head that this is too soon, but then I remember what he said: *when it's right, it doesn't matter how fast things move.*

Plus, I really do want to know what his tongue is capable of.

With a single nod, I lift my butt off the bed, and he pulls my sweatpants off my legs, leaving only the boy shorts I'm wearing. Embarrassed to have him down there, I lay my head back and cover my eyes with my arm, but I should've known Lachlan wouldn't let that fly.

"Eyes open," he demands softly. "I want you to watch me make you come." I can't help how nervous yet excited I am. I've only had one guy attempt to go down on me before, but nothing really came of it. We were young and he wasn't very experienced.

Lachlan loops his fingers around the sides of my panties and tugs them down, leaving me completely exposed. With the blinds shut, it's not too bright in here, but there's definitely enough light shining through that I'm able to watch him without issue, which means he can see all of me: every stretchmark, every flaw, every imperfection. The thought has me wanting to put my clothes back on and run away.

As if Lachlan can sense the vulnerability in my thoughts, he says, "You look absolutely fucking stunning, lying in this bed with your legs spread open and ready for me." His words have such a calming effect on me. My shoulders slump, my body relaxes. "Good girl," he murmurs just before he spreads me open and begins to lick up my center. Not able to see what he's doing, I prop myself up on my elbow for a better look, just in time to see Lachlan's tongue dart out and lick my clit, eliciting a moan from me as my pelvis pops up in shock at how mind blowing it feels.

He eyes me curiously, so I answer his silent question. "This is…kind of my first time," I admit, sheepishly. My answer must be one he likes because he grins like a Cheshire cat before dipping his face back down and licking up my slit again. I continue to watch as Lachlan licks and sucks and nibbles my clit, working me up into a frenzy. I've made myself come many times over the years, but my vibrator sure as hell isn't capable of these functions.

When I feel my orgasm reaching the precipice, I throw my head back against the pillow, close my eyes, and allow myself to just feel what Lachlan is doing to me. And with one more flick to my clit, I'm coming so hard my toes curl into my sheets and my pelvis lifts from the bed.

"Oh. My. God," I scream as Lachlan continues to suck and lap up my juices that are flowing down my center, until I've completely come down from my high.

When I open my eyes, he's lying next to me on his side with the goofiest grin on his face. I try to recall a single time Rick smiled like that at me after sex, but I can't, and it's in this moment, I finally accept Lachlan is not Rick. He's not going to put me down or call me names. He's not going to blame me if I don't orgasm fast enough, or tell me I'm broken. For some crazy reason, Lachlan wants me. And while I have no clue where this will go or how long we'll last, I'm done fighting it.

And with that conclusion, I blurt out the first thing that comes to mind. "Thank you." Lachlan throws his head back with a laugh, and I groan inside. I just thanked him for eating me out. Fabulous.

"You're welcome," he says through his laughter. "I don't think I've ever been thanked for going down on anyone before." He gives my cheek a kiss before he stands. "I don't have any clothes here, so I'm going to run home to shower and change, and then I'll meet you at the soccer game." Grabbing his shirt from the nightstand, he pulls it on over his head, and I mentally pout.

"What's wrong?" he asks. Shit! I must've been actually pouting.

"I was just wishing you could stay shirtless forever," I say, shocking myself at how honest and open I've become. Lachlan is bringing the old Quinn out in me, and I must admit, I've really missed her.

"I will if you do," Lachlan says with a grin, nodding toward me. How did I forget I'm still naked? Grabbing the blanket, I wrap it around my shoulders and get out of bed.

"I'll see you at nine," I say before I head into the bathroom.

Once I'm showered and dressed, I head downstairs to grab some coffee before I head out. Willow and Jax are both sitting at the table, in their Forbidden Ink shirts, drinking coffee and talking.

"Morning," I say, passing by them, going straight to the kitchen.

"Morning," Willow chirps, but Jax doesn't say anything. After I've made myself a cup of much needed coffee, I walk back out to the dining room to find them whispering in hushed tones.

"Everything okay?"

"Yeah," Willow says, at the same time Jax says, "I saw Lachlan leave...this morning."

"Oh, yeah, he spent the night." I sit at the table with them and take a sip of my coffee.

"Well fucking aware," Jax murmurs.

"What's that supposed to mean?" I ask, confused.

"Nothing." He shrugs, taking a sip of his coffee.

"No, tell me," I push, not liking my brother's attitude. This is the first guy I've allowed in my bed in years, and we didn't even have sex!

"Fine, what I meant was...in the future, try to keep it down." His nose scrunches up and his body visibly shivers. It takes me a second, but once I understand what he means, I flush with heat.

"Oh my God!"

"Hey! That's exactly what you were screaming earlier," Willow says with a giggle that has Jax hitting her with a hard glare. "Sorry, not funny?" She laughs some more.

"You don't think that maybe you guys are moving a little too fast?" Jax accuses. "You only met him like two weeks ago."

"You are aware I'm a grown woman, right? I'll be forty in a few months."

"I just don't want to see you rush into anything," Jax says in his brotherly tone. "He's young, Quinn."

"I'm ten years younger than you," Willow says with a frown.

"You're supposed to be on my side," Jax hisses, and I laugh.

"I appreciate you looking out for me, but I've thought a lot about this for the last couple weeks, since the day I met Lachlan and he asked me out, and I want to see where things go with him." And then I add, "And I'm going to find a place for Kinsley and me."

"What?" Jax glowers. "Why?"

"Because it's time. We were only supposed to stay here until I got back on my feet. Thanks to the money I received from Rick's death, even if my photography business wasn't doing well, which it is, I can afford my own place."

"We'll miss you," Willow says, "but we understand." She pats my hand with hers and stands. "Come on, grouch," she says to Jax, who is now pouting like a child.

"Are you guys coming to Kinsley's soccer game?"

"Of course." Jax huffs. "And since you're taking her from us, I'm going to have to make more room in my calendar to see her."

"You know I'm going to find a place close by. Don't act like that," I tell him. "I'm not taking Kinsley away from you. I'm giving you guys some privacy, while trying to finally become independent. Wherever we move won't be far, and you know you can take her anytime."

"I'm sorry," he says, "I know you're right, but that doesn't mean I have to like it."

Eleven

LACHLAN

When I get to the soccer field, I locate Quinn right away, and then I notice, sitting with her are both her brothers and their significant others. And surrounding them are a shit ton of little girls running around. Unsure of how Quinn feels about public displays of affection, when I get over to them, I go straight for Kinsley, who is standing near them but kind of off to the side.

"You ready for your game?" I ask, kneeling down next to her.

"You came!" she exclaims, throwing her tiny arms around me. "I'm really nervous," she admits softly, reminding me of her mother.

"That's okay. It happens to the best of us," I tell her. "But don't worry, once you're out there, the nerves will go away and you'll kick ass." I'm well aware I've just cursed, but I'm hoping it will distract her.

She lifts her head from my shoulder and backs up. "You owe me a dollar."

"Damn it," I say, reaching into my pocket.

"Now two!" She laughs, bouncing on the balls of her feet in anticipation. I hand her the two dollars, and she runs them over to her mom, her nerves gone for the moment. "Can you hold these, please?"

"Sure," Quinn tells her daughter.

Everyone wishes Kinsley good luck and then she runs out onto the field.

"Hey," I say, having a seat next to Quinn on the blanket.

"Hey," she says back. When all of the other adults around us go quiet, Quinn says, "What?" with an exasperated huff.

"You could at least introduce us to your friend," Celeste says with a knowing smirk, as if she hasn't met me several times when she's come by the shop to visit her husband, and sometimes to even help out.

"Umm…what are you guys looking at? You already know Lachlan," Quinn says, sounding annoyed.

"Well, yeah," Willow says, "But not as your…" She looks over to me. "What exactly are you?" She quirks her head to the side, and I bust out laughing.

"He's my…friend," Quinn answers, at the same time, I say, "I'm her boyfriend."

Everybody laughs as Quinn's eyes bug out of her head. "Baby," I whisper, leaning into her so only she can hear me. "What I was doing to your pussy with my tongue only a few short hours ago definitely makes us more than friends."

Quinn gasps, her sexy neck turning that beautiful shade

121

of pink I love, and Celeste chokes on the water she's drinking. Oops…at least, I didn't think anyone could hear me. Oh well.

"Did I mention I'm moving out of the townhouse?" Quinn says to no one in particular, in an attempt to change the subject. Celeste gasps, and Jase curses under his breath.

"And in with Lachlan?" Celeste clarifies.

"What? No!" Quinn says, realizing her comment was vague and made everyone jump to conclusions. "I'm moving on my own, with Kinsley."

Jase's shoulders drop in relief, and I chuckle. "Damn, would it be so bad if she was moving in with me?" I joke, and Jase and Jax both glare my way, which only has me laughing harder.

"We'll be talking later," Jase says, pointing a finger in my direction. Quinn's eyes widen in shock, maybe fear, but once I lean over and squeeze her thigh, she calms.

We spend the next hour watching Kinsley play soccer. None of the kids are really good, but I guess you can't expect them to be at five years old. One kid makes a goal, and another blocks one. Kinsley runs back and forth, kicking the ball a few times. A kid from the other team kicks a goal, and another one attempts one, but it gets blocked. When the game is over, the kids crowd around the coach who tells them they did a good job and passes out drinks and snacks for them.

I'm watching Kinsley open her drink and snack, when I hear Quinn yell, "Oh no!" She jumps up from her seat on the ground and rushes over to Kinsley. Concerned something has happened to her, I follow her over.

"Kins, sweetie, you have to remember," Quinn says, her voice laced with worry.

"I'm sorry. I only forgot for a second," Kinsley tells her with an adorable pout.

"What's wrong?" I ask, coming up next to Quinn.

"Kinsley is allergic to raw fruit." Quinn holds up the juice box. "It doesn't contain a lot of natural fruit, but I'd rather not take the chance. When she was a baby, I gave her fresh peaches and her lips puffed up. I rushed her right to the emergency room, but by the time we arrived, she had rashes all over her and was having trouble breathing. I'd never been so scared in my life. After running tests, they said she has OAS, meaning she's allergic to certain types of fruit."

"So she can't eat any fruit?" I ask. I had no idea a kid could be allergic to stuff like that.

"If it's cooked she can, but not raw," Quinn clarifies. "She has an emergency Epi-pen I keep in my purse, and one at school, in case she eats something by mistake that causes an allergic reaction."

"Too bad you're not allergic to vegetables," I joke, giving Kinsley a playful wink.

She laughs. "I'm allergic to carrots!"

"Only raw," Quinn adds with a laugh. "It's mostly fruits, but she is also allergic to carrots."

After everyone tells Kinsley how amazing she played, she thanks everyone for coming and hugs a couple of her cousins. I let Jase and Jax know that I'll see them at the shop later since I only work a half day on Saturdays.

Once everyone has left, and it's only the three of us, I pull Quinn into my side and whisper, "Can I take you ladies to lunch?" so Kinsley can't hear. A slow smile creeps up on her lips and she nods. Inside, I'm fist bumping myself. Every time she says yes, it feels like another victory in my book, another step to completely winning her over.

We head over to a café nearby to eat lunch. Kinsley spends the entire meal going over her game play by play, asking us what we thought and what she thinks she can do better next time. Afterward, Quinn offers to drop me off at the shop, since she and Kinsley are going to go meet with a friend of hers who is a realtor to show them some houses.

When I step into the shop, both Jase—who rarely ever works on the weekends—and Jax are waiting for me. "Back office," Jase grunts. Willow, who is pretending to dust the front desk or some shit, looks up and mouths *Good luck*.

"Make it quick," I tell them, "I have an appointment at noon."

"What are your intentions with our sister?" Jax asks, getting straight to the point once we're seated.

"To get to know her."

"You're aware she's almost forty, right?" Jase adds.

"So, what? She's too old to date? To fall in love? You planning on making her live the rest of her life alone?" I quip. When they both look at me like I have a third eye, I say, "Look, I like Quinn and Mini-Q, and I have every intention—"

"Wait, who's Mini-Q?" Jase asks, cutting me off.

"Kinsley." I smile. "You know? Because she's a mini version of her mother." I picture them both at lunch earlier, and how they rolled their eyes at the same time when I cracked a cheesy joke, and the way both their eyes lit up over the sundae I surprised Kinsley with for playing a good game. One has black and the other blue, yet when they smile, they sparkle similarly.

"True." Jase nods in agreement. "Okay, go on."

"I like them both, and I want to get to know them. I can't promise I won't ever hurt Quinn because I don't know what the future holds, but I can tell you right now, I would never do anything to intentionally hurt either of them. She told me about that fucker, Rick, and—"

"She told you about him?" Jax asks, shocked.

"Yeah…and if he were still alive, I would fucking kill him with my bare hands." Jase and Jax both grin.

"All right," Jase says, "I like you, and it's obvious you like our sister, but if you hurt her…"

"I know," I tell him, not needing him to finish his sentence. If I hurt her, I better be ready to find another job. But the fact is, if I hurt that woman in any way, I would never stay where she would have to see me. The last thing I want is for Quinn or her daughter to ever be hurt or sad in any way, let alone me being the cause of it.

Twelve

QUINN

I'm sitting on my couch with my phone in my hand, trying to decide what to do. After we left from having lunch with Lachlan, the plan was to meet with my friend Jenn, who is a realtor. I took photos of her wedding a few years back, and we hit it off. Unfortunately, she texted and apologized, asking if we could please reschedule for tomorrow due to a last minute emergency. I texted her back that I understood and told her tomorrow would be fine.

Then Kinsley begged me to spend the night again with her cousins. When I called Celeste, she told me she invited her over and forgot to mention it. Apparently they're going to the movies to see some new Disney flick. I offered to join, but Celeste told me to enjoy another night to myself.

I've thought about texting Lachlan to see what he's up to, but I don't want to appear too clingy. It's not like we're dating, and even if we were, I imagine couples his age aren't attached at the hip twenty-four seven. Although, he did refer to himself as my boyfriend to my family, so there's that...

Putting my phone away, I grab my iPad and pull up the book I'm currently reading. I'm not even through the current page when the front door swings open—much like it did last night—and in walk Jax and Willow.

"Hey!" Willow says, stopping in front of me. "Kinsley asleep?"

"She's actually sleeping over at Celeste and Jase's again."

"Wow! Two nights in a row with no Kinsley. What are you going to do with yourself?" she jokes. "You should come out with us." Instantly, my head is shaking of its own accord, but Willow raises her hand to stop me. "It's been over ten years since you've been out. I remember when I first started at Forbidden Ink... before Rick. You used to be the life of the damn party."

"That was a long time ago." *I was still in my twenties...Practically a lifetime ago.*

"So what?" She waves her hand dismissively. "Put on a sexy dress and some heels, and come out with us."

"I was actually thinking of texting Lachlan," I admit.

"Well, then you can surprise him because he's going to be there," Jax says, coming back down the stairs in a fresh outfit. "His cousin Declan surprised him by flying back in today from Ireland, and we all decided to go out to welcome him home."

"You know his cousin?"

"Yeah," Jax says. "He hangs out with everyone."

"I don't know..." What if he gets annoyed that I showed up there without letting him know? What if he's out with someone else? The thought makes my stomach sink. Just because we're getting to know each other and he gave me the best orgasm of my life this morning doesn't mean I can just show up and stake a claim on him.

"Stop overthinking this," Willow says. "C'mon, let's get dressed. You can put on a little makeup and brush your hair." She laughs at her own joke as she grabs my hands and pulls me up.

"I should at least text him so he knows I'm coming," I insist.

"Okay, so text him. Let's go!"

An hour later, dressed in a black off the shoulder dress and black heels with makeup on my face, and my hair curled into loose waves, I walk into Assets, an upscale night club in the Upper East Side. I texted Lachlan to let him know I was coming, but he never texted me back. I'm assuming he couldn't hear his phone over the bass of the speakers in this place.

Following Jax and Willow through the throng of people, I glance around the club for Lachlan, seriously hoping I didn't make the wrong decision in coming here. Any time I would offer to accompany Rick on his trips or to his business dinners, he would get a huge attitude, telling me I was too clingy, and if he wanted me to go, he would ask. I know now that a lot of the reason for his reaction was because he was cheating on me, but I still can't help but question everything I do now. Lachlan is young and carefree. The last thing he probably wants is an older woman dampening his fun.

"Stop overthinking this," Willow repeats as we approach a table that is filled with people. Immediately, I spot Evan and Gage, who work at the tattoo shop. From working there as their receptionist on and off for years, I've become good friends with both of them. Since I don't know who the other men and women are, and I don't see Lachlan anywhere, I head over to Gage, who smiles when he spots me walking over.

"Well, look who it is!" he shouts. "Am I seeing shit, or is it really Quinn Crawford in a dress, at a club?" He stands and embraces me in a hug.

"Yeah, yeah!" I laugh, and it feels good. I forgot what it was like to go out, without my daughter, and act like someone other than a mom. "How about you come with me to get a drink?" I might as well get a little bit of alcohol in my system to help me let loose.

"Gage!" a petite, brown-haired woman squeals, sidling up next to him and putting her arm around his waist—clearly staking a claim. "Who's this?" She bats her mascara-covered lashes, and I stifle a laugh. I'm probably a good fifteen years older than her. She must know I'm hardly competition.

"I'm Quinn," I say politely, "Jax's sister." I nod toward my brother who is leaning over and taking a shot from the center of Willow's chest. *Gross!*

"Cool!" she exclaims. "I'm Courtney, Gage's girlfriend." Realizing I had no idea Gage has a girlfriend, I suddenly feel like a horrible person. Even after Rick died, I didn't really make a huge effort to stay in touch with the people I used to be close to. Sure, I see Gage when I visit the shop—which isn't really often because I'm always working or taking care of Kinsley—but I haven't taken the time to find out how his life is going, what he's been up to. I was so relieved to be out from under Rick's hold, yet I never took the time to put the pieces of myself back together again like I promised myself I would do. I'm functioning, I'm mothering, I'm working, but I'm not actually living.

"It's nice to meet you," I tell her. I'm about to excuse myself to get a drink when Evan comes over and gives me a hug.

"It's been awhile, woman!" he yells over the music.

"I know," I agree, pulling back.

"Aren't you going to introduce me?" an Irish accented voice says. When I look over, I spot a guy, similar in features to Lachlan—same green eyes and ginger hair, but a much shorter beard. He's also a bit shorter than Lachlan, but not by much. His accent is a tad bit more pronounced than Lachlan's, but still nowhere near as heavy as the Irish people in Sons of Anarchy.

"Declan, this is Quinn, Jax's sister." Declan's eyes widen fractionally, and I briefly wonder if Lachlan has mentioned me.

"Nice to meet you," he says, just as a woman comes over and puts her hand on his forearm. She looks almost identical to him, only more feminine. "This is my sister, Riley. She's in town, visiting."

"Hey, I'm Quinn." I give her a small wave.

Another female comes over on the other side of Declan and gives his cheek a kiss. "Hey, baby, I was looking for you."

"Sorry, I came over to meet Jax's sister, Quinn." He tilts his head my way. "This is Venessa." When he doesn't give her a label, she frowns but doesn't say anything.

I give her a five finger wave as well. "I'm going to go grab a drink from the bar. Does anyone want anything?"

Everyone who's paying attention shakes their head no, so I head over to the bar by myself. I'm halfway to it, when I spot Lachlan standing over in the corner of the bar with a young, blond woman. He's leaning against the side of the bar, and she's standing extremely close to him. Her hand is resting on his forearm, but he's not touching her. I can only see their profiles, but they look to be in the middle of an intense conversation.

My first instinct is to run and hide, and that really pisses me off because that's what the Quinn post-Rick would do, and I don't want to be that woman anymore. At the same time, I don't want to be the young Quinn who would've confronted him right here, making a scene. So instead I do what I think the thirty-nine-year-old Quinn should do. I continue my walk over to the bar and order a drink. I'm generally a whisky kind of girl, so when the bartender asks what I would like, I tell him just to give me a double of whatever they have local, on the rocks.

After he hands me my drink, and I hand him my card, I take a sip. The whiskey goes down smooth, and I wonder which one it is.

"Excuse me?" I yell to the bartender before he walks away after dropping off my card and receipt. "Can you tell me who makes this?" I point to my glass.

"Bryson… That's Rye," he shouts back. Bryson? Where do I know that name from? I glance over at Lachlan, who is still in the same spot, still talking to the same woman, and it hits me. That's his last name. Hmm. Could it be?

"Thank you." I write down a tip, sign the paper, and take my drink back over to the table. Declan, Riley, and…what was her name? Oh! Venessa…are sitting at the table, but everyone else is on the dance floor. I decide I'm going to enjoy my drink and then head home—that way it won't feel like Lachlan has chased me away, and I can call it a win.

"What are you drinking?" Declan asks when I sit across from him and Venessa and next to Riley.

"Whiskey." I smile and take a sip. "Bryson Rye," I add. Declan's eyes widen, confirming my suspicions. Someone in Lachlan's family owns a distillery. I want to ask him about it, but I would rather learn about Lachlan and his family from Lachlan himself.

"Quinn?" I recognize the voice without even having to look at him, and if I'm honest, I'm scared to look. If I see that girl attached to his side, I know it's going to hurt like hell. Not that I didn't see this coming from a mile away, but with all the convincing he's been doing, I guess a part of me started to believe what he was selling. Stupid me.

"That's me," I say, taking another sip before turning to look at Lachlan. "In the flesh." When our eyes meet, I see the girl he was talking to is standing next to him, shooting daggers my way.

"What are you doing here?" he asks, and the walls I've kept erected for the last several years, the same ones I now realize I've lowered to let Lachlan in, fly back up. This is exactly why I haven't dated, why I've chosen to focus on raising my daughter. Because no matter how much I want to leave Rick in the past, he's still very much in the present.

Haunting and taunting me from the dead. Controlling my thoughts and actions and feelings.

"I…" I take a deep breath, reminding myself that Lachlan isn't Rick, and I'm no longer in a position to allow any man to make me feel weak. I'm allowed to be here. I'm a grown woman, and this is a public place. Sure, I came here with the hope of seeing Lachlan, but my brother and Willow and Gage and Evan are also here. I don't *have* to be here for him.

"Where's Kinsley?" Lachlan asks before I can answer his first question.

"She's at my brother's for the night." My eyes flicker from Lachlan to the woman standing by his side. Her hand brushes up against his arm, in an attempt to get his attention, and it makes me realize one thing: Despite every reason why I shouldn't be, I'm already falling hard for him. The question is, will he really be there to catch me like he said he would be?

Thirteen

LACHLAN

I can't take my eyes off of Quinn. The few times I've seen her, she's either been dressed professionally or dressed down—in sweats or jeans. She rocks both like a beautiful boss. But right now, even though she's sitting at the table, I can tell she's in a dress. One of her shoulders is exposed, showing the thin black lacy strap of her bra. I know it's her bra because it's the same one she was wearing last night. She's also wearing makeup. Not that she needs it, but the bit of color around her eyes make them appear mysterious. And her hair...it's no longer in her signature messy bun thing she's always sporting. It's down in waves. My gaze momentarily drops to her legs, which are half under the table, one crossed over the other. She's wearing tall as fuck heels. Jesus, she's fucking sexy.

When my eyes meet hers, I notice her pouty lips are glossy and...frowning. Why is she frowning? Just as I'm about to ask what's wrong, a hand touches my forearm and it all clicks. Shea is here, and Quinn must've seen us. Fuck!

"Lachlan, are you going to introduce us?" Shea asks, and Quinn's frown deepens.

"I was actually just leaving," Quinn says, downing the last of whatever she's drinking. "Have a good night." When she stands, I'm able to see her entire body. Her black dress covers all the important parts, yet shows off every single gorgeous curve. The top half is loose, but the farther down you go, the tighter the dress gets. As she saunters past me, my gaze falls to her backside. The woman can definitely fill out a dress like no other.

"Lach!" Declan yells, snapping his fingers in front of my face, and snapping me out of my thoughts. "She just walked away."

"Fuck!" I yell. I was so busy fantasizing about her, I blanked out. I start to chase after her when Shea grabs my arm and holds me back.

"You're not seriously going after that *woman* are you?" Her face contorts into a look of disgust, and I can spot her jealousy from a mile away. She came to the states in hope of getting back together, and she was pissed to learn I've moved on. Even if I hadn't met Quinn recently, I wouldn't be willing to give Shea and me another chance, but knowing there is another woman, pisses her off.

"Hell yeah, I am," I say, pulling my arm out of her grasp and running after Quinn. I'm searching everywhere for her, when I spot her talking to her brother and Willow at the bar. Jogging over, I stop in front of them. Quinn's back is to me, so she doesn't see me coming, but Jax and Willow do and both are glaring.

Not wanting to startle Quinn, I call out her name, and she turns around. "Can we talk, please?" I plead, but I can see it in her face, she's not going to give me the time of day. If I want her to listen, I need to act quick and talk fast. "What you saw wasn't what it looked like." When she flinches at my words, I internally groan. I sound like every guy who's ever been caught cheating, and Quinn has been cheated on. Damn it!

"That came out wrong." I place my palms up in a placating manner. "That woman you saw is my ex, Shea." Quinn's eye widen slightly, but she does a good job at staying emotionless. "She showed up here without me knowing. Her best friend is Declan's sister, my cousin, Riley. I was already here when they arrived, and she cornered me at the bar, asking to get back together. I told her no. I even told her about you."

"You don't have to explain anything to me," she says so softly I can barely hear her over the loud thumping of the dance music. "We aren't together or even dating. Hell, I don't even know *what* we are. You can talk to whoever you want." She keeps her voice devoid of any emotion, but I can see the hurt in her eyes. I promised to never hurt intentionally, and while this isn't intentional, she's still hurting because of me. Because of my drama. Drama she doesn't need to deal with.

"I disagree," I tell her. "Everything that happened with us last night and this morning means we are definitely something." Her eyes flit from me to her brother. I forgot he and Willow were even standing there.

My sole focus is fixing this shit with Quinn. I'm not about to lose her before I've even gotten her, and especially not over my fucking ex.

"We'll let you two talk," Willow says, pulling Jax away.

Stepping closer to Quinn, I say, "We might not have officially placed a label on us yet, but that doesn't mean nothing is going on. I don't just go around eating women out. I told Willow I'm your boyfriend because that's what I want to be." I take another step toward her and grip the curve of her hip. "You're the only woman I'm talking to." I brush my lips across hers, tasting the fruit-flavored lip gloss she's wearing. "You're the only woman I'm kissing." I lean into her and nip the bottom of her earlobe, eliciting a shiver out of her. I love the way she reacts to me. "You're the only woman I want, Q." She exhales deeply. "Don't leave, please." I bring my face back up to hers. "You're standing here in this club, looking sexy as fuck in that black dress and those heels. Dance with me."

She takes a long moment to answer, but just as I'm beginning to lose hope, she nods once. "Promise me one thing."

"Anything." And that's the truth. I've only known this woman for a short time, but I would do anything for her.

"If you ever decide you don't want me anymore, or you want someone else, please let me go." She bites down on her bottom lip, and her eyes go glossy. She didn't ask me not to cheat on her. She didn't ask me to tell her if I do. She asked me to let her go. Because her fucknut of an ex strung her along while he cheated on her. She felt trapped when all she wanted was to be set free.

"It's never going to happen—"

"Lachlan, please," she cuts me off, begging, and fuck if I don't want to slam my fist into something right now.

"But," I say emphasizing the word to make it clear I wasn't done, "if I ever do, I promise to let you go." The words taste sour on my tongue, but I know she needs to hear them. And when her shoulders visibly sag in relief, it's confirmed. "Now will you please dance with me?"

Her eyes dart behind me, and I look back to see what—or who—she's looking at. I spot Shea standing by the table staring at us with her arms crossed over her chest.

"Ignore her. Come dance with me." Taking her hand in mine, I guide her out of sight of the table and over to an empty-ish area. The club is crowded as hell. It's a popular place, and it's Saturday night, but here in the corner, it's not *as* crowded.

Pulling her into my arms, I glide my hands down her curvy sides and land on her ass. Fuck, I love her ass. Quinn's hands link together behind my neck as she begins to grind her front against mine. Needing to taste her again, I bring my mouth to hers, tasting the lip gloss again, but when my tongue delves between her parted lips, I can taste the whiskey on her breath, and I know it's my family's. It has a very distinct taste to it, and the thought that she was drinking my family's whiskey has me wanting to take her right here and now. She moans softly into my mouth, finally kissing me back. My tongue sweeps past her teeth once again, finding hers. Tasting. Teasing. Our tongues find a rhythm as our kiss deepens.

Needing to be even closer to her, my thigh pushes her

legs farther apart, and I run my knee along the apex of her thighs, against her heat. "Oh, God," she groans into my mouth. I continue rubbing my knee forward and backward. Teasing. Tormenting.

"Lach," she moans, and I know she's coming. Her legs shake, and if I wasn't holding her, she would probably collapse. Our kiss breaks, and her head lands on my shoulder, her teeth biting down gently as she comes undone right here on the dance floor. And fuck if it isn't the hottest thing I've ever witnessed.

"I've made you come twice now," I whisper into her ear. "You're most definitely mine." She doesn't say anything, but I can feel her nod into my shoulder. "Let's get you home." Another nod.

After Quinn uses the restroom, we head back over to the table to let everyone know we're leaving. I feel bad that it's Declan's first night back and I'm bailing on him, but there's no way I'm asking Quinn to hang out with Shea. But when Declan gives me a slight head nod, I know he gets it.

"I'll see you back at home later," I tell him.

"I'll get Shea and Riley set up in a hotel," he tells me.

"Thanks, man."

I snag a cab, and even though Quinn insists she can get home on her own, I ride with her back to her place. When we arrive at her house, I ask the driver to wait a second, so I can get out and walk her to her door.

"Thank you for the dance," I tell her with a grin that makes her laugh. Pushing her up against the door, I lean in and nip her bottom lip. She giggles, and her hands, which are as soft as her lips, touch my cheeks.

"Thank *you* for the dance," she murmurs before deepening the kiss.

Wanting to be a gentleman, and still trying to take shit slow, I reluctantly pull back, breaking the kiss. "Call me."

She nods in understanding. "Okay."

Fourteen

QUINN

It's Saturday night and Kinsley is in bed. She was feeling a bit under the weather and conked out early, giving me some time to finally work on my edits. This week has been literally one failure after the next. After the horrible-turned-amazing evening with Lachlan at the club, I met with Jenna Sunday morning. When we sat down and went over my finances, I learned that even with Rick's money, I can't afford a home where my siblings live. Well, I could, but it would mean having to use the money from my savings, and since I don't make enough to afford the house with my income, I would eventually run out. I had no idea Cobble Hill was so expensive. In order to buy, or even rent, I'll have to be willing to move to another area, and that will mean Kinsley switching schools. I thanked Jenna for taking the time to go over it all with me. I know a lot of realtors would just want the commission. I told her I would think about it, and she offered to send me over several listings that are in my price range.

The rest of the day was spent visiting several of those listings, to which Kinsley whined and cried that she loves her school and would die if she had to leave it. Yes, she actually said she would die. When we got home, she told Jax, who assured her she wouldn't have to switch schools. Which caused Jax and me to get into our first fight ever when I told him he had no right to tell her that.

My week did get a bit better when Celeste called in need of a last minute photographer when hers canceled due to a family emergency. I spent the day with Celeste and Skyla—who co-owns Celeste's company, Leblanc, Inc—it's made up of several mini-companies which focus on clothing, makeup, and jewelry. I was thrilled to learn how much I would make from doing the shoot, and it made me see that I might need to branch out to more than just weddings and family shoots. While I love doing them, I need to think about providing for my daughter, and weddings and engagement shoots just don't bring in enough. When I brought it up to Celeste, she told me she would hire me in a heartbeat, and that the only reason she never suggested it was because she didn't think I wanted to go in that direction. She's already scheduled me for several upcoming shoots.

Thursday took a nosedive when my daughter's teacher called to let me know that Kinsley punched a boy in the stomach and would have to go home until Monday. I learned he's been picking on her, and she had enough. I explained that we don't put our hands on anyone, and Kinsley said she understood. I also let her teacher know of the situation.

When I told Kinsley there would be no electronics or soccer this weekend because of the choice she made, she cried and went straight to her room. Sometimes being a mom is hard.

Friday, I photographed a wedding, and Ember watched Kinsley. She's a college student at NYU and has been babysitting Kinsley for the last couple years. And that leads me to tonight. I'm in my comfy cotton pajamas, exhausted as all hell, and determined to get these edits done, so I can look at some more of the listings Jenna sent over. When the doorbell rings, I set my laptop down and walk over to the front door to answer it, and standing there, looking sexy as all hell in his Forbidden Ink T-shirt and jeans, is Lachlan.

And no, he wasn't mentioned in any of my recollection of the week. Why? Because when I texted him Sunday night, asking if he could talk, he texted me back: **No.** I was a bit thrown by his clipped response, but didn't want to assume anything, so I texted him back: **Later?** And when he responded with another **No,** I took the hint.

I thought about asking him why, but I was too upset. And if I'm honest, I was afraid he would tell me it's because of his ex, Shea. He had promised to let me go if he decided to be with someone else, so maybe that was his way of doing so. On the other hand, he could've texted a bit more explanation. But if he doesn't want to talk to me, then I'm not going to beg. I spent years begging Rick to love and want me, and the only thing it did was make me look pathetic and give him more power. So, instead, I responded with two letters of my own: **OK**

"Hey," he says, giving me a nervous half-smile.

"Hey," I say back. "What's up?"

"Can I come in?"

"Sure." I open the door for him, even though I don't want him here. He steps into the house and walks straight to the living room.

"Is Kinsley here?"

"She's upstairs sleeping."

"Okay, so, I just wanted to say…" He digs his hands into his pockets, and his arms stretch out, the muscles flexing. It reminds me of last Saturday, when we had finished eating and Kinsley asked if she could feed the ducks some bread. She said her feet hurt from playing soccer, so Lachlan picked her up and placed her on his shoulders. She giggled and kicked, and he carried her like she weighed nothing.

My gaze goes from his muscles to his eyes and see he's staring at me with his brows raised. Shit! While I was drooling over his arm-porn, did I miss what he said to me?

"Can you…umm…" I clear my throat. "Can you repeat what you said?"

"I said, even though things didn't work out with us, I want you to know that I really did like you. I think you're beautiful, and I hope that, despite what we did last weekend, we can still be friends."

"You could've just texted that," I say, not understanding why he felt the need to come here. But maybe *this* is his way of letting me go. He still could've done it through text, though.

"I would've, if I had your number." He gives me a confused look. "I asked Jase for it, but he told me if you wanted me to have it, you would've given it to me, so I figured I would just come over and say what I needed to say in person."

This doesn't make any sense. "I texted you my number Saturday night when I was on my way to the club...and Sunday." Grabbing my cell off the coffee table, I pull our message thread up and show him. "You never responded to my text Saturday night, and you made it clear on Sunday that you didn't want to talk."

"Quinn," Lachlan says slowly, taking the phone from my hand. "I didn't text you that. I never got a single message from you." He clicks around on my phone, then I hear it ringing. A few seconds later, someone answers.

"Hello." We both look at each other, confused.

"Who's this?" Lachlan asks.

The person on the other line giggles, clearly a child, and then there's shuffling. "Hello?" an older voice comes on the line. "Who's this?"

"My name is Lachlan. Who answered your phone?"

"I'm sorry, do I know you?" the woman asks.

"No, I think I called the wrong number," he says before he hangs up. I look over his shoulder as he pulls up his name on my contact list and curses under his breath. "I gave you the wrong number." He backspaces the last digit which was a nine and inputs a six. He hits call, and less than a second later, his phone is ringing in his pocket.

"I thought you changed your mind about us," he says, handing me back my phone.

"I thought the same thing," I admit. "When you...well, the fake you...responded like that, I thought maybe you didn't want me anymore. I thought about asking you why, but..." I take a deep breath, preparing myself to give him more truth. "I used to beg Rick to be with me. To stop putting me down and to love me." Tears fill my eyes before I can stop them. "I thought that maybe after everything…and with Shea being back…" I release a harsh sigh.

"Fuck, Q." Lachlan pulls me into his arms, and for the first time in a week, I finally relax. "I didn't know." Stepping back, he picks me up and carries me over to the couch, setting me down into his lap. "Shea is staying at a hotel. I haven't spoken to, or seen, her since the club. What did I tell you Saturday night?"

"I know what you said," I say, willing the tears to stop, "but I figured that maybe once you stepped back, you realized you didn't want me after all. People can change their minds. I mean, she's really freaking pretty and skinny and all girly, and I'm, well, I'm…" I wince as I say the words, not able to even finish my sentence. Even though I've been thinking them, saying them out loud makes me sound so ridiculously jealous and insecure.

"Finish your sentence," Lachlan demands.

"You know what I'm saying."

"I want to hear the words," he pushes. "Say them. Finish the damn sentence."

"Fine! I'm fat. Shea is skinny, and I'm fat! Why would you want me, when you could have her?"

Lachlan takes a calming breath, and then says, while looking me in the eyes, "This has to stop. I hate what that fucker did to you, and I'm sure it was worse than what you've said. But I'm not him, and you aren't overweight or ugly. I'm not saying there's anything wrong with an overweight woman, but you are so far from fat, it's ridiculous."

He cups my cheeks with his hands. "You. Are. Gorgeous. No more comparing yourself to my ex. She doesn't exist in what we have going on here. Got it?"

Before I can verbally answer him, Lachlan presses his lips to mine, and I sigh into his mouth, completely content at being in his arms and kissing him.

When the kiss ends, Lachlan glances over at the laptop and leans over to grab it. "Did you take these pictures?" On the screen are photos of a newlywed couple standing in the garden where they were married. She's dressed in an elegant, white gown, and he's in a tux. The image is of them laughing together.

"I took it without them realizing," I tell him. "She had just tripped in the grass over her high heel and he caught her."

"It's a really good picture," Lachlan says, clicking from image to image. "It's like you can feel every emotion through their expressions." He stops at one where the husband is looking at his wife, but she's looking down at her dress, fixing it.

"It's easy when two people are in love."

"Still, it takes someone who knows what they're doing to capture it."

"It's like you and tattoos," I point out. "You take an idea, sometimes a crappy drawing, and turn it into a masterpiece."

Lachlan grins. "You know…" He sets the laptop back down and twists me around so I'm straddling his lap. "Your daughter trusted me enough to tattoo her." He waggles his eyebrows.

"One, she's five, so she trusts easier. She hasn't experienced real life yet. And two, I haven't gotten a tattoo done since…" My throat clogs with emotion when I think of the last tattoo I got. When I came home and *he* saw it and lost it on me. I don't even realize I've turned my face away from Lachlan in shame until his cool fingers are gently touching my chin, and he's bringing my face back up to look at him.

"Since you were with him." Lachlan finishes my sentence for me. "Fuck him, Quinn." He brushes his thumb down my cheek and then across my bottom lip. "Fuck. Him. You're a beautiful woman who should be covered in art if that's what you want. And one day, you're going to trust me enough to let me ink *my* art on your body."

Lachlan reaches around behind my head, grips my hair, and covers my mouth with his. My body melts into his touch, and if I were listening to my hormones, I would not only let him ink me, but let him do whatever the hell he wants to do to me. But I've learned the hard way that I need to be smarter than that. I need to listen to my heart, but also my head. My body might trust Lachlan, but my head and heart aren't completely there yet.

The kiss is slow and gentle. His strong calloused hands cup my jaw, and his tongue massages mine. I lift his shirt, sliding my palms over the ridges of his abs. His skin is hot, and I crave his warmth. When I let out a soft moan, it seems to spur him on. His hands leave my face, and we break our kiss just long enough to pull each other's shirts over our heads.

His lips find my neck at the same time my fingers thread through his hair. He trails soft, open-mouthed kisses down my neck and chest. Then he pulls the cups of my bra down, one and then the other, exposing my erect, pink nipples. Wrapping his beautiful lips around one, he sucks it into his mouth, and the sensation zaps straight to the apex between my legs. My thighs clench, and my butt grinds down, revealing the large bulge in his pants.

Lachlan's lips move to my other breast, sucking and licking my nipple. I haven't the slightest clue how it is that he's sucking on my breast yet it feels like my pussy is on fire. When I grind down again, needing relief, he bites down on my nipple and I yelp, which reminds me we're sitting in my living room, where my brother and Willow can walk in at any time, or my daughter can come out of her room and find us.

"Lach," I try to say through a moan. When he bites down on my other nipple, sending waves of pleasure straight to my core, I grab his face and push him back. "We can't do this out here."

He looks around as if just now realizing where we are. Picking me up, he takes me upstairs to my room, closing the door behind us. Laying me on the center of the bed, he tugs my pants and underwear down my thighs, and then gripping my ankles, pulls me to the edge of the bed, so my legs are dangling down.

My brain goes mushy, my only thought being how much I want and need this man.

Bending over me, Lachlan's lips softly caress mine before he travels south, laying kisses along the center of my chest, one to each breast, my belly, and finally the hood of my pussy. He leans in and inhales deeply. My breathing becomes embarrassingly labored, my chest rising and falling quickly. I'm in shock that he just smelled me...there! *Who does that?*

Spreading me wide, Lachlan stares at my pussy for a long minute. "Fuck, Q, you smell so good, and you're so damn wet." He swipes his finger down my center and brings it to his lips, wrapping his mouth around the glistening wet digit, and licking it clean. And I about come on the spot. *Who is this man?*

A whimper escapes my lips, and Lachlan grins, staring back down at me. "You taste delicious." He swipes his finger back down and licks it again. "So perfect," he murmurs.

"Lachlan," I groan, unsure what I'm even wanting to say.

"What's wrong?" His brows furrow. "Do you want to know what you taste like?" When I gasp in shock, his mouth tips into a half-smile that has my insides heating up. How can one look, a simple touch, affect me in such a big way? He runs his middle finger down my center once again, this time slowly, then brings it to my mouth. "Open," he commands, and I do. My lips wrap around his long digit, and I suck on my own arousal. My eyes stay glued to his, and his are glued to my mouth. When I pull back, he licks his lips. "Perfect, right?" It's a tad tangy, and not all that sweet—not really a taste I would personally find delicious—but if he thinks it tastes good, more power to him.

He backs up slightly without waiting for a response, places my legs on top of his shoulders, and then his hot mouth begins to lick me so skillfully, with so much precision,

I'm squirming in pleasure, silently begging for my release within seconds. His fingers push inside me, massaging my insides intimately, and then I'm coming. Bright lights behind my lids burst through the dark as my body comes completely undone.

When I open my eyes, Lachlan is wiping his mouth and beard with the back of his hand, a satisfied grin splayed upon his lips like he's the one who was just pleasured. And then it hits me that he's now made me come three times without even asking or suggesting to be pleasured back. And that thought has me wanting to satisfy him the same way he's satisfied me.

Sitting up, I turn my body around so I'm on my stomach and my head is in the direct line of his crotch. Lachlan, the intelligent guy he is, catches on quickly, and his eyes go wide. "Quinn," he whispers as I pull him closer to me.

"My turn," I murmur, unbuttoning and unzipping his pants.

"Okay, but there's something you need to know."

"Not now," I say, on a mission to please him. Pushing his jeans and boxers down, his dick, hard as a steel pole, springs free and hits his stomach. It's thick and smooth, neatly trimmed, with only a single vein running along the underside. I've only been with a few guys, so I don't have a lot to compare it to, but it's perfect. And then a small sliver of metal catches my eye, and I gasp.

"You're…you're…"

"Pierced."

"Holy shit," I breathe, entranced by what I'm seeing. "Can I touch it?"

Fifteen

LACHLAN

"Can I touch it?" she whispers, and I have to will myself not to come from her words alone. This woman, she has no idea how fucking beautiful and sexy and goddamn motherfucking perfect she is. The way she tastes and smells. The sound she makes when she comes all over my fingers and tongue. I can't get enough of her. Sure, I'm a guy who's attracted to a woman, so of course I want nothing more than to sink into her hot, tight cunt. But at the same time, I'm completely content to just make her come. Every time I give her attention, she soaks it up like she's dying of thirst. She eats up every compliment like she's starved. And all I want to do is nourish the fuck out of her by bringing her pleasure and giving her the happiness she deserves.

"Yeah, you can touch it," I tell her, taking a small step forward. She's lying on her belly, her elbows holding her up with her plump ass and smooth back on display. Her bra is still on, but her tits are spilling out of it, exposing her pink nipples. Her legs are cross-legged, dangling in the air. If I wouldn't look like such a perv, I would pull my phone out and snap a picture of her so I never forget how she looks right now. So goddamn beautiful, and all. Fucking. Woman. How she can even begin to compare herself to Shea is fucking stupid. Yeah, Shea is skinny and blond, and she's definitely easy on the eyes, but she isn't even in the same league as Quinn.

Tightening her fingers around my shaft, Quinn runs her sexy mouth across my Prince Albert piercing. A smidge of precum drips out and lightly coats her lips. I watch as her curious tongue darts out to taste it just before she parts her lips and gives the head of my dick a soft kiss. I groan, and she smiles a shy smile. Gently closing her mouth around my piercing, she tugs on it playfully, glancing up at me from under her thick lashes. Her tongue darts out and licks my slit, and I nearly come on the spot. Watching her explore my body is a fucking turn on. Not just because she's touching me, but because I can see it in her eyes as she becomes more comfortable with herself, with me.

"I want to suck you," she says, "but..." She sighs softly, and her eyes fill with liquid. What the hell just happened?

"Hey." I pull her up so she's kneeling on the bed. "What's going on?" My eyes dart back and forth between hers.

"I don't want to bring *him* up..." Her gaze drops down, and she doesn't even have to finish for me to know this is about that piece-of-shit.

"Tell me," I insist. "We can't get past it if I don't know."

"He said I wasn't good at it. I think…" She inhales then exhales. "I think maybe he cheated on me because I wasn't good at satisfying him." She bites down on her bottom lip, and it takes everything in me not to punch the drywall in. What *man* makes a woman feel like she isn't perfect? Makes her feel as though she can't do anything right? Single-handedly takes her confidence and self-esteem and destroys it? A piece-of-shit asshole who needs to bring his woman down, in order to make himself feel better, that's who.

"Quinn," I start, but she cuts me off.

"Could you just maybe…if I do something you don't like…can you tell me, please?" she pleads. And I can hear the words she doesn't speak. *So you don't resort to cheating on me.*

"Look at me," I implore, needing her to understand how serious I am. "I will never cheat on you. Ever."

"You can't possibly…"

"No!" I boom, and regret it when she winces. "I'm sorry," I say softer, gliding my hands down the smooth flesh of her hips and pulling her into me until she's so close, my dick is nestled between her legs. "There is not a single, tiny, minute possibility of me ever cheating on you. You are mine, and I am yours. And as long as you keep letting me come around, you are it for me. I don't care what you say or do. I don't give a shit how badly you piss me off, or if you push me away a million times. I will never touch or look at another woman besides you. Got it?"

"Got it," she says with a nod.

"Now, listen carefully," I say, grabbing two fistfuls of her ass and rocking my hips against her heat. "You simply *choosing* to wrap your perfect lips around my dick makes me the luckiest fucking bastard in the world. Everything you do once you're down there is merely a bonus." I shoot her a playful wink and her cheeks tinge that beautiful shade of pink I love.

"Okay." She concedes with another nod. "Sorry…" She winces. "I just totally killed the mood, didn't I?"

"You didn't kill anything, baby." I have Quinn kneeling on her bed, with her heavy tits hanging out of her bra, and her entire lower half bare and rubbing against my hard dick. "Feel this." I grind my dick against her. "It's hard as granite. That's what you do to me." I press my lips to hers briefly, then tell her to lie down. "I want to make you come again."

"No." She shakes her head. "You already did it three times. It's my turn."

"This isn't a game, Quinn. We're not keeping score."

"I know, but I want to."

"Keep score?" I tease.

"No." She giggles. "Make you come." She pushes me back slightly, then climbs off the bed, dropping to her knees. And without any warning, she damn near takes my entire dick down her throat. She gags softly, and the sound almost has me shooting my load straight down her throat. She pulls up briefly then sucks me back down. And with renewed confidence, my girl sucks my dick like she's out to win a fucking award for Best Head Ever Given.

When my balls begin to tighten, and my dick starts to swell, I know I'm close. Not wanting to come down her throat—for her sake, not mine—I entangle her hair in my fingers and pull her mouth off my dick. Her lips come off with a pop, and a bit of saliva drips down her chin. The sight has me losing my mind, and before I can stop myself or warn her, my cum is shooting out and covering her luscious tits.

She watches with fascination, and once I'm done, she leans forward and licks the head clean. "You taste better than I do," she says with a wink, and I know without a shadow of a fucking doubt, I'm keeping this woman for eternity.

Once we're both cleaned up, we go back downstairs to watch TV. Quinn is snuggled into my side with her head on my chest when the front door opens and in walks Jax and Willow. Willow smiles, and Jax grimaces. I laugh at how cranky he is over me dating his sister. I know he supports us being together, but he refuses to show it. When Quinn doesn't acknowledge them, I glance down and see her eyes are closed and she's sleeping.

"Night," Willow whispers.

"Keep it down," Jax adds.

I finish the episode we're watching of Gilmore Girls—yeah, yeah, I know…not very manly, but in my defense, I needed to know if Rory and Dean end up hooking up even though he's married. Spoiler alert: they do—and I'm about to carry Quinn up to bed, when I hear a child cry out. Remembering Kinsley is here, I wake Quinn up.

"Kinsley's crying," I tell her, already standing to go to her. She quickly shakes off her sleep and flies up the stairs behind me. When we get to her room, I let Quinn go in first.

"Oh, Kins!" Quinn rushes to her side.

"I threw up everywhere," Kinsley cries.

"Shh…it's okay," Quinn tells her. She places her hand on her forehead, then turns to me. "Can you grab me the thermometer? It's in the top drawer."

"Yeah." I rush out of the Kinsley's room and into Quinn's. She has two nightstands and a dresser. She didn't specify which top drawer, so I open her dresser drawers first but don't find anything aside from some shirts and her pajamas. I move to the nightstand on the side of the bed she sleeps on and open the top drawer, finding nothing but her underwear in there. I'm about to close it, when I spot something. Grabbing it out of the drawer, I examine it for a moment. It's rose gold and has a power button, but when I press it, it doesn't turn on. It has a thick handle and a silicone top to it. It almost looks like something a doctor uses to check your ears.

"Lachlan!" Quinn yells out.

"Coming!" Uncertain if this is it, I check her other nightstand just to be sure, and when I only find a couple baby photos of Kinsley in the drawer, I figure this must be it.

"Hey, is everything okay?" Willow asks, stepping out of her room.

"Kinsley isn't feeling well," I tell her, walking toward Kinsley's room. "Quinn is in there with her."

"Oh, no! Let us know if she needs anything."

"Will do."

When I get inside Kinsley's room, Quinn is removing her soiled clothes. "Here ya go." I hand her the thermometer. "I couldn't get it to turn on." I shrug. "Thermometers have gotten a whole lot more techy since I was a kid."

Quinn laughs and turns to grab it. When she spots it in

my hand, she jumps to her feet, her entire face glowing red. "Oh my God!" she shrieks. "That's...that's not a thermometer." She snatches it from my hand. "I said the top drawer in the kitchen, not my bedroom!"

"Umm..." I say, having no idea why she's freaking out right now. "You didn't specify, actually. I just assumed." And then it hits me. Why is she blushing like I just walked in on her...

"What is that thing?" I ask, trying to get another look at it.

"Can you just go grab the thermometer, please? I'm going to get Kinsley bathed, and I need to change her sheets."

"Okay, want me to put that back?" I nod toward the *not*-thermometer.

"No!" she screeches. "I will."

Doing as she says, I find the correct thermometer, and while I can now recognize it as the actual thermometer, the item I grabbed is very similar in size and shape. The only major differences are the color and there's a screen on this one. After I give Quinn the correct thermometer, I grab Kinsley's soiled clothes and sheets and bring them down to the washer and turn it on. Then, I find the linen closet and locate some fresh sheets so I can make her bed. By the time I'm done, Kinsley and Quinn are coming back into her room.

"How you feeling?" I ask Kinsley who tries, and fails, to smile.

"I don't feel so well," she admits. "Can I go back to sleep, Mommy?"

"Are you sure you don't want to sleep in my bed?" Quinn asks.

"You know I like my own bed." Kinsley pouts.

"I know," Quinn tells her. "Here's the trash can in case you wake up again, and if you need me, just call out and I'll come running."

"Okay." Kinsley lays down and Quinn gives her a kiss on her cheek. "Will I able to go to school Monday?"

"Probably not," Quinn says with a frown. "But we'll see."

"Fine." Kinsley huffs and rolls over.

"Night, Mini-Q," I say. She rolls back over and gives me a small smile.

"Night, Lach."

When we step out of her room, Quinn walks next door to her room, and I follow. "Thank you for changing her bed," she says, grabbing her shirt and pulling it over her head. "I just need to change real quick. I don't know if any throw up got on me, but just in case." She sticks her tongue out and scrunches her nose.

"Not a fan?" I laugh.

"I hate throw up. Blood, I can handle just fine. But throw up." She mock shivers, then pulls a new shirt over her head. "I can't handle it, like at all."

"I should probably get going," I tell her, and she nods.

"Okay." She cuts across the room and encircles her arms around my neck. "Seriously, thank you." She presses her mouth to mine. "Where did you put the sheets? I need to throw them in the washer."

"Already in there," I say, giving her another kiss.

"Mmm." She moans. "A man who does well under pressure, changes puked-on sheets without being asked, *and* puts them in the washer. I feel like I've won the lottery." She giggles, and the sound goes straight to my chest.

"Speaking of which, what was that thermometer-looking thing I gave you by mistake?" When her cheeks stain pink again, my mind goes straight to the gutter. "Wait a second!" I laugh, removing her arms from around my neck and walking over to the nightstand.

"It's not in there!" she exclaims. "I left it in the bathroom."

"Was that... a vibrator?"

"Lachlan, stop!" she screeches, and I laugh harder.

"I've seen vibrators before and none of them looked like that. That was like some high-tech shit."

"It's a clitoral stimulator," she says matter-of-factly. When my lips upturn into a grin, she huffs. "When you're a single mom, and your pussy may as well be a graveyard, you have to bring in the big guns."

"A graveyard?" I ask, slightly turned on that she just said *pussy*.

"You know...because it hasn't gotten any action in so long, it might as well be dead."

I bark out a laugh at that, shaking my head. "You're fucking nuts." Then I think of something. "Have you used it since we started..." I waggle my eyebrows.

"No," she says pointedly.

"Damn right, you haven't. Because that techy shit can't compare to the orgasms I give you."

Quinn laughs. "That techy *shit* can make me come in

under a minute." She raises her brows.

"Challenge accepted." I pick her up by her ass and throw her onto the bed., peeling off her pants and underwear. Once she's completely bare to me, I give her a smirk. "Start counting now."

"Lachlan…Lachlan, you have to wake up," Quinn whispers. I glance around the room, taking in my surroundings. I'm at her place, in her room, in her bed. We must've fallen asleep. Grabbing my phone from the nightstand, I check the time. It's five in the morning.

"We fell asleep," she says softly. "You have to go before Kinsley wakes up."

Nodding in understanding, I give her a kiss on her cheek, then roll out of bed, throwing on my shirt and jeans, then slipping on my shoes.

"I'll walk you out," she offers, but I shake my head.

"No, go back to sleep." I lean over the bed and give her a kiss to her forehead. "Want to do something later?"

Her face lights up with a bright smile. "Yeah." But then she frowns. "Actually, no. Kinsley will most likely wake up still sick."

"How about I go home, shower and change, and then come back with breakfast? We can rent some movies and make it a lazy day so she can rest."

"That sounds perfect," she says, pulling me back down

to her for a kiss.

A couple hours later, I return with breakfast from a deli nearby. Kinsley and Quinn are both up, and Kinsley is lying on the couch, looking like someone told her that her favorite puppy has been killed.

"You okay, Mini-Q?"

"I feel blah," she says. "Mommy said you're going to watch movies with me. Can I pick it out?"

"Of course."

"Okay." She grants me a bright smile that's identical to her mother's. "I want to watch Mary Poppins." I have no clue who Mary Poppins is, but I tell her that sounds great. After Quinn gets the food sorted and we eat, we spend the entire rest of the day watching movie after movie together. In between, the girls share their likes and dislikes. They tell me about the trips they've taken and want to take. I share with them a little bit about my family and friends. About my time in Boston. We have lunch and dinner together.

It's such a simple kind of day. We didn't really do anything, yet at the same time, it's also absolutely perfect. A day I hope to repeat many more times in the future.

I've just finished a two-hour-long session and am stretching my arms over my head, when Jax walks through my door. "Hey man, got a minute?"

"What's up?" I stand and walk to the back to get a drink.

"I wanted to talk to you for a second."

Glancing at my phone, I see it's a quarter to five. I don't have any more clients scheduled, so unless someone walks in, in the next fifteen minutes, I'm done for the day. It's Saturday, so I'm off tomorrow, and looking forward to hanging out with Quinn and Kinsley.

This last week I've been hanging out at Quinn's place every second I'm not working or sleeping. I never spend the night, but we have dinner together if I'm off early enough, or dessert, if I get there after dinner. After Kinsley goes to bed, we hang out on the couch, talking, and eventually make our way to Quinn's room, where we make out like teenagers, but never take things further. I've learned that Quinn is submissive by nature until I coax her and make her feel comfortable enough to take charge, then she spreads her wings and flies. I know it's because of her ex. He probably got off on clipping Quinn's wings instead of letting her fly high. I can tell she's waiting for me to take things to the next level sexually, but I'm not going to do so until I know she trusts me—trusts what we have. So, every night after I've made sure she's satisfied, I kiss her goodnight and go home.

Thankfully, Shea has returned back to Ireland with Riley, so I don't have to worry about Quinn bumping into her, or Shea causing any problems.

I sit on the couch and shoot a text to Quinn to see if she wants me to pick up take out on my way over. Now that Kinsley is feeling better, I'm thinking we can order pizza or something. We've been eating healthy while she's been sick, mostly soup and foods she won't throw up. She was home from school through Thursday with the sitter, but went back to school yesterday, and was back to her usual self in time for her soccer game this morning. Her mom only let her play half the time, which bummed Mini-Q, but her scoring a goal during her time made up for it.

Jax sits next to me. "Willow and I have decided to move out of the townhouse." My head snaps up. They're moving? Is Quinn moving too?

"Quinn's staying," he says, answering my thoughts. "She's been looking for a place, but she can't afford anything in Kinsley's school zone."

"She hasn't mentioned anything to me about moving." We've talked about her work, mine, Kinsley, a lot about her past, but thinking about it, we don't ever discuss the future.

"She probably didn't want to say anything until she found a place. We bought the townhouse during the recession and fixed it up. It's now paid off, thanks to Quinn who insisted on paying it off when she sold her ex's condo and moved back in with us. She's been through enough. It doesn't make sense for her to have to find another place and switch Kinsley to a new school that might not be in a good area, when Willow and I can live anywhere." Jax shrugs like it's no big deal, and it makes me wonder something.

"Why didn't you guys get Quinn away from that asshole?" My question isn't meant to come out as an accusation, but even to my own ears, I hear the blame dripping from my words.

Jax sighs, scrubbing his hands over his face. "I know she was with him for four years, but it feels like it all happened so fast." He exhales harshly. "One minute she was dating him and the next she was living with him. He was rarely home, and when he was gone, she would come over. She would never complain or say anything bad about him. Her smile never faltered." He looks at me dead in the eyes. "I didn't see it, and I hate myself every day for it. I thought she was just busy doing her own thing. I should've looked deeper, asked more questions. It wasn't until her wedding when I knew something was wrong."

"What happened at her wedding?"

"Quinn is several years younger than us. She got her first tattoo at sixteen. I shouldn't have let her, but…" He shrugs, and I nod. We're tattoo artists. "She walked down the aisle in this hideous, frumpy-looking dress, man. It was white and expensive, but it wasn't Quinn. It covered every tattoo on her body." He curses under his breath. "She was proud of her tattoos before she met him. She used to wear clothes that showed them off. I used to yell at her all the time to put on more clothes." He laughs. "But she wouldn't listen. She lived in cut-off jean shorts and tiny shirts. An older brother's nightmare. When Celeste asked her why her dress covered them all up, she said she's older now and they look immature and trashy. She should've been beaming at her wedding, but she looked awkward and nervous."

"She's not proud of them now," I tell him. "Her tattoos…You know she's only gotten one tattoo since she's been with him? And it says, 'this too shall pass.'"

"Yeah, Gage tattooed that one. I don't think she wanted us to know, but Gage was worried about her. They used to be good friends. She wouldn't discuss anything with us. When she gave up her photography business to stay home, I could tell she was devastated, but she made excuses, saying it was for the best because they planned to start a family, and she wanted to be home with their kids. Looking back, that's all those four years with him were…one excuse after the next."

"I've never hated someone so much in my life," I admit. "Every time she questions herself or gets nervous. Every time she makes a comment about being fat or ugly. I want him to rise from the dead, so I can slowly murder him all over again."

"Yeah, well, I'm just glad he died before finding out about Kinsley. I can't even imagine what would've happened if she had to raise a baby with him. She said she thought about running, but the guy was loaded. He would've found her and fucked her over."

"Hey!" Willow exclaims, joining Jax on the couch. "Whatcha guys talking about?"

"Us moving this weekend." Jax throws his arm over Willow's shoulders and pulls her into his side. "We found a nice two bedroom condo and are renting to buy." Jax tells me. "We want to make sure it's what we want before we commit."

"Nice, need any help moving?"

"That's actually why I wanted to talk to you. Quinn is going to throw a fit when she learns we're moving, so we aren't going to tell her."

"So, you're what? Going to move out while she's gone?" I wince, imagining how pissed Quinn is going to be when she comes home and finds all their stuff gone.

"I know it sounds bad, but trust me, it's the only way. Otherwise, she'll try to move out first," Jax says.

"And let me guess…you want to use me as a distraction to keep her busy tomorrow while you move your stuff out."

"Bingo," Willow chimes in. "You guys are practically inseparable anyway."

"Fine, but when this shit creeps down, you better let her know, you made me." Jax and Willow both laugh.

When Quinn shoots me a message, saying that Kinsley wants to get a pumpkin to decorate, an idea forms. "I think I can actually give you tonight and tomorrow," I tell them. "I'll text you in a little bit and let you know for sure."

Sixteen

QUINN

"Are you going to tell us where we're going?" I ask Lachlan for the fourth time in twenty minutes, well aware I sound like my five year old, but too nosey and nervous to care. When Lachlan texted and asked if I trusted him enough to let him take us away, I didn't even have to think about it. I trust Lachlan with everything in me. And I loved that he was including my daughter. So, I packed Kinsley and me a bag, texted Jax to let him know we wouldn't be home tonight so he wouldn't worry, and waited for Lachlan to go home and get his stuff and then come to my house. He insisted on driving so I could relax, and I didn't argue.

"Nope," he says for the fourth time. "You'll see when we get there."

"Mommy," Kinsley says, looking up from her coloring book. "Can Lachlan come to my birthday party?"

"Your birthday is coming up?" Lachlan asks.

"Yep!" Kinsley squeals. "I was born on Halloween!"

"When's her birthday party?" he asks, his eyes darting from the road to me.

"Next Sunday," I tell him. "We always do it the weekend before Halloween, so it doesn't interfere with trick-or-treating."

"How long have you known about it?"

I'm not sure where he's going with this… "Invitations went out a few weeks ago."

"You haven't once mentioned it."

"It's not really a big deal." I shrug. "It's usually just her friends from school and family."

He nods once. "Got it."

When he goes quiet, I think about how I worded what I said. "I didn't mean it like that. I just didn't think you would be interested in going to a child's birthday party. I'm sure there are tons of adult parties going on with it being the weekend before Halloween." Lachlan's jaw ticks, and the act brings back memories of when Rick would get mad at me.

"Lachlan," I say softly, trying to keep my composure. "Can you tell me what's wrong, please?" This is when Rick would yell at me, blame me, and call me names. Mentally, I prepare myself for it, so I'm shocked when Lachlan takes my hand in his and brings it up to his lips, giving each of my knuckles a kiss. We don't show a lot of affection in front of Kinsley, but a few days ago when she asked if Lachlan was my boyfriend, we told her he was, and she seemed okay with it. I have no clue how this is all supposed to work, so I'm just going with my gut and taking it one day at a time.

"We'll talk later," he says.

"But…" I need to know what I did, so I can make it better.

"Not now," he insists, his eyes darting back to Kinsley. "I promise we'll talk later." He gives me a comforting smile that calms my nerves.

The rest of the drive is spent with Kinsley telling Lachlan all about her upcoming party, who's going, what the theme is, and what she's going to be for Halloween. He listens intently to every word she says, and responds as if whatever she's talking about is the most important thing he's ever heard. A little over an hour later, we're pulling up to what I assume is our destination. The sign reads: Westchester Bed and Breakfast.

We drive down a dirt road, and when we turn the bend, the most gorgeous cottage comes into view. It's two stories tall with a beautiful wrap around porch on the bottom floor, complete with bench swings. Lachlan parks the SUV and then goes around to the back to get our stuff out.

"We're sleeping here?" I ask dumbly.

"Yep. Grab Kinsley, and I'll grab the stuff."

The second we walk in, Lachlan's name is called, and a young, petite, blond-haired woman comes scurrying out from behind the counter to greet him. "Ay, my sweet boy," the woman says in a similar accent to Lachlan's, only much, much heavier. "It's been too long. How's your ma? Your da?" She hugs him tightly then backs up. "I feel like I haven't seen them in forever."

"They're good. They decided to stay in Galway through the holidays," he tells her. Then he turns to me and Kinsley. "This is my girlfriend, Quinn, and her daughter, Kinsley.

Ladies, this is my cousin Kiara. She owns this place with her husband, James."

"It's nice to meet you." I extend my hand to shake hers, a little shocked I'm meeting someone in Lachlan's family, and a lot giddy that she's so sweet.

"Kinsley, here, wants to get a pumpkin," Lachlan tells her.

"Yes!" Kinsley hops up and down. "Can we?"

"Well, Lachlan has brought you here during the perfect weekend," Kiara says, bending slightly so she's closer to Kinsley's level. "Tomorrow is the annual fall festival. There will be bounce houses, face painting, fresh popcorn, hay rides, and…there will be thousands of pumpkins to choose from."

Kinsley's eyes light up. "Thank you, Lachlan!" She runs over to him and hugs his waist. "I want to get a pumpkin so big!" She stretches her arms out wide as far as they can go, and Lachlan laughs.

"Whatever you want," he says, but when I shake my head, he adds, "as long as your mom says it's okay." His last comment has me laughing and Kinsley pouting.

"Let's get you guys settled in." Kiara walks back behind the desk and grabs a couple of keys from the hanging board. I love how old-school this place is. I love New York, but I also miss all of the country comfort that you find in North Carolina. "Quinn and Kinsley, you're in room 201, and Lachlan, I've put you right next to them in 202. They're on the second floor." She hands us our keys. "Here's an activity guide for tomorrow. Breakfast is served from six to eight, and lunch from eleven to one, but I imagine you will be at the festival during that time. If you need anything, just dial zero."

"Thank you," I tell her, taking my key at the same time Lachlan takes his.

To me, she says, "Kevin isn't here right now. He's running around, getting everything ready for tomorrow. It's an all weekend event. But please find us tomorrow, so I can introduce you." Then to Lachlan, she says, "I know he would love to see you."

"Sounds good," he tells her at the same time I nod.

Lachlan takes our suitcases up the stairs, and we follow him. When we get to my room, I unlock the door and let Kinsley run in. When I see it's not a single room, but a suite with a living room, and two bedrooms, I say to Lachlan, "We could've shared a room."

"If you don't feel Kinsley is ready to see me wake up in her home, she's not ready to share a hotel room." He kisses my forehead. "I'll hang out like I always do and then head over to my room to go to sleep." *Oh, this man...*

Kinsley picks her room, and since we haven't had dinner, we venture out to get something to eat. The entire town is as adorable as the B & B is, reminding me of Gilmore Girls. When we get back, Kinsley takes a bath and puts on her pajamas. She's excited to have a TV in her room and asks if she can lay down and watch a movie. I can tell by her yawn, she will be out within minutes.

"Would you mind hanging out while I shower real quick?" I ask Lachlan. He gives me a mischievous look, and I almost ask him to join me, but my self-doubt rears its ugly head, and I chicken out. We haven't even had sex yet. I think

Lachlan is trying to takes things slow for my sake, but a small part of me wonders if maybe he isn't as attracted to me as I am to him. I immediately chide myself for thinking like that. I've been working on being more positive lately and thinking like that is not a step in the right direction. I know Lachlan is attracted to me. I can see it in his eyes, in the way he kisses me and loves on my body. And if that's not enough, he makes it a point to tell me every day how beautiful I am.

"Sure," he says, eyeing me up and down. "I'll be right here." He kicks his Vans off and sits on my bed, leaning back against the headboard.

My intent is to shower quickly, but once the hot water is raining down on me, I take my time, washing my body and hair and shaving my legs. When I get out, I wrap the plush towel around my body. After brushing my hair and teeth, I'm about to drop my towel to get dressed when I realize I didn't bring a change of clothes in here with me. Taking a deep breath, I step out into my room.

When Lachlan's eyes leave his cell phone and land on me, his brows rise, and if I'm not mistaken his pupils might even dilate slightly. "I forgot my pajamas," I tell him, going straight to my luggage. After sifting through it twice, it's apparent I completely forgot to pack my pajamas. Damn it!

"Everything okay?" Lachlan asks.

"I forgot to pack something to sleep in." I pout. I only brought one outfit for tomorrow, and the clothes I wore today aren't exactly comfortable to sleep in. "Any chance you brought an extra shirt I could sleep in?"

"Sure," he says, but the devilish grin on his face contradicts his words. And when he stays seated, but leans forward and removes his shirt, I know why.

"I meant a clean shirt!" I say with a laugh.

"Beggars can't be choosers," he volleys back, extending his hand that's holding his shirt.

When I reach out to grab it, he doesn't let go. Instead he yanks on the material, tugging me toward the side of the bed. When I'm within his reach, he leans over and lifts me, plopping me down onto his lap so my legs are straddling either side of him. A laugh as I look into his gorgeous, flirty, emerald eyes.

"Mmmm…" He reaches around and grabs my towel-clad butt, pulling me closer to him. "I like this." He fingers the knot holding my towel together. With one pull, he could expose me completely. Sitting this close to him, I want to nuzzle my face into his neck, but I also really want to talk to him, so I decide to go with the latter.

"Can we talk?"

He looks up, meeting my gaze, and nods. "Yeah."

"In the car, you seemed really upset…"

Threading his fingers through my damp hair, he grips the back of my head and our mouths meet for a brief moment. In return, my arms snake around his neck and my fingers weave through his messy hair. The kiss lasts long enough for me to taste his cool, sweet breath, but ends far too quickly, leaving me wanting more. "I know it's going to take time," he begins, "but I can't help feeling like every time we take one step forward, you take two back."

When I attempt to pull my hands away, Lachlan's fingers wrap around my forearms, holding me in place. "No." He shakes his head, so I keep my arms around his neck. "I need you to stay with me, Quinn. I need you right next to me every step of the way."

I swallow thickly. "I hate this," I admit. "I hate the way I feel around you… and about you."

When his brows furrow in confusion, I explain. "You're twelve years younger than me, Lach. You're a single, good-looking guy with a good career. You could have your pick of any woman you want." I'm fully aware I'm back to being negative, but he needs to understand where I'm coming from. How different our lives are. "I just…I don't understand why you're sticking around. Why you would even want to go to my daughter's kiddie birthday party when you can be out living your adult life. Going drinking and dancing at the club." I inhale and exhale slowly, waiting for Lachlan to respond.

For a few seconds, he rakes his gaze over my face, as if he's trying to memorize my features. I begin to worry that maybe I've pushed him too far with my honesty and negativity. I worry what he's going to say in response to my question—my accusation.

But then he brings my face to his and whispers, "Because I'm falling in love with you," and my entire world feels like it's spinning. *He's falling in love with me…*

"What can I even give you?" I blurt out. "I have nothing to give."

"All I want and need is you."

Seventeen

LACHLAN

The second I tell her what I'm feeling, I regret saying the words. Not because I don't mean them. I do. I am one hundred percent falling in love with Quinn Crawford and her little girl. No, I regret them because I told myself I would take things slow, so she feels safe and secure. I swore I wouldn't throw caution to the wind. And confessing my love for her isn't exactly driving cautiously—foot tapping lightly on the brake while keeping at a slow and steady speed. It's more like pressing the gas pedal all the way to the floor and gunning it, ignoring the rising RPMs, and saying fuck it, with the windows down as I fly around the bends without once slowing down. It's risky as hell, and can easily send her running scared.

So I'm shocked as shit when Quinn responds to everything I've just laid out for her by attacking me. Her mouth crashes against mine, and her tongue delves between my lips. Her hands tug on the strands of my hair, and her hot cunt grinds against the bulge that's quickly thickening in my pants.

My hands, of their own accord, pull her towel apart and yank it from her luscious body, leaving her completely naked and vulnerable. When she doesn't try to cover herself up like she usually does, I smile on the inside. One step forward…

"I need you," she murmurs against my lips, her words sending warmth through my veins and setting my body on fire. Flipping her onto her back, my hands land on either side of her head, my arms caging her in. I kiss all over her body, worshipping every perfect inch of her: her face, her neck, her delicious tits, her delicate collarbone. Frantically, she undoes my pants, and I push them down, along with my boxers. Our mouths fuse together as I bury myself to the hilt in her slick, hot cunt. It's never felt like this before. This perfect, this real, this fucking raw. This woman is it for me. I can feel it in every fiber of my being. She and her daughter are all I need in this life to be happy.

A small whimper escapes Quinn's lips, and I swallow it down as I deepen our kiss, massaging and sucking on her tongue, tasting and devouring her.

Mine. She's all fucking mine.

"Lachlan," she whispers, letting me know she's close. My piercing is making sure of it. Her hips rise to meet mine, thrust for thrust, and I lose myself in this woman. *My* woman.

Breaking our kiss, I find the crook of her neck, trailing kisses downward and over her collarbone, licking and suckling on her skin. I don't want this to end. I want to stay buried deep inside her for the rest of my life.

Too soon, though, her fingernails dig into my back, and her walls clench around my dick. Her legs, which are wrapped around my waist, shake as she comes completely undone, taking me with her.

When we've both somewhat come down from our high, I reluctantly pull out of her. "Take another shower with me," I whisper, not wanting to let her go yet. She nods in agreement.

Once the water is hot enough, we both step into the massive shower that comfortably fits us both. There are two shower heads, so we're both standing under the water. I watch Quinn for a moment consider how to hide her body. Her hands come up, and she's not sure where to put them, but when I smile her way, she relaxes, and I feel like we've just taken another step forward together. While we wash each other's bodies, we talk and kiss and laugh.

So simple. So fucking perfect.

When we get out and dry off, I give her my shirt to wear. When it drops over her head, the front is taut against her heavy tits, and her nipples poke through the thin material. The bottom goes to just below her underwear, and when she walks around the bed to get in, I can see the bottom of her ass cheeks peeking out. She looks fucking incredible. And all mine.

"We should probably have the obligatory safe sex conversation," she says, laying on her side. I'm so distracted by her in my clothes, her thick thighs bare and begging to be felt up, it takes me a second to put together what she's just said. But once I do, I bark out a loud laugh at the formality in her words. She sounds like my mom… And that makes me laugh even harder because she is a mom.

"I know you're older than me…" I give her a wink so she knows I'm joking. "But my parents already gave me the sex talk when I was a wee lad."

She smirks, but doesn't laugh. And of course she rolls her eyes. "And did they explain to you what happens when two people have sex and don't use protection?"

"Yeah…they make a baby…or catch crabs." I grimace at that last part. My parents really did have the talk with me, and my dad really did mention catching crabs. I was scared for months that I would have sex and some girl would be covered in red-clawed sea critters waiting to pinch my balls off.

"Oh, good," she continues, "so you do know the risks. Well, just so you know, I haven't had sex in over five years, unless you count my vibrator or dildo, neither of which can spread venereal diseases, so I'm clean." My brows rise at her mention of a dildo. I didn't see that in her drawer…

She keeps going, so I don't have time to conjure up the image of her lying, spread eagle on her bed, fucking herself with a dildo. I stow the thought away for later, though. "And since it took me nearly four years to get pregnant, we're most-likely okay, but in the future, we should probably use protection. I'm old, but I haven't hit menopause yet."

I'm almost positive there was a joke and maybe even some sarcasm mixed in with what she just said, but since I'm not exactly sure which parts are which, and I think overall she's being serious right now, I don't crack a joke. What I do, however, is imagine how sexy she would look with her

179

belly swollen with my child. How beautiful she would look rocking our baby to sleep. Jesus effing Christ, we've only been doing this thing for a few weeks. I shouldn't be okay with her falling pregnant, let alone fantasizing about it.

And holy hell, would my mom kill me if I knocked up a woman out of wedlock. But I can't help it. I don't care if it's been a few days, weeks, or months. I know what I want, and it's to spend my life with this woman. I want us to be a family. Maybe I should suggest we get married. Then we wouldn't have to use protection, and if she ends up pregnant, it would be all good.

When I look at her, looking at me, I notice her brows are furrowed, and her lips pursed together into a thin line. Is she scared of getting pregnant by me? I know she's in her late thirties, but a lot of couples have kids later on in years. Oh, shit! Maybe she's worried I'm not clean.

"I'm clean," I assure her. "I haven't been with anyone in months, and I was checked." I don't comment on being okay with her getting pregnant or that I just thought about making her my wife. She might run for the hills.

"I can make an appointment with my doctor to get on birth control."

"All right," I say, trying not to sound too disappointed. "Until then, I'll make a better effort to use condoms." I edge closer to her and hitch her top thigh above mine. "Even though I really, really enjoyed the feel of my dick inside you raw."

"Lachlan!" She slaps my chest playfully, her face and neck heating up.

"What? It's the truth." My hand moves between her

legs, and I rub my fingers up and down her pussy over her underwear. "I could feel everything. How slick and warm you were." Fuck, I can't get enough of this woman. I slip my fingers inside and flick her already swollen clit. She lifts her leg slightly to give me better access, and when I push two fingers inside, I find her soaking fucking wet.

"I know you liked it too," I tell her. "The way you could feel my piercing rubbing and coaxing that orgasm right out of you." I add a third finger, pushing them in and out of her tight cunt, and Quinn's breathing becomes labored. "It won't feel like that with a condom, you know."

Grabbing her by her hips, I pull myself up into half-sitting, half-lying position, bringing her with me, so she's straddling my thighs. I yank my dick out of my boxers and pump it a few times while Quinn watches with hooded eyes. "You know you want me inside of you with nothing between us." I continue to stroke my dick, but this time, I push the material of her panties to the side and rub my head up and down her center, massaging her clit with my piercing.

Quinn moans softly, grinding herself against my shaft and hand. And before I can taunt her anymore, she's rising and guiding herself over my dick, filling herself completely with me. Her hands go to my shoulders, and I watch in wonderment as she rides me, circling her hips and rocking back and forth, finding the spot she needs to get off. With one hand still on her hip, my other lifts her shirt over her head, exposing her body. As she fucks me, her tits bounce up and down in rhythm, taunting and teasing me to touch them. I capture one with my mouth, biting down on the hardened peak.

181

"Oh, fuck," Quinn groans, pushing herself up then sinking all the way back down. Her moans get louder the closer she gets to finding her climax. Leaning my head back against the headboard, I watch her continue to ride my cock, completely okay with being naked on top of me, exuding the kind of self-confidence that only a few short weeks ago was nowhere to be found. She's not worried about her weight or her looks, whether or not she's perfect. She's not concerned with our age difference or anything else. It's just the two of us, lost in the moment. *Three steps forward...*

"Come on, baby," I murmur. She's so close, but she's not quite there yet. Wanting her to get off before I do, I push my thumb against her clit. She's soaking wet, which makes it that much easier to take her over the edge. With only a few swipes of my thumb, Quinn is coming all over my cock, taking me along with her.

When she finally stills, her head lulls forward onto my shoulder. I can feel her body shaking with laughter. "That's the exact *opposite* of what was supposed to happen," she says through her laughter.

"Really? Because it was exactly what I was hoping would happen."

Mine. All fucking mine.

There's a knock on the door, and my eyes pop open, trying to remember where I am. I'm at the B & B, but when I glance over, I spot Quinn lying next to me. Shit! We fell asleep in her room, and I never went back to mine. As I'm scrambling out of bed, throwing my jeans on, the door opens and Kinsley steps into the room.

"Is Mommy asleep? I'm hungry." Her hair is up in a loose messy bun just like her mother wears, and she's half asleep. She also doesn't appear to be at all concerned that I'm in her mom's room.

"She is," I whisper, grabbing my shirt off the floor and throwing it on since Quinn never put it back on last night. "How about we let her sleep in, and I'll take you downstairs to get breakfast?"

"Okay." A smile tugs at her lips. "Can we bring her back food?"

"Of course. Go get dressed."

Once Kinsley is dressed, and I leave Quinn a note letting her know where we are, we head downstairs to eat. My cousin Kiara and her husband, Kevin, are walking around and talking to the guests. When they spot us, they come over to say hi.

"And who is this little girl?" Kevin asks to Kinsley, who I notice is hiding slightly behind me.

"This is Kinsley; Kinsley, this is my cousin's husband, Kevin."

"Nice to meet you," he says. Kinsley smiles shyly, but remains quiet. "The food is along that back wall. Take as much as you'd like and grab any open table."

"Sounds good, man. Thanks." I clasp him on the shoulder then head over to the buffet with Kinsley. "Can you make your own plate or do you want me to make one for you?"

"I can do it." She rolls her eyes. I hand her a plate, and she goes to town piling an assortment of foods onto her plate. Once there's no sign of a plate left, we find a table and start to eat.

"What are you looking forward to doing the most?" I ask her to make conversation.

She shoves a bite-size waffle into her mouth, and once she's swallowed, says, "Finding a pumpkin and decorating it. I hope there's a hay maze too! I saw one on a show and it looks fun. I also want to get my face painted."

I take a bite of my fruit-filled pastry and groan at how delicious it tastes. The peaches are fresh and sweet, and the pastry is flaky and baked to perfection. Kiara has always been an exceptional baker. When she lived in Ireland, she owned a small bakery that did very well. As I'm taking another bite, I look over at Kinsley. who is about to take a bite of the same pastry I'm eating. I don't even know how I remember, but the next thing I know I'm screaming for her to put the food down. She drops the pastry onto her plate, but she's already taken a bite.

"Shit!" I yell, not caring that I'm causing a scene. "Spit it out." I'm out of my chair and over to her with a napkin, trying to wipe the food out of her mouth. Kinsley is now in tears, and I'm terrified she's having an allergic reaction.

"Someone call nine-one-one," I yell.

"Lachlan!" I look over and see Quinn running over to us. "What's wrong?" she asks me. Then to Kinsley, she says, "Why are you crying?"

"She ate a pastry. It has peaches in it. I'm trying to get it out of her mouth." My heart is pounding so hard, it feels like it's about to thump right out of my chest. Am I having a heart attack?

"What's wrong?" Kiara comes over and asks.

"Kinsley is allergic to fruit," I tell her, "and she took a bite of the pastry. It has fruit in it. Call nine-one-one. She can die."

I glance around, confused as to why everyone is remaining so calm when there's a little girl whose throat could be closing right now.

"Lachlan, it's okay," Quinn says. "She's okay."

When I look back over to Kinsley, she still has tears in her eyes, but she's not hyperventilating or having trouble breathing. "She was crying," I point out.

"Because you scared me," Kinsley says with her brows knitted together. "I didn't know it had fruit in it," she tells her mom.

"It's baked," Quinn says, picking up the fruit I removed from Kinsley's mouth. "She's only allergic to raw fruits."

"Oh," I breathe, suddenly feeling really damn stupid because I knew that. "I-I'm sorry. I..." I look over to Kinsley. "I don't know what I would do if something happened to you, Mini-Q." The ache in my chest is still there in full force. If something would've happened to Kinsley, I don't think I would survive it. I've already grown to love that little girl as if she's my own.

Quinn takes my hands in hers and leans on her tiptoes to give me a soft kiss. "You have nothing to be sorry about," she murmurs against my lips. "Thank you."

"For what?" I just caused her daughter to cry and demanded people call for help for no reason.

"For caring about my daughter enough to remember about her allergy. When I walked in and saw how scared you were..." A single tear slides down her face. "I was terrified that something happened to my daughter. But there you were, taking charge, doing exactly what I would've been doing. Thank you."

She steps back and sits down at the table next to Kinsley. "Lachlan didn't mean to scare you, sweetie. He was worried the fruit would make you sick."

Kinsley nods in understanding. "It's okay. But can I eat it? It's really good."

Everyone laughs, and Quinn nods back. "Yes, you can eat it." She glances up at Kiara and Kevin, who are standing next to the table. "Sorry about all that. Kinsley is allergic to raw fruits."

"We're just glad she's okay," Kiara says. "One of the guests did call nine-one-one, but she's called them back to let them know it was a misunderstanding. All the pastries that have fruit inside have been baked with the fruit in them." She turns her attention to Kinsley. "Are you ready for a fun day at the festival?"

"Yep!" Kinsley exclaims, already over what happened. I sit back down, but I can't eat or speak or think. I'm still freaking the fuck out. I have no clue how Quinn manages to let Kinsley out of her sight for even a second.

As if she can hear the chaos in my head, Quinn looks over to me and smiles softly. "Are you okay?"

"I don't know how you do it."

"Do what?"

"Parent."

Quinn chuckles. "One minute, one hour, one day at a time."

"I would put her in a bubble and never let her out," I admit half-jokingly, which has Quinn throwing her head back in laughter.

"You'll make a wonderful father one day," she says, patting my arm.

Thankfully, the rest of the day goes more smoothly than breakfast. We pick out a couple of pumpkins and decorate them, get lost in the hay maze, where I'm able to sneak a few kisses with Quinn. Kinsley gets her face painted like a princess, and fills her belly with every kind of junk food imaginable. All too soon, it's time to head home. Kinsley sleeps the entire drive to my place, where Quinn gets out and kisses me goodbye before getting behind the wheel to head home. I text Jax to give him a heads up, and he lets me know everything of theirs is out and the house is ready for the girls.

Quinn calls me a little while later to let me know that Jax and Willow moved out. She cries over how generous and kind they are, and curses me—jokingly—for knowing about their plan the entire time. When Kinsley calls for her to tuck her into bed, we say goodnight.

Later that night, as I'm lying in bed, I wish I were with Quinn and Kinsley. Declan is over at his girlfriend's place, so my house is quiet. I want to be on the couch with Quinn cuddling into my side, in bed with her, stealing all of the blankets. I want to wake up and have breakfast with the two of them. The more time I spend with them, the more I miss them when I'm not with them. I fall asleep trying to think of a way to make Quinn—and Kinsley—mine, sooner rather than later.

Eighteen

QUINN

"I can't believe that after all these years we still can't keep a receptionist around longer than a couple months." I laugh as Jase complains of another temp not working out at Forbidden Ink.

"The only one who stuck around was Evan." Celeste cackles. "And that's only because I hired him."

"Yeah, because he's a tattooist!" Jase laughs, wrapping his arm around his wife.

We're sitting in the backyard of my townhouse under a tent that's been erected for Kinsley's birthday party. There are several kids from her class, as well as all of her cousins, running around and playing. There's a bounce house and a blowup slide, along with a new swing set. Earlier, they hit the piñata shaped as a Troll that Jax tied to a tree, and fought over the candy like they were participating in the Hunger Games. Now it's time for cake, but I can't seem to locate

Kinsley—or Lachlan—anywhere. A little while ago, she asked to show him her new swing set, but I don't see them over in that area anymore.

"Any chance you can work at the shop in the afternoons this week?" Jase begs. "Skyla and Celeste both switched on and off last week. We have a few people coming in to interview this week."

"Of course," I tell him. "The only thing I have this week are the shoots Monday and Tuesday for Leblanc, and a wedding shoot Friday."

"You're a lifesaver," Jase says, leaning over and giving me a kiss on my cheek.

"You know I love the shop."

"Plus, it now has Lachlan there." Willow waggles her eyebrows playfully.

"You and Lachlan?" Olivia gasps. "Isn't he a bit...young?" At her words, my face feels like it's being set on fire. While my family knows about Lachlan and me, and have seemed to accept it, Celeste's friends, Olivia and Giselle, didn't know. I know it's stupid to keep us a secret, but I'm still getting used to the age difference myself, and when you look at us, you can clearly tell there is one.

"So, what?" Giselle says, defending me. "Let the woman get her groove back."

"I'm not judging!" Olivia frowns and throws a chip at Giselle, then turns to me. "I was just shocked, that's all. I think the last guy I saw you with was Rick and he was older and...well, a lot different looking." Nobody besides my family knows anything about what Rick put me through, but hearing his name and having him be compared to Lachlan makes me want to throw up. Although, she is right. Rick was a good five years older than me, and obviously without a single piercing or tattoo.

"Lachlan is nothing like Rick." Jase grunts. "Thank fucking God."

Celeste puts her hand on his arm to calm him and says, "How are things going with you and Lachlan? When I was at the shop last week, he couldn't stop talking about you." She smiles softly. "He seems very taken with you."

"They must be doing good because Lachlan hasn't been home in weeks," Declan pipes up with a chuckle. Everyone's eyes swing to me, and I stand, suddenly feeling the need to flee. This entire conversation is just too much.

"He's gone before Kinsley wakes up," I say by way of explanation, not wanting to be judged.

"Hey, you don't have to explain yourself," Giselle says. "You do you, girl. Lachlan is definitely a looker." She waggles her eyebrows and her husband, Killian, growls. Everyone laughs.

"Yeah, and I bet he's stellar in bed!" Skyla cackles. "I read in Cosmo, a man is in his prime from twenty-six to thirty-four."

"Hey!" Jase and Jax both yell in unison. "Don't be talking about men and when they're in their prime!" Jase adds. "You're too young for that crap."

"Dad, I'm almost twenty-three." Skyla laughs. "But sure, we can pretend I'm not having sex." She rolls her eyes, and Celeste and I both cover our laugh with a cough. That girl will be giving Jase a run for his money as long as he's alive—and probably even once he's dead.

"I'm going to go find the birthday girl so we can do cake," I tell everyone, heading over to find Lachlan and Kinsley. When I spot them both in the bounce house, Lachlan is sitting against the side of the knitted wall, and Kinsley is bouncing up and down in the middle. I'm about to yell for them when Kinsley drops to her knees, her usual happy face, frowning.

"Do you have a mom and a dad?" she asks Lachlan. Curious as to where this is going, I step to the side, so I can hear them but they can't see me. Kinsley has been told her dad died before she was born, but she never brings it up.

"I do," he tells her.

"Where are they?"

"They live here, but they're in Ireland right now, visiting family. It's where I'm from."

"What's Ireland?" She tilts her curious head to the side.

"It's a country in another part of the world."

"My dad is dead," she says matter-of-factly. "When someone dies, they never come back. Ever." Her eyes are wide and her head is nodding slowly.

"That sucks," Lachlan says, even though I know he doesn't give a shit that Rick is dead. He's stated on several occasions that if he wasn't, he would gladly kill him.

"My friend Fiona's dad died too."

"I'm sorry. Death sucks."

"Yeah, he had…" She puts her tiny finger to her chin and taps it a few times. "He had cancer. I don't know what that is, but Fiona said it made him die."

"Cancer sucks for sure," Lachlan says.

"Yeah, but Fiona's mommy married another guy and

now he's her new daddy." Oh shit! I step into view, but I'm too late when Kinsley adds, "Can you marry my mommy and be my new daddy?"

"Hey guys!" I squeak out. "It's time for cake!" Lachlan and Kinsley both turn toward me, and I wince at how awkward I sound. Lachlan gives me a curious look, telling me he knows I heard what she asked.

"Okay!" Kinsley cheers, jumping out of the bounce house and running toward the picnic table with her cake on it.

"You heard."

"Yeah, sorry about that."

Lachlan climbs out of the bounce house and walks over to me. "You have a very observant and smart daughter. You have nothing to be sorry for. It would be my honor if one day you made me your husband and Kinsley viewed me as her father."

"Lach… We've only been…" My breathing picks up slightly. His admission has me at a loss for words. I don't know what to think or feel.

"I'm not saying now. I'm just saying that if one day it happened, I would be the luckiest fucking man in the world." He slants his mouth over mine, kissing me with such passion, I feel it all the way down to my toes. "I wasn't lying when I said I was falling in love with you."

"I'd like to get my belly button pierced," the bubbly, bleach-blond bimbo asks, twirling her hair around her finger.

"And I'd like to get my clit pierced," her equally bleach-blond bimbo friend adds with a giggle.

I've only been helping out at Forbidden Ink for a few hours and I'm already the hell over it. One thing I've learned is that because Lachlan is the newest hire, he handles the majority of the walk-ins, which includes the piercings…which are usually women. I already knew this rule, but I didn't think about the fact that at the moment *he's* the new guy.

So far today, he's pierced a woman's nipples and the hood of her pussy, tattooed a chick's hip bone, where she insisted on taking her pants off, leaving her in her barely there panties. Two of the women have left me their number to give to Lachlan, and one asked for his number right in front of me. He didn't give it to her, mentioning he had a girlfriend, but it still had me bristling. This is a freaking workplace for crying out loud!

I glance down at the schedule for today and see that Jax has an opening at the same time Lachlan does. "Sure, just have a seat and someone will be with you shortly."

Stomping back to Jax's room, I knock once, and he announces to come in. "How's it going?"

"Why must you guys pierce private parts?"

"Because we're a tattoo and *piercing* shop," he says with a confused look. A few seconds later, though, his lips tip up into a knowing smirk.

But before he can call me out, I say, "Well, you have two women who need to get *pierced*."

Jax laughs. "I don't pierce."

"You *can.*"

"But I don't," he volleys back, his smirk never faltering.

"Just because you're a part owner doesn't make you exempt from doing the gritty work once in a while," I snap. "Everyone else is busy."

"Everything okay in here?" Lachlan asks, and my back straightens. Oh, jeez, Jax, please don't embarrass me…

"Yeah, everything is good." Jax's smirk turns into a full blown grin. "My sister was just asking me to do a couple of walk-in piercings."

"I can do them, man," Lachlan offers. "I'm wide open."

"Really?" Jax laughs. "Quinn, here, said everyone else was busy." Damn him! What happened to the brother who treated me like a princess?!

"Quinn," Lachlan says, giving me a perplexed look. "I am open, right?"

"Yeah." I clear my throat. "Sorry, I forgot," I say dumbly. After glaring at my brother, who just cackles louder, I stomp out of the room past Lachlan.

"Hey, wait!" Lachlan grabs ahold of my arm. "What's going on?" He guides me into his room and closes the door, sitting down on his stool and pulling me into his arms. My body immediately relaxes, and I'm able to finally think clearly.

"I'm jealous," I admit.

"Of what…who?" He looks confused, but not mad. He never gets mad. Every time a weakness of mine plows through, he handles it with such patience. He may be several years younger than me, but he never acts like it.

"Of the women you're piercing and tattooing." I huff. "I swear you see more vagina and boobs than a gynecologist!"

Lachlan bites down on his bottom lip to stifle his laugh. "You know you're the only woman I want." He pulls my head down to his level and kisses me.

"Why do you put up with me?" I groan, fully aware I'm acting like a crazy person. "I'm such a hot mess."

"Because you're *my* hot mess," Lachlan says with the most adorable boyish grin. "Speaking of which, I talked to Jax. He and Willow are taking Kinsley Saturday night. I'm finally taking you out on a proper date."

"Really?" I beam. "Where?"

"It's a surprise."

When I pout, he laughs softly. "How about I do those piercings you mentioned and then we pick up some takeout and head home to relieve the sitter?" *Home*...the word coming out of his mouth sounds so right.

"That sounds really good."

After the blond bimbos leave, I head back to Lachlan's room. He's cleaning up his station, so I hop onto the tattoo chair and lie back while he finishes up. "I hope that chick's clit gets infected," I say half-jokingly, and Lachlan chuckles.

"You're so adorable." He throws several empty containers of ink into the trash.

"And that stupid girl who got those stupid seahorses on her hips. I hope when she gets pregnant and fat, they expand into killer whales."

Lachlan just laughs harder. "When are you going to let me tattoo you?" he asks, leaning over and kissing me. His lips are soft yet demanding, so damn perfect. My fingers tug on his strands of hair, trying to pull him on top of me. He chuckles into my mouth, but doesn't obey. "Not here, babe," he says, pulling back.

"See? You're already denying me. It's because you saw like fifteen pussies today, isn't it?" I pout, and Lachlan snorts in laughter. "It's not funny. You never say no to me."

"You want me to fuck you right here with your brothers in the other room?" His hand glides up my thigh and under the bottom of my shorts and panties, landing right on the hood of my pussy. "Fine," he murmurs, leaning over and slamming the door. Subconsciously, I know this is a very bad idea, but my hormones and jealously have taken over, and I just want to feel Lachlan inside of me.

He pulls my shorts and underwear down and then yanks my body so I'm sideways on the chair. He unbuckles his pants and pulls his dick out, stroking it a few times to get it hard.

"Flip over, baby," he commands. I do as he says, flipping onto my stomach and spreading my legs so my ass is in the air and I'm open for him. "Jesus," he growls. "This ass." He slaps my ass cheek and then pushes into me from behind.

Entwining his fingers into my hair, he yanks my head back and drives into me before he pulls back out. "Fuck, you're so tight. We're going to have to make this quick," he groans. "Rub your clit, baby." I bring my hand down to my clit and do as he says as he sinks back inside of me oh so slowly.

"Fuck me harder, please," I beg, needing more. And

with another hard smack to my ass, Lachlan starts to fuck me deep and fast. His piercing is nudging and stroking my insides, and it feels so freaking good. His lips find my shoulder, and he bites down hard. All too quickly, my orgasm slams into me. My legs shake, and my head lands on the edge of the cool leather seat. I ride out every wave of my orgasm as Lachlan finds his own release.

With his dick still inside me, he leans forward and whispers into my ear, "You're mine, and I'm yours, and whatever the fuck you need from me to understand that, I'll *always* give you. Even if it means I have to fuck the jealousy right out of you."

Nineteen

QUINN

I've changed my outfit no less than a dozen times. Since Lachlan refused to tell me where we're going or what we're doing, I have no clue how to dress. I haven't been on a real date in years—since a year after Kinsley was born and I attempted to date, only to quickly realize I wasn't anywhere near ready.

It's the first week of November, and a small cold front has come through, so I decide on a pair of dark blue ripped skinny jeans, a mauve off the shoulder sweater, and a pair of black heels. I figure with the heels, I can at least look a little dressed up if we're going somewhere nice. After straightening my hair, I grab my purse and head downstairs. It's so weird living here without Jax and Willow, but I also love having my own place. I would feel bad about them leaving if they weren't now living in a super gorgeous condo only a few blocks away from their shop.

There's a knock on the door, and since Kinsley left a little while ago with Willow and Jax, it has to be Lachlan. After applying a smidge of lip gloss, I swing the door open to find the most stunning man standing on my front stoop. His hair is messy as usual, but his beard has been trimmed so it's short and neat, exposing a bit of his chiseled jaw. He's dressed in a white button-down shirt with his sleeves rolled up, showing off the intricate tattoos that cover his forearms, and jeans that mold to his muscular thighs. And in place of his signature Vans, he's sporting wheat-colored boots.

When he clears his throat, my eyes swing back up to meet his sea-foam green eyes, and that's when I notice he's holding a gorgeous bouquet of white, pink, and purple flowers. My heart thumps rapidly against my ribcage as I take in the man in front of me—the man I was hellbent on not giving a chance to in the beginning because of something as stupid as our age difference. Who has turned out to be everything good in my life, giving me the confidence I never thought I would find again. Reminding me every day of how beautiful I am. Loving my daughter as if she's his own. And I know in this moment, I have hopelessly and irrevocably fallen in love with Lachlan Bryson.

"You look absolutely stunning," he says, his eyes remaining locked with mine. "These are for you." He hands me the flowers. "They're Gillyflowers," he says, and if I'm not mistaken, he looks almost embarrassed. "The florist said they mean happy life."

"You asked what the flowers meant?" I bring them up to my nose and inhale the fresh scent of them. I've never been given flowers before.

"Yeah, well, there were a lot of options." He shrugs. "And I've never bought flowers before."

"They're beautiful. Let me put them down and then we can go."

After putting the bouquet of flowers into a vase I find under the sink, I lock my door, and we head down the driveaway. "We can take my car," I offer. Lachlan shakes his head no, and that's when I notice there's a metallic blue BMW parked in the driveaway. "Is that your vehicle?" I don't know a lot about cars, but I do know that it looks to be on the expensive side.

"Yeah, I haven't really driven it since moving back to New York," he admits, opening the door for me so I can get in. The inside is gorgeous, all black leather and new-age electronics. I know he makes a decent living working at Forbidden Ink, but I'm not sure how he could possibly afford a vehicle like this and live in such an expensive condo. Suddenly, I feel like there's still a lot I don't know about Lachlan.

We drive for about twenty minutes, until we arrive in downtown Brooklyn. Lachlan parks and we walk over to a restaurant called O'Connor's. From the outside, it looks like one of the typical hole-in-the-wall restaurants that New York is littered with, but once we step inside, I'm amazed by the extravagance of the place. Elegant wood-panel walls, finished with crown-molding and high-vaulted ceilings are the first things I notice as we approach the hostess. When I glance around, I see an expansive bar off to the side. The back wall is mirrored glass, and the bar top is black shiny marble.

"Lachlan!" The woman manning the hostess stand comes around and gives Lachlan a hug. "It's been a while. Does Declan know you're here?"

"Yeah, he made a reservation for me," he tells her. I didn't even know Declan works here. Actually, I don't really know much about him or any of Lachlan's family. I know Lachlan's parents are in Ireland, and I think someone in his family might own a distillery. I know one of his cousins owns the B & B, but other than that, I don't know anything else.

"Perfect! Follow me to your table." She takes us to a small table in the back, away from the other tables. "Your waiter will be right with you." She hands us each a menu.

Once she's out of hearing range, I set my menu down and look at Lachlan. "You know, I was just thinking that you know my family and friends, but I feel like I don't know a whole lot about you."

"That's actually what tonight is about," he admits. "With my parents out of the country, I realized I haven't shared a lot about myself with you, so tonight our date will double as a crash course in everything Bryson." He winks playfully. "Starting with my best friend and cousin, Declan O'Connor."

"Hey, man!" Declan comes into view and clasps his hand on Lachlan's shoulder. "Quinn." He nods with a smile. "Welcome to O'Connor's."

"Wait!" I exclaim, putting the pieces together. "You own this place?"

"That I do." He grins. "Every Irish family needs at least one pub."

I can't help the laugh that escapes past my lips. "This is

hardly a pub." It's an upscale restaurant. I peeked at the prices on the menu, and they're no joke.

"Eh, semantics," Declan jokes, before bidding us a good dinner and excusing himself, just as the waiter comes over to take our drink order. Lachlan orders a water, so I do the same.

"Where I'm taking you next has alcohol," Lachlan explains.

"And where's that?" I have a feeling I know, but I want him to tell me.

"Not falling for that." He laughs.

"So, Declan owns a pub, and your cousin Kiara owns a B & B. Any other family members own any restaurants or hotels in the area?"

"Nope, although, my aunt and uncle own a corner store in Galway."

"Is Galway where you're from?"

"It's where my parents were raised."

When I grin, Lachlan asks, "What?"

"It's like that song by Ed Sheeran…Galway Girl."

Lachlan laughs. "I'm a guy."

"Yeah, but I bet you dated tons of Galway girls." I waggle my eyebrows, and he shakes his head.

When the waiter returns with our drinks, we order our food. I get the scallops, and Lachlan gets the steak. We spend the rest of the meal with Lachlan telling me about his aunts and uncles and all of his cousins.

"Declan and I are leaving the weekend after Thanksgiving for our cousin Emily's wedding," he says, taking a bite of food.

"That will be fun. In Ireland?"

"Yeah."

"How long will you be gone for?" I take a sip of my water, trying to ignore the sinking feeling in my stomach at the memory of every time Rick would let me know he was leaving. Lachlan isn't Rick, though, and I have to remember that.

"I told your brothers I'll be gone for five days: Thursday through Monday." He sets his fork down. "And I was hoping you would join me." My heart skips a beat at his words. He's inviting me to go to Ireland with him. To meet his entire family.

"Wow… Five days in Ireland sounds like a dream, but I have Kinsley." Just the fact that he invited me means the world to me. I want to explain that to him, but I don't want to bring up Rick and taint the moment.

"You can bring her," he says, as if it's a given, and my heart constricts at how amazing he is.

"That's so sweet of you, but she has school."

"She'd only miss a few days." He shrugs. "Just think about it, please. I would really love for you guys to meet the rest of my family. "

"Okay, I'll think about it."

After we finish dinner and say bye to Declan, Lachlan drives us to the next stop on our date. When we arrive, the parking lot leading up to a beautiful two story brick and mortar house is empty. I look for a sign but can't find one. I must've missed it when I was looking at the video Jax sent me of Kinsley playing the Wii.

Taking my hand in his, Lachlan guides us past a large

yard and up the wooden steps. He unlocks the door, and switches on the light. As I take in my surroundings, I'm not sure exactly what I'm looking at. I expected to see the inside of a home, but it's definitely not that. The two stories are completely open with mahogany wood walls and matching floors. There are several barrels turned sideways in the middle of the room, and when I walk to the wood railing and look down, I spot a... distillery?

"Is this where whiskey is made?" I glance at a barrel and read the logo branded on the side: Bryson Distillery. I was right! His family does own one. How cool!

"Yeah, gin too." He grins. "Come, take a look." He walks over to one of the barrels and shakes it back and forth. That's when I notice the barrel isn't like a normal barrel. It has a glass bottom so you can see the liquid sloshing around. Lachlan points to a small hole in the wood. "Put your nose up to it."

I do as he says and the aroma of the whiskey hits me hard. "Mmm...that smells good." I beam up at him. "I drank your whiskey at Assets," I admit. "It was delicious. I can't believe you guys make this!"

"I know. When I kissed you, I could taste it on your tongue." He grins devilishly. "C'mon, let me show you around. I had Salazar close the place early so I could give you a private tour." He winks and threads his fingers through mine.

"Who owns this place?"

"My family."

"I know that." I smack his arm playfully. "But I mean, your parents? Or extended family?"

"My parents and I own it."

We take the stairs down to the first floor and Lachlan explains each piece of equipment and how the process of making whiskey and gin works. He's so charismatic about it all, I have to wonder why he's tattooing instead of working here when he said he owns the place with his parents. I save my question for later, though. Right now, I'm enjoying getting the full tour. When we make it back upstairs, we walk through a shop of sorts that sells all of their drinks as well as some other goodies such as shot glasses and magnets.

"Is your whiskey and gin in a lot of stores?" I ask curiously.

"We're in most stores, bars, and restaurants on the East Coast," Lachlan says with pride. "When my dad moved here from Ireland to expand, his dad wasn't thrilled. He didn't believe he could make a living selling whiskey and gin in the United States, but my dad was determined. My mom said he would go from business to business offering free bottles for them to try. Over the years the business grew bigger and bigger, and now we're one of the largest distilleries in the east."

"That's amazing." Lachlan opens the door for me and we enter an open area with an expansive lacquered wood top bar and several matching tables and chairs. He steps behind the bar, so I follow him.

"Hop up." He grips the curves of my hips and lifts me onto the top of the bar. He separates my thighs and leans in to kiss me. When his lips start to move gently against mine, I sigh into his mouth. Reveling in his touch and his warmth. I can't remember a time before Lachlan came into my life when I felt so completely content. Now, I feel that way all the time.

"Whiskey or gin?" he asks, pulling back and taking his warmth with him.

"Usually I would say whiskey, but I'm curious about the gin."

"All right, one Red-Headed Ginger coming right up." He grants me a panty-melting, lopsided grin that has me cracking up with laughter. I watch as he pours the different ingredients into a metal cup, adds the ice, and then shakes it all together. He pours it all into a Collins glass when he's done, and hands it to me.

I take a sip of the red-tinted drink, immediately tasting orange and lemon. It's the perfect mixture of sweet and sour. "This is delicious," I tell him, taking another sip.

"Let me have a taste," he says, but when I try to hand him the glass, he sets it aside and pulls me closer to the edge so he's standing between my legs, his stomach right up against my center. And then his mouth is on mine. He kisses me like he's dying and I'm his lifeline. With every brush of our lips, I'm bringing him back to life. And he has no idea that he's doing the same to me. I'm finally living, and it's all because of Lachlan. "You're right," he murmurs against my lips, "it does taste good."

And then he's unbuttoning and unzipping my jeans. I lift up slightly, and he yanks them down my legs. My heels fall off, making a clacking sound against the tiled ground. "Let's see if you taste as sweet as the drink," he whispers, spreading my legs so I'm completely open and on display for him to do as he pleases. A few weeks ago, I would've shied away from something like this, begged him to close my legs, but now I welcome everything Lachlan does to me because I know when he looks at me, he sees me as beautiful, regardless of all of my flaws.

I close my eyes, waiting to feel his warm breath on me, so I'm shocked when, instead, I feel something cold and wet hit my center. When I look down, I see a piece of ice between Lachlan's lips. His head moves up and down, the freezing cold ice running along my slit and landing on my clit. When he swirls it around my already swollen nub, my body nearly convulses.

"Lachlan," I moan, having no clue what I'm even calling his name out for.

"What do you need, baby?" he purrs, pushing the melting ice into me. When I squirm, he chuckles softly. "Hold still." And then his tongue is hitting my clit, and he's lapping and licking me like I'm a popsicle on a hot day that needs to be devoured before it melts completely. With every swipe of his cold tongue, I'm pushed closer to the edge, and then I'm falling. My legs are shaking, and I'm writhing against him as warmth spreads throughout my entire body.

Before I've even come down from my orgasmic bliss, Lachlan is lifting me off the bar top and setting me on my feet. I faintly hear his pants unzip before he knocks my legs apart and thrusts deep into me. And then, once again, I'm coming completely undone as I lose myself to Lachlan Bryson. And I know in this moment, as he fucks me into oblivion, there is no turning back.

Fuck our age difference.

Fuck my being overweight.

Fuck Rick.

Fuck the rest of the world.

The only thing I can think about is spending the rest of my life being well and truly fucked by this perfect man.

"When's your birthday?" I ask Lachlan. We're lying in bed with our bodies entangled around each other. My head is resting against his chest, and he's drawing circles on my bare back. The sun is rising and we haven't slept a wink, but I can't find it in me to close my eyes. In a few hours, I'm going to have to get up and meet Willow, Jax, and Kinsley at the park for her soccer game, and I'm going to regret not getting any sleep. But right now, I just want to lay with Lachlan and learn all there is to know about him. I've been asking him random questions in between our heavy make out sessions—some of which end with him inside of me—and I love how he's an open book with me.

"On Christmas."

"Really?" I lift my head to look at him.

"Yep."

"That's cool. Kinsley and your birthday are both on holidays."

"It's not as cool as it seems," he says, his voice serious. "People always tried to give me one present for Christmas *and* my birthday." His lips turn down into an adorable pout, and I crack up laughing.

"Poor baby."

"Damn right. When's yours?"

"March fifteenth." I groan.

"What's wrong with your birthday?" He laughs.

"I'll be the big four-oh."

"Eh, don't fret. You're like whiskey, you get better with age." His chest shakes with laughter at his own joke.

"Ha ha, easy for you to say. What are you turning? Twenty-eight?" I roll my eyes, and even though he couldn't possible know I did so, he laughs and says, "One day your eyes are going to get stuck like that."

"Wow, you're just full of jokes, aren't you?"

His response, of course, is to tilt my face up and kiss me. "We should start getting ready soon. Kinsley's game starts in a couple hours. I imagine you're going to need coffee and something to eat."

"You don't have to go," I tell him. "We were up all night and you have to work today."

"I'll take a quick nap later, but I'm not missing her game." He gives the tip of my nose a kiss and shifts me off him so he can get up. "Shower with me?" He waggles his brows.

"Sounds perfect."

Twenty

QUINN

"I'll make the mashed potatoes, and you can make that cornbread casserole everyone loves." I'm having lunch with Celeste, Olivia, Willow, and Giselle, so we can discuss Thanksgiving, which is in a few days. We've decided to do one dinner at Celeste and Jase's place since their house is the biggest and has the largest dining room.

"Okay, great." Celeste types something into her phone.

"I'll bring the green bean casserole and sweet potatoes," Olivia adds.

"Perfect." I check the items off my list.

"I'll have my mom make the deserts," Giselle says. Her mom owns an upscale restaurant here in New York. The food is delicious!

"Jax and I can bring the rolls," Willow says with a laugh, and we all join in.

"I think that covers everything." I check my phone and

see it's almost time for Kinsley to get out of school. Her babysitter, Ember, took the week off to visit family, and the backup one has moved out of the state, so I've been picking Kinsley up every day myself. Today is her last day of school before Thanksgiving break. With the snow falling, making the roads slippery, I need to leave shortly so I'm not late to get her. A text vibrates on my phone, and when I click into it, it's Lachlan: **I miss you. Send me a pic.** I shoot him back a text, telling him I'm at lunch with everyone, but he texts back he doesn't care, which makes me laugh.

"What's so funny?" Celeste asks.

"Every time I'm not around Lachlan, he's begging me to send him pictures."

Giselle laughs. "Killian does the same thing!"

"Really?" Olivia asks. "Do you send them?"

"Of course, gotta keep his spank bank filled with me," Giselle quips.

"I would be so afraid of them getting lost in cyber space," Olivia says.

"I send them to Lachlan, but only ones of me clothed. He's asked for some nudes, but I feel like I'd need to edit them beforehand," I say, only half-joking.

"Oh! You should do a boudoir shoot," Celeste says. "That way he gets his nudes and they're done tastefully."

"That's actually a really good idea," I admit. "Lachlan's birthday is coming up. I could give them to him as a gift."

Celeste's face splits into a wide grin. "Well, look at you, getting all risqué in your old age." She winks teasingly. "You know Adam's husband, Felix, right? I think you've met him before." Adam is a model and one of Celeste's best friends, and Felix, his husband, is a huge well-known photographer. "Want me to see if he's available?"

"That would be great. Thanks," I tell her, feeling both excited and nervous.

"Have you decided yet, if you're going to Ireland with him?" Willow asks.

"Ireland?" Celeste questions. "You guys really are getting serious, aren't you?"

"He told me he's falling in love with me," I admit. "He asked me to go with him for a wedding."

"You should go!" Willow says. "You deserve a mini vacay."

"I do want to go, but I feel bad leaving Kinsley with you guys. He said I could bring her, but I hate for her to miss any days since she'll be out for Christmas break shortly after."

"That's what family is for," Celeste points out. "You have all of us. I bet Skyla would even stay with her if you wanted her to. It's okay to lean on us, you know." Hearing her say the words, knowing my family has my back, solidifies my decision to go.

"You're right. Thank you. I'm going to tell him yes." I send Lachlan a text, asking if the invitation is still available to join him in Ireland. A few seconds later, my phone rings. "Hello."

"Does this mean you guys are coming?"

"This means I'm coming."

"No Kinsley?" I can hear his disappointment through the phone.

"She has school, but my family said they'll watch her."

"I'll book our flights tonight," he says with a smile in his voice. "If you change your mind about her, just let me know."

"Will do."

We hang up, and when I place my phone down on the table and look up, I see four sets of eyes smiling at me. "What?"

"You are so in love with him," Celeste says in a sing-song-y voice.

I don't even bother to deny it. "I so am."

"Good morning, beautiful." Lachlan's words are accompanied by a kiss to my cheek. I snuggle deeper into his side, hiding my face so we don't have to wake up. I have no idea what time it is. The only thing I'm sure of is that I don't want to leave this bed ever. And then it hits me. Lachlan is in my bed...in my house...and Kinsley is home. Oh, God! We fell asleep again! We've been getting more and more careless lately. Lachlan keeps waking up a little later. And judging by the light shining in through the windows, unless a miracle has occurred and Kinsley is still asleep, she's going to see him leaving.

"You have to go," I stress.

Lachlan's body stiffens. "Shit!" he hisses. He shoots up into a sitting position and my head drops onto the pillow. "I set my alarm." He grabs his phone and swipes it open. "Damn it, I'm sorry, I set it for p.m. by mistake. You go down and distract her and I'll sneak out."

That's when I remember today is Thanksgiving. "You're coming back, though, right? For dinner?"

"Of course." He cups the side of my face and presses his lips to mine. "Declan said he and Venessa would be going as well, so I'll probably drive them over since I still have my vehicle."

"Okay." I pout, not thrilled that I won't see him until later.

"What's wrong?"

"What if I talk to Kinsley about us? She already knows you're my boyfriend."

Lachlan is already shaking his head.. "No, you said you weren't comfortable with her seeing a man wake up here unless you knew it was forever. One day I'm going to make you mine, forever, and then we will explain why we're all living together. Until then, I need to do a better job at sneaking out."

My shoulders droop in relief at how perfect this man is. "Okay, I'll go distract her." I give him a chaste kiss, despite wishing I had the time to devour him. "See you later."

I find Kinsley in her room, still in her pajamas and playing with her Barbies. I close her door partially so Lachlan can sneak out without her seeing. We spend the better part of the morning playing and then Kinsley helps me make the mashed potatoes to bring with us for dinner.

We arrive at my brother and Celeste's place, and I see Lachlan's BMW is already parked in the driveway. When we walk in, Kinsley immediately spots him sitting at the dining room table and gives him a hug. She and Lachlan have become close the last couple months, and it warms my heart to know she has yet another person in her life who loves her. I take a moment to say hi to all of the guys—and Declan's girlfriend—who are sitting on the couch watching football.

Both Nick and Killian are yelling at the screen, and I can't help but laugh. They both played several years in the NFL and always have a lot to say when a game is on.

After I'm done talking to Killian about the new ink he just got done, I walk over to Lachlan. "Hey you," I say, leaning down to give him a kiss. "Whatcha doing?" I look around and see several of the kids are drawing and painting turkeys.

"Painting my turkey." Lachlan laughs. "Hey, Mini-Q, want to draw one?"

"Yeah!" she exclaims, jumping into the empty seat next to him. He hands her a plate and explains how to trace her hand and then cut it out. I watch as she follows his directions to a T. When she starts drawing and painting the actual turkey, though, she frowns, her gaze flickering between Lachlan's finished turkey and hers. "Mine sucks." She pouts.

"Hey," he admonishes, cheekily. "You said a bad word. You owe me a dollar." The room erupts into a fit of laughter—well, everyone but Kinsley, whose brows knit together as she pulls a dollar bill from her pocket.

"Fine, but it's a waste of time because you'll curse soon and have to give it back." She slaps the dollar bill into his palm with an adorable glare. "My turkey looks so bad, and yours looks perfect." She crosses her arms over her chest. "It's not fair. You make tattoos, so you can draw." She huffs loudly.

"You're being kind of rude," I tell her. "Are you in need of a nap?" Every day after school, she goes home and takes a short nap to help her unwind from her day. We were busy cooking and playing today, so she never took one. It's about that time.

"I'm not a baby, Mom," she whines, her eyes darting around at all of the kids at the table.

"I didn't say you were," I point out.

"Why don't I help you draw it," Lachlan says, taking over, "and then you can paint it."

"Okay," she whispers, covering her mouth to hide her yawn. "Thank you."

Leaving them to do their own thing, I head into the kitchen to deliver the potatoes. Celeste and Skyla are standing at the double oven, taking the two birds out, Giselle is getting all the sides in order, buffet style, and Olivia and Willow are gathering up the plates and silverware.

"What can I help with?" I ask, and everyone waves me off.

"I heard you're going to Ireland with Lachlan," Sky says, walking over to me. "Go you, Aunt Quinn!" She laughs, and I roll my eyes. "I told Dad and Mom, I can watch Kinsley at your place, so she can sleep in her own room. I can take her to school in the morning and pick her up."

"Have I told you how much I love you?" I take Skyla's face between my hands and kiss her nose. It's hard to believe she's going to be twenty-three next year, which makes me realize Lachlan is closer in age to Sky than he is to me.

"What's wrong?" Sky asks.

"Nothing." I fake a smile, pushing down the self-doubt.

Lachlan told me he's falling in love with me. He spends the night, every night. No man jumps through the hoops he does, just to get laid by a woman twelve years his senior.

"Okay." She gives me a look that says she isn't quite buying it, but doesn't argue. "What time are you leaving Thursday? Do you need me to spend the night on Wednesday?"

"That would be great," I tell her, wrapping my arms around her for a hug. "I'm so proud of the woman you've become."

"Oh, stop!" She laughs. "I'm twenty-two and just recently moved out on my own."

"And you go to FIT fulltime, and will be graduating in May, while helping to run a multi-billion dollar company," I point out, which has Sky blushing with pride. "Like I said, I'm very proud of you."

Dinner is served, and everyone grabs a plate, piling food high, and then finding a seat at the expansive table. The kids have a separate table right next to us. Jase gives a small speech about being thankful for everyone here, and I can't help the tears that come. I don't know what I would do without my family. Jase and Jax have been there through everything: a dead father, a deadbeat mother, a cheating husband. Helping me to raise Kinsley. And now here they are supporting me as I find love.

"Hey, you okay?" Lachlan leans over and asks softly, giving my thigh a comforting squeeze.

"Yeah, just getting emotional." I laugh it off. "Thank you for being here." I press my lips to his cheek. "I love you." I still in my place, realizing what I said right after the words come out.

Lachlan turns to face me. "Do you mean that?"

"Yeah." I nod once. "That wasn't how I wanted to tell you, but yes, I do mean it. I love you."

He grins the most beautiful boyish grin, and cupping the side of my face with his hand, he says, "I've been waiting for you to catch up, beautiful. I love you."

Twenty-One

LACHLAN

"You have your cell phone?"

"Yes." She nods.

"Passport?"

"Yep." She nods again.

"Laptop to do edits during the flight?"

"Oh! I forgot that."

I chuckle as I watch Quinn run back upstairs, for the third time, to grab her laptop. It's four in the morning, and since our flight to Dublin leaves at seven, we have to get going, so we can get through security. Flying out of JFK is always a hassle, but during the month of December, it's exceptionally crazy. Luckily, it's the week after Thanksgiving and a few weeks before Christmas, so it shouldn't be too horrendous.

"Got it!" she whisper-yells, not wanting to wake up Skyla or Kinsley. "Oh! I need the adaptor!" She takes off running her sexy ass back up the stairs again, while I get the pleasure of watching. While she's up there, I spot Kinsley walking down the stairs, rubbing her eyes with her tiny fists.

"Everything okay, Mini-Q?"

"Yeah, I heard Mommy running around and I wanted to say bye." Her tiny mouth curls down into a sad little pout. "I'm going to miss you guys."

"We're going to miss you." I glance up the stairs and don't spot Quinn, so I kneel down in front of Kinsley and whisper, "I got it."

Her eyes widen. "Can I see? Please!"

Pulling the box out of my pocket, which reminds me that I need to stick it in my luggage before we go through security, I hand it to her.

"It's so pretty," Kinsley murmurs with a giant smile on her face. She's staring down at the three carat, platinum, princess cut engagement ring I purchased the day after Quinn told me she loved me—that was after I spoke to Kinsley and asked if she would be okay with me asking her mother to marry me and the three of us becoming a family.

She hands it back to me. "I really want to go with you guys," she says with tears brimming her lids, breaking my heart. If it were up to me, she would be getting on that plane with us, but Quinn is her mom, which means it's up to her, and I have to respect her decision.

"I know, but your mom doesn't want you to miss school. After I ask her, I promise we'll Facetime you on your iPad, though. Okay?"

"Okay," she agrees.

"Kins, you're awake?" Quinn comes jogging down the

stairs with her laptop under her arm and her cord in her hand.

"I wanted to say bye." Kinsley wraps her arms around her mom's waist. "I'm going to miss you so much," she says with heavy emotion clogged in her throat. It takes everything in me not to beg Quinn to let her go with us. She might not be my daughter, but I've grown to love her as if she's mine, and I hate the idea of her being upset in any way.

"Oh, sweetie. I'm going to miss you too. I'll Facetime you every day. I love you."

"Okay, love you more."

"C'mon, Kins," Skyla says, making her presence known. "Since you're up early, why don't we get ready and go to breakfast before school? We can go to our favorite donut shop." She waggles her eyebrows, and Kinsley's frown turns right side up.

"Okay! Bye, Mom! Bye, Lachlan," she yells, running up the stairs.

"Thank you," Quinn says to Skyla, giving her a hug.

"You're welcome. Have a good trip." She smirks at me, and I stifle a laugh. She was sleeping on the couch, so my guess is she heard Kinsley and I talking, and she knows I'm planning to propose.

The six hour flight to Dublin was spent with Quinn wrapped up in my arms while we talked, flirted, an even made out.

Purchasing first class tickets was the best decision I could've made. With only the two of us sitting next to each other, the flight was actually enjoyable. Since Ireland is five hours ahead of New York, we arrive at six p.m., and after renting a vehicle—where I splurged and got a BMW M5—the same model as mine, only newer—we drive the two hours from Dublin to Galway.

When we pull up to the Glenlo Abbey Hotel, Quinn is lying back in her seat, but when she spots the two-story manor that's situated on several acres of lush green property, she pops up and gasps. I chose this hotel because I knew she would love the restored castle. It was originally a church, and then it was bought and turned into one of the most luxurious hotels in Galway. Tourists, who aren't even staying here, will make the drive just to get a look at the castle in person. I imagined Quinn taking a million pictures here.

"Lachlan," she breathes, "this place is amazing! This is where we're staying?"

"It is…but only for two nights. My mom asked that we stay with her the night before the wedding and the next night."

"We could've stayed there the entire time."

"I know, but I wanted some time with you alone."

We pull around to the side of one of the bays, and park, so we can go check in. Quinn, as I expected, pulls her camera out of her carry-on and starts snapping pictures as we walk up the steps. "I can't believe how gorgeous this hotel is. It looks like an old church."

"It's a restored church," I tell her. "Wait until you see the inside."

We're greeted by a butler who takes our luggage and guides us to the front desk. When I give the woman my name, she confirms we're staying for two nights in the Grand Suite. I hand her my credit card, and when she gives me the total, Quinn gasps. I was hoping she wouldn't know the Euro to US dollar rate conversion, but judging by the look on her face, she knows. Quinn and I haven't talked money—not what she or I have. I know she's well off by the car she drives and the designer labels she wears, but we haven't had an actual conversation about it. Truth be told, I don't really give a shit about money, which is why I rarely spend any, and is probably the reason I have so much of it.

After taking the key, and being told our luggage will be brought up shortly, we head upstairs to our room. Quinn is quiet the entire time, and I know she's itching to ask how in the world I'm able to afford luxuries like a BMW, a condo in Hell's Kitchen, first class tickets to Ireland, and a hotel that costs a night what some pay a month for their mortgage.

When we step into the suite, Quinn stops in her place to take it all in. The entire suite is over six hundred square feet with a separate living room and bedroom. In the living room, the furniture is elegant with mahogany wood and gold trim, giving the room an enchanting feel to it. The bedroom has a large king size four poster bed with crisp white sheets and is topped with a plush duck feather duvet—and no, I don't actually know this shit. I read about it when I was booking it.

"Lachlan, I don't want to sound like some gold-digger—" Quinn scrunches her nose up adorably— "but how are you able to afford all of this?"

"I'm a damn good tattoo artist," I joke, and she laughs.

"I'm kidding…I sell drugs." When her eyes bug out, I crack up laughing. "I'm kidding! I'm an only child." I shrug. "Since I was old enough to walk, I've helped my parents with the distillery. I worked there all through high school. When I turned eighteen, my parents gave me one-third ownership of the business. I told you I owned it with them."

"Yeah, you did. I guess I didn't consider what that means."

"It means I get a five figure quarterly check for as long as we're in business. Whenever they need me, like when my dad had his stroke, I'm there."

"Wow, that's awesome," she says. "I love that you're so involved in your family's business. If I could tattoo, I would've opened Forbidden Ink with Jase and Jax, but drawing is not my forte." She laughs.

Taking her hands in mine, I pull her into me until we're almost flush. "Family is important to me. Sure, having money is a positive since we need it to survive, but being with family, spending time with them is what's important. I could've worked fulltime for my parent's distillery, but they knew inking was my passion. I didn't ask or expect them to give me a percentage of the business, but they did it because they wanted to make sure I'm always taken care of. The same reason your brothers wanted you to have that townhouse instead of selling it. It's part of being in a family. And one day I would really like for us to be a family."

Quinn nibbles on her bottom lip and nods. "I want that too."

Because of the time difference between home and here, Quinn isn't the least bit tired. I warned her she'll regret it tomorrow, but tonight she can't sleep, so we spend the next few hours lounging in the spa tub, talking about this weekend and the wedding, who she'll be meeting, planning our day tomorrow, Facetiming Kinsley, and getting fully acquainted with our comfortable as fuck bed.

The morning comes too soon, and while I want to stay in bed—and in Quinn—all day, I also don't want to waste the time we have here. So, after ordering breakfast from room service, I wake her up so she can jump in the shower and we can start our day. After we eat, we head out. We're planning to have brunch with my entire family tomorrow morning, but I already told my parents that today and tonight would be just Quinn and me.

We drive to the center of the city, to Eyre Square, and get out. It's not spectacular, just a typical downtown type of area with places to shop and eat, but it's a nice day out, and the walk over to the Salthill Promenade, which runs along the northern shore, makes it worth it.

"Lachlan! This country, this city, is seriously so beautiful," Quinn gushes as she takes picture after picture of everything she sees. As she watches everything and everyone around her, I watch her. I love seeing her excitement, her love for the city my family is from.

After checking out all the different shops, we eat at a

bistro in the square and then walk hand-in-hand along the sidewalk that leads to Salthill. The closer we get to the beach, the more nervous I get. Quinn of course notices and asks if everything is okay.

"Everything is perfect," I tell her honestly.

When we get to the shoreline, we walk a bit farther until we're alone. Quinn takes pictures of the water, the pier, and the rocks. She gushes over everything, from the smell of the salty air to the beauty in the way the water hits the rocks. Briefly lowering her camera, she turns to me with the most beautiful smile and says, "Thank you for bringing me here," and my heart feels like it's about to explode. She's the best mom, the most selfless, caring woman. She loves with everything she has, and she has no idea how much she deserves, how much I want to give her. What I want—and plan—to give her, if she'll agree to spend her life with me.

She turns back to take more pictures, and I pull the ring box out of my pocket and get down on one knee. It takes her a second before she looks back over at me, but when she does, when her eyes glide downward and she sees that I'm kneeling with an open ring box in my hand, her camera falls—which is thankfully hanging around her neck—her hands go to her mouth, and she gasps loudly.

"The moment I saw you walk through the door of Forbidden Ink, I knew you were the one. Not only were you the most beautiful woman I've ever met, but your sass was a damn turn on."

Quinn's hands remain covering her mouth, but I can see her shoulders shake with laughter, and the curve of her lips turn up around her hands.

"You were dressed all professional, but I knew, under those conservative pants and blouse, was a tattooed, sexy woman, waiting to break out of that shell she was hiding under." Tears shine in her eyes. She knows what I'm talking about, but I'm still going to tell her. She needs to hear how I feel about her. "I instantly fell in lust with your luscious curves and perfect tits...those dark, soulful eyes and pouty lips. And the way you blush over every emotion. I knew I needed to make you mine. And that was all before I even got to know you." I chuckle softly.

"I know we've only been dating for a few months, but I've fallen in love with you, Quinn, and I can't imagine there ever being a day that I'm not in love with you. All I want to do is spend every moment with you. When you cry, I want to make the tears go away. I want to be the one who makes you laugh, and be the one by your side while all of your dreams come true."

Twenty-Two

QUINN

I'm standing on the edge of the water, listening to Lachlan tell me all of the reasons he's in love with me and wants to marry me, and the tears are threatening to come with each word he speaks. But then he stands and bridges the gap between us. With the ring box still in his hand, he closes it and pushes it back into his pocket, so he can take my hands in his. I'm confused why he put the box away, until his eyes lock with mine, and he continues to speak.

"But I didn't just fall in love with you," he says, his voice so strong, not wavering in the slightest. "I also fell in love with your daughter." And the tears that were threatening to fall, spill down my cheeks. "How could I not, though?" He laughs softly. "She's literally a mini version of you. And I want nothing more than to make her mine. When she asked me that day in the bounce house, if I married you, if I could be her dad, I wanted to tell her that I would love nothing more than to be her dad, but I knew I couldn't do that. It wasn't my place to make that promise before I made a promise to you. It killed me having to wait for you to catch up, but I'm a patient man." He chuckles. "Kind of," he adds with a shrug.

"My point is, I knew one day we would get here, with me asking you to marry me, but I also knew I would have to wait a little while for you to get to this point. On Thanksgiving, when you told me you loved me, I knew we were *both* finally at the same place." His smile shines so bright, it's almost blinding. "You're everything I could ever want and need. I want you and Kinsley and me to be a family. And I promise you, I will spend every day for the rest of our lives loving the both of you with all of my heart." He pulls the ring box back out and opens the top, the ring sparkling in the sun, and takes it out. "Will you marry me?"

There's only one answer to give him. There's only ever been one answer, but I have a couple things I need to say before I tell him yes. "When I met you, I didn't realize how insecure I was. I didn't understand the damage my ex-husband did to me. I thought I was healed. I was happy and living my life. I had my business and my family and Kinsley. But it wasn't until you, that I understood how unhappy I really was. With myself. I read once somewhere that nobody can make you happy. You have to make yourself happy. And I fully believe that. But what I also believe is that through you loving me, despite all of my imperfections, I've learned to love myself. And once I was able to love myself, it allowed me to fall in love with you."

I don't even realize I'm crying again, until Lachlan

reaches up and catches my falling tears. "Thank you for loving me unconditionally, and for loving my daughter as if she were your own." I brush a soft kiss to his lips. "Yes, I will marry you."

The corners of Lachlan's lips curve into a soft smile as he takes my left hand in his and slides the ring onto my finger. "You just made me the happiest guy alive."

After Facetiming Kinsley like Lachlan apparently promised, and learning my daughter already saw the ring and knew Lachlan was going to propose, we spend the rest of the morning exploring Galway. In the afternoon, we take a ferry over to Aron Island and explore over there. I'm absolutely in love with Ireland, with Galway. Everything is so lush and green and breathtakingly beautiful. The people are friendly, and there is so much to see and do. We end up having dinner at the hotel, and after making love, we fall asleep with Lachlan's body wrapped around mine. I told myself he wouldn't move in until after we're married, and since I can't see myself lasting much longer going to bed and waking up without him, I imagine the engagement will be rather short.

"What if they don't like me?"

"They're going to love you."

"But what if they don't?"

"They will."

Lachlan and I are driving over to his parents' place—

because apparently they visit so often, they own a home here—and it's just hit me that I'm engaged to a man whose parents I've never met. My mind has been running wild all morning. What if they're like Rick's parents and stuck up? Or hate me like Rick's parents hated me? What if they think Shea is better suited for him? Or what if they think my tattoos look trashy? Okay, that's probably a dumb thought since their son is covered in them, but what if they're sexist and think ink should only be on men? What if they find out I have a daughter and are against blended families? They are still married after all.

I haven't asked Lachlan any of these questions, though. Mostly because I don't think he would tell me the truth. He loves me, and because of that, I think he would do anything to protect me, even if that means lying to me. But also because I'm afraid of what his answers might be if he does tell me the truth. My line of questioning also tells me something about myself… I'm still a work in progress. And with that thought comes one I've been thinking about more often lately. Maybe it's time I find someone to talk to. A professional. I want to be the best version of myself for Kinsley and Lachlan, but in order to do that, I need to be whole. And being whole means being healthy—emotionally and mentally. And while I feel like I've made strides in the right direction, I still have a long way to go.

We pull up the driveway, and even though I shouldn't be, I'm in shock by the extravagance of his parents' home. It's two stories with a three car garage, a huge wrap around porch and second story balcony, complete with a freaking running fountain in the front yard.

"Tell me everyone's names again," I beg, suddenly feeling nervous over meeting his entire family at once. I've spent a lot of time with wealthy people like Rick's parents and know firsthand how unforgiving and judgmental they can be.

"My mom is Evelyn, and my dad is Matt," Lachlan says for the third time with the patience of a saint. Every time I do or say something that I know would've aggravated Rick, I hold my breath, waiting for Lachlan to behave in a similar way, but every damn time he proves me wrong, making me fall that much more in love with him.

"My mom's brother is Anthony, and he's married to my Aunt Tracy. They have two daughters. You met Kiara, who's here with her husband, Kevin, and then there's Emily, who's getting married to Steven. My mom's sister's name is Patricia, and she's married to my Uncle Thomas."

"They're Declan's parents," I add, trying to remember.

"Yep, and Riley is his sister."

"Who's best friend's with Shea," I mutter, needing to remind myself that she will be here because she's close with his family. Her mom is best friend's with Lachlan's mom, of course.

Lachlan smiles softly and turns my face toward him, leaning over and kissing me tenderly. "I love you," he murmurs against my lips.

"I love you too." I inhale and exhale, allowing his words to run through me like a soothing balm to my nerves.

"You ready?" he asks.

"Yes."

The minute Lachlan turns the ignition off, the large oak

door swings open, and out runs a petite orange-haired woman. She's light-skinned with tiny freckles dotting her skin. When we step out, she wraps Lachlan up in a hug and her eyes briefly land on me. They're green just like Lachlan's. She must be his mom. She smiles sweetly, and my nerves come down a couple notches.

"Ay, my boy, it's so good to see ya!" Her Irish accent is thick—thicker than his cousin Kiara's—and I immediately fall in love with it, just like I've fallen in love with everything about this country.

Just as they finish hugging, an older version of Lachlan steps outside to join the party. Lachlan gives him a hug as well. Unsure of what to do or say, I stand here, waiting for Lachlan to lead.

Once the three of them have finished hugging each other, they step over to me, and Lachlan introduces us. "Mom, Dad, I would like for you to meet Quinn, my fiancée." Lachlan grins, and I choke on my saliva, shocked that he just threw it out there. *Way to ease the family into it, buddy...*

His parents, though, don't appear to be surprised, like at all. Instead, they both smile warmly. His mom embraces me in a hug first. "We're so glad to finally meet ya," she says sweetly. "Lachlan, here, hasn't stopped talking about you and your wee one."

"Congratulations," his father says, giving me a friendly hug. "It's so wonderful to meet the woman who's stolen our son's heart."

"Thank you, it's nice you meet you, too," I say politely, in shock at how nice they are.

"You ladies go in, and Lachlan and I will grab your things."

The second we're through the front door, I can hear all of the voices. I must've been too nervous to notice the cars in the driveway, but just as Lachlan said, everyone is here. One by one, they each introduce themselves to me, and I take a deep breath when I don't see Shea here.

Evelyn tells us that they were just finishing getting brunch ready, and everyone heads to the dining room. Since it's the next room over, I don't get a good look at the house, but I do notice the striking crystal tear-drop chandelier hanging in the foyer. The living room is to the right, and looks like it's never even been sat in. The dining room is to the left. In the center is a large sweeping staircase, which leads to the second floor. When we enter the dining room, the huge rectangular wood table takes up the majority of the room. Intricately carved wood bench seats run down the length of the table with a matching armchair on each end.

As if Lachlan can sense how nervous I am, he pulls me to sit next to him and starts making me a plate of food. He's naming each of the foods, asking if I would like some, since I have no idea what any of this is, when the sound of the front door shutting, reverberates through the room, and in walks Shea. She's dressed in an adorable yet sexy olive-colored romper with her perky breasts peeking out on the sides. Her blond hair is down in perfect beach waves, and she's wearing cute nude heels.

She walks around the table with a bright smile on her face, greeting everyone with the confidence and self-assurance I wish I had. *You used to,* I remind myself. *You just have to allow yourself to get back there.*

When she gets to Lachlan, who has an empty spot next to him—although, it's not the only empty spot—she leans down and gives him a chaste kiss on his cheek. I can see him give her a disapproving look out of the corner of my eye, but he doesn't say anything to her.

She also makes it a point not to say anything to me. Simply sitting down next to Lachlan and making conversation with Riley, who is sitting across from me, as she loads her plate up with food. When Lachlan asks me if I'd like cheese on my eggs, Shea's eyes swing over to us, her brows knitting together as she watches us.

"That's sweet, Lach. You're making your girlfriend a plate." She says it softly, so only Lachlan and I can hear over the chattering that's going on all over the table. And then she adds, "But wouldn't it make more sense for her to make yours?" She grins evilly, looking right at me. "You are young enough to be her second child." She snorts at her own joke, and I want to hide, because just as she said the last part, the table got quiet and everyone heard.

My heart starts picking up speed, my fight-or-flight kicking in. Of course, flight wins out—it always does—only I'm stuck on this bench between Lachlan and his mom with no way to get out without asking Lachlan and Shea to move.

Just as I'm seriously considering jumping over the back of the bench, Lachlan's hand lands on mine, squeezing it tightly. Calmly, yet loud enough for everyone to hear, he says, "I will not tolerate you speaking to, or about, my fiancée negatively. This is my home, and I will ask you to leave. I don't care who your mother is."

Without waiting for her to answer, he leans in so only I can hear, and whispers, "I'm sorry."

Unable to speak without risking my voice cracking with emotion, I nod my okay, refusing to look over at Shea, then reach over and grab my plate that Lachlan's still holding. There's only a couple items of food on there, and I know I'm still going to be hungry later, but I hate what she said about him making my plate. I shouldn't let it bother me, but she hit on one of my biggest insecurities about us—our huge age difference.

Lachlan's brows furrow, knowing he wasn't done making my plate, but I ignore him and start eating. The entire time we're eating, his gaze flicks over to my plate. I know he wants to add more to it, or tell me to, but he also knows it will only embarrass me.

His mom tries to make conversation, asking me various questions, but I'm too closed off to converse. I answer her every question, but they're short and cut off. The worst part is I know what I'm doing, and I hate it. I hate being weak. I want to be strong. I want to snap back at Shea and tell her to fuck off. I want to display my engagement ring, so she can stare in envy. And in my head, I totally do. Too bad, in my head doesn't count. It's moments like these that I'm reminded of how much further I need to go to get back to being the person I used to be. The person I was before Rick. And then I curse Rick for doing this to me, and myself for allowing him to do this to me. And then I chastise myself for once again letting Rick into my thoughts. It's really a vicious cycle that needs to be stopped.

When brunch finishes, Lachlan excuses us so he can

show me to our room. Refusing to let me help with the luggage, he carries both upstairs to the guestroom we'll be sharing. The room is beautifully decorated in cream and powder blue. There's a large king size bed in the corner, and the coziest looking reading nook I've ever seen under the window—complete with several fluffy pillows. Lachlan mentioned going out tonight for the bachelor party with all the guys, and since I didn't want to be that woman that prevents him from having a good time, even though the idea of me being here without him makes me feel sick, I told him he should go. Well, now I know exactly where I'll be tonight. Relaxing on that comfy bench, reading my book.

Lachlan sets our bags down and closes the door behind us, then pulls me over to the bed and sits me down on the edge, separating my legs and stepping in between. He grips my chin and lifts my head, so I'm looking at him. "Do not let that bitch get in your head," he commands, his voice taking on an edge I've never heard from him before.

And then his mouth is crashing down on mine, his tongue pushing through my lips and swirling against my own. The rough way he kisses me leaves my head spinning. My body heating. My insides sizzling.

He pulls me into a standing position, ripping my shirt off my body, reaching behind to unclasp my bra. We're ravenous, both of our hands working in a frenzy to remove every article of clothing from each other's body.

Lachlan drops to his knees and pushes me back onto the bed. His hands grip my knees and spread my thighs. His tongue delves between my pussy lips, licking and sucking on my clit. It feels so good that I release a heady moan, one that quickly reminds me where we are.

But I don't care because when Lachlan's mouth is on my body, everything else fades away. The entire world around us could be falling apart, but as long as he's touching me, I wouldn't even notice. I wouldn't even care.

And then his fingers are inside of me. Pushing in and pulling out. In and Out. In and Out. Deliciously slow and deep. A complete contrast to the way he was just devouring me with his mouth. Craving his roughness again, my hips push down on his fingers, meeting them thrust for thrust.

I can't get enough of him. Of the way he gives me all of him. Every ounce of himself is mine for the taking.

His pace picks up, pushing in deeper, harder, hitting that magical spot inside me. The man knows my body better than I do at this point. And with another thrust in, I'm exploding around him. My legs trembling. And then my entire body goes limp.

He doesn't even let me come down from my climax before he's dragging me up the bed and placing me on top of him. I have no clue how I'm supposed to ride him with numb legs. His fingers grip the sides of my ass, and he lifts me up and onto his stiff, pierced cock. He's so deep this way, my back arches. He grabs my hands and places them on the back of the headboard, on either side of his head. My body jerks forward, my heavy breasts going right into his face. He catches one with his mouth, sucking on the hardened peak. All the while, he continues to fuck me from the bottom. Powerful thrusts that have him in me so deep it feels like he's in my stomach.

Every. Piece. Of. Him. Is. Mine.

My legs finally get some of their feeling back, so I take over, riding him, trying to show him through my movements how much I need him. When he notices, his hands travel from my hips to my breasts, massaging and kneading them. And then his thumb hits my clit, flicking the swollen nub, and I detonate, coming so hard, my hands fall from the headboard, and my body slumps forward. My face nuzzles into the curve between his neck and shoulder, and Lachlan's face does the same. He kisses and suckles on my neck as he spills his warm seed into me.

I should probably get off him, so we can get cleaned up. I can feel his cum running out of me, but I can't move. I don't want to. I've come to the realization that Lachlan has imbedded himself within me. I'm no longer just me, I'm a part of him. When I'm with him, I feel beautiful, wanted, loved. I feel whole. He took all of the broken pieces and somehow managed to put me back together. And then it clicks. There's no way he found all my pieces. I know for a fact Rick took several of them with him to the grave. Which means there's only one reason I'm complete. Lachlan replaced all of the missing pieces with his own. The puzzle is only complete because he took pieces of himself and gave them to me. And I know the second we pull apart, I'll no longer feel as put together. I don't just love him, I need him. He completes me. Without him, I'm not whole. I'm not me.

Twenty-Three

QUINN

"I love you so much, sweetie! Be good for Auntie Sky!" I wave through the phone, and my daughter waves back.

"Okay, Mommy! Love you too! See you soon! Bye!"

With one last kiss to the screen, Kinsley hits the end button, and her adorable face disappears. I drop my phone on the bed with a sigh. Lachlan's only been gone for a few hours, but I really wish he was already back. I imagine my need to be near him isn't healthy, but I don't really care all that much. Especially when he's out having a good time at the bachelor party that Declan is throwing for the groom, Steven. He said tonight was perfect since Emily insisted they sleep apart the night before the wedding. She's here, along with all of the other women, including Shea. I tried to hang out with everyone downstairs. I didn't want to be that person. The one who seems stuck up because she doesn't socialize, but when Shea droned on and on about all of the fun times she, Declan, Lachlan, and Riley used to have, I excused myself to call my daughter. Now I'm dying of thirst and my stomach is growling, and the last thing I want to do is go down there, but it's going to have to happen.

Tiptoeing out the door of our room, I quietly glide down the stairs. I inhale a deep breath when I hear voices and deduce they're coming from the family room—the room just past the dining room and kitchen. When I get to the kitchen, I peek in, and once I see it's empty, I scurry over to the fridge to find something to eat and drink. The sound of women laughing and chattering rings through the house, but I ignore it as I quickly cut up some strawberries and make myself a roast beef sandwich. That is until I hear Shea's whiny voice mention Lachlan. Then I stop what I'm doing and listen.

"I can't believe he's seriously going to raise someone else's child," she says in her heavy Irish accent. Why does she have to have such a beautiful accent just to spew such nasty words?

"He's always wanted a house full of children," another woman adds. It sounds like Riley, but I could be wrong.

"Yeah, of his *own* kids," Shea volleys back, disgust evident in her tone. "What is she, like forty? She's not having any more kids. They'll never last," she hisses. "Lach and I are meant to be together, and once he learns we're on the same page, he's going to drop her like a bad habit."

"So, you've changed your mind?" a different woman asks.

"I didn't really think it was that important to him..."

"But have you changed your mind?" the same woman repeats.

"Lachlan will—" Shea's sentence stops abruptly. There's a quiet moment, and then she says, "Oh, Evelyn, you're back! Where were you?" I almost vomit at how different her tone is. What a fake bitch.

"With us leaving right after the wedding, I wanted to visit my garden one last time," Evelyn says sweetly. "What were you ladies talking about? I thought I heard Lachlan's name."

"We were just talking about how good Lachlan is with his nieces and nephews," Shea says, her voice so saccharine, I'm going to get a toothache just from listening to her speak.

"He was definitely meant to be a family man," Evelyn says, motherly pride and fondness for her son in her tone.

"I bet you can't wait to one day be a grandmother," another woman says, but I'm not sure who it is.

"Oh, yes," she gushes. "I can't wait to have my own grandbaby to spoil."

My heart drops at her last word: *grandbaby*. She wants a grandbaby, and Lachlan wants his own children. He's meant to be a family man.

Having lost my appetite, and not wanting to hear another word, I drop my food into the trash, grab a bottle of water, and go back upstairs. I grab my iPad to read, but the idea of reading about someone else getting their happily ever after makes me feel that much worse.

As I cuddle into my blankets, I think about everything Lachlan has done to make my life better, everything he's given me, and the whole time, I didn't stop to think about his life. What his needs and wants are. Shea insinuated they broke up because she wasn't ready for a family, and it makes sense because Lachlan is a natural born father. He's amazing with Kinsley. While I don't think he'll end up with Shea, she still makes a valid point. I am turning forty. It took me nearly four years to get pregnant with Kinsley, and I was younger. The odds of me getting pregnant go down every year, and then there are the risk factors that increase the older the woman gets.

Lachlan deserves to have a family of his own. He deserves more than to only ever raise another man's child. Sure, he'll probably deny it when I ask him if that's enough for him, but what happens one day when reality hits and he resents me? He'll either stay with me out of guilt or leave me.

My mind goes to my father. He's not someone I ever try to think or talk about. But right now, it doesn't surprise me he's who pops into my head. He was with my mom for years, but when she couldn't conceive, he started to cheat on her. Jax and Jase were both born and then a couple years later I came. But by then he was fully living a double life...well, actually three lives, if you include his *other* wife no one knew about. He chose my mom over the others and sought custody of Jax and Jase, proving their mom to be unfit. She ended up committing suicide.

I feared Rick would do the same thing to me when I found out I was pregnant—try to prove me to be unfit. Only he died, and I was able to raise Kinsley on my own. Would

Lachlan cheat on me if I couldn't get pregnant? Would he seek another woman to fill in the gaps I'm not capable of filling in? I want to say no, but I've seen what men are capable of doing.

Unable to fall asleep, my mind races with every doubt and insecurity, every worst case scenario and what if, until the tears are racing down my cheeks as I mourn the loss of Lachlan and me and our future.

Just as my eyes are finally closing, the door creaks open. I know it's Lachlan without seeing him. I can feel his overpowering presence, and it takes everything in me not to lose it.

After he shuffles around the room, the bed dips down as he climbs in behind me, his strong arms wrapping around my torso. I let my lids flutter shut, reveling in the warmth his body and touch radiates. He snuggles closer to me and nestles his face into the back of my hair. "I know you're awake," he murmurs. "I can practically hear your mind spinning, and your body is stiff with tension." He runs his hand down the curve of my hip and over my thigh. "My mom said you've been in the room all night. Did something happen?"

I inhale deeply and exhale slowly, trying to decide what to do or say. I never want to lie to Lachlan. So, I answer his question with one of my own. "Do you want your own kids?" I stay lying with my back to Lachlan, and I'm surprised when he lets me. His fingers still on my thigh, and I feel him tense up. I already know his answer, but I wait for him to say it.

"No," he murmurs, and I close my eyes, the silent tears

breaking out from under my lids and falling.

He lied to me. His answer should've been yes, but he said no. He chose to protect me with a lie, instead of breaking my heart with the truth. And by doing so, I now know what needs to happen next.

Twenty-Four

LACHLAN

Over the next two days I watch helplessly as Quinn pushes me away. She attends the wedding with me, speaks politely when spoken to, smiles at the right time—although every one of them is fake—laughs when someone says a joke, and takes tons of pictures of everything around her. But I can feel it, she's retreating back into her shell.

When she asked me if I wanted my own kids, I knew something was wrong. She wouldn't have asked that out of nowhere. Something was said, probably by fucking Shea. I don't know. I tried to further explain my answer after I said no, but Quinn wouldn't let me. She complained of a stomachache and retreated to the bathroom, locking it behind her. When she finally came out, I tried again, but she cut me off, telling me she was tired and wanted to get some sleep.

On the plane ride home, she faked sleeping for half the

trip. The other half, she plugged in her headphones and worked on edits. I can literally feel her slipping from my fingers, and I have no idea how to fix this. I don't know what to ask, what to say.

Because we live in different parts of the city, after we get our bags from luggage claim, she insists we take different cabs home. I try to argue, but when she says she just needs some space, that she misses Kinsley and wants to spend some alone time with her, I know I'm stuck.

As she gets into the cab, she kisses my cheek and gives me a sad smile, and I can feel it in my bones, I've lost her before I ever truly had her. I close the door, in shock, and watch as the cab drives away. I take the next cab home, staring at my phone, wondering if I should text or call her. Debating if she just needs space. But then when I'm home and in my room, as I'm pulling my jeans off to change into a pairs of sweats, a diamond ring falls out of my front pocket, hitting the wood floor with a clink, confirming what I already know.

I've lost her.

Twenty-Five

LACHLAN

I wake up, and for the first time in days, Quinn isn't lying next to me in bed. Her perfect, warm body isn't pressed into my side, and her leg isn't thrown over mine. Her hair isn't fanned out across her face and pillow. She's not waking me up and hurrying me out the door, so I can go get breakfast and come right back to eat with her and Kinsley.

I throw my legs over the side of the bed and turn my alarm off since I'm up before it's gone off. After showering and getting dressed, I head out to the kitchen to pop a K-cup into the Keurig so I can make myself a cup of coffee before I go to work. As I listen to the water heat up and then the coffee brew, I ignore the otherwise deafening silence. Kinsley's giggles are missing. The way she clacks her fork and knife against her plate. Quinn's voice isn't yelling across the house for her daughter to hurry up and eat so they aren't late. She's not begging me to make her a cup then kissing me when I hand it to her, already made.

Declan makes his presence known, half-asleep and scrubbing his face as he grabs a mug from the cabinet and moves mine to the side so he can make his own coffee. He flew back in yesterday along with my parents and Quinn. Nobody knows that Quinn and me have…fuck…what have we done? What did she do? Are we on a break? Did we break up for good? She gave me back the engagement ring. Does that mean she ended our engagement?

Grabbing the mug, I take a sip of the black coffee. When I notice Declan is silent too, I ask if everything is okay with him. Better to focus on someone else's issues instead of my own.

"I caught Venessa with another guy last night. I wasn't supposed to return until later in the week, but as you know I changed my flight last minute to get home to her." He shrugs nonchalantly, but it's an act. He cares about her.

"Are you sure it's what it looked like?"

"Yeah, unless shoving her tongue down a guy's throat can somehow be misconstrued." He takes a spoon out of the drawer, then slams in shut.

"Quinn ended our engagement last night," I admit.

Declan whips his head around to face me. "Are these women fucking possessed?"

I just shrug a shoulder and chuckle humorlessly.

"You're not going to just let her end it, are you?"

I've thought a lot about this since I found the ring last night. "She asked for space, so I'm going to give it to her. I don't want to. Hell, if it were up to me, I would throw her over my shoulder and lock her in my bedroom." I laugh without any humor. "Quinn is so fucking insecure, man." I take a sip of my coffee. "I've tried everything to convince her that she's perfect, that I love her, that she's the one for me. But it feels like with every mole I whack, another one pops up in its place." I hate this feeling of defeat.

"What happened to make her end things?"

"I'm not certain, but I think while we were at the bachelor party, the women were talking. When I got back, she asked if I wanted my own kids."

"Have you asked your mom? You know, she was there."

I didn't even think about that. But Declan is right. "I'll do that. Thanks."

On my walk to work, I call my mom and she confirms the women—specifically Shea—were gossiping about how much I love kids and want my own family, but she says that Quinn wasn't in the room, and she wasn't either during the beginning of the conversation. So maybe she overheard? Or she left before my mom walked in? I want to call Quinn and ask her, but that will go against giving her space. So instead, I go to work and lose myself in tattooing.

On Wednesday I wake up to my phone buzzing. I jump up and snatch it off the nightstand, praying it's Quinn. Only it's my mom, who apparently has been shopping. Not wanting her to judge Quinn, in case we get back together, I haven't told my mom that Quinn called off the engagement. There are several pictures of little girl toys. Barbies, a Barbie mansion, tons of dolls and other shit. Under all the images is a message from my mom: **Christmas is in three weeks! I would like to meet my granddaughter before then!**

Not having the heart to tell her she may never meet Kinsley, I text back: **Ok.** Then I get out of bed and repeat everything I did yesterday. Only today, the ache in my chest hurts like a bitch. I consider calling Quinn several times throughout the day, but I don't do it. Space. She needs space. But fuck if I don't need her.

On Thursday I call in sick, never leaving my bed except to eat and drink and piss. I'm fucking hurt and pissed at Quinn for doing this shit to us. All I want is to be with her. I turn off my phone and shove it in my drawer so I don't call or text her.

On Friday I wake up and power my phone back on. It immediately dings with a text from Jax letting me know the new receptionist he *just* hired has called in sick and Quinn is filling in. He also added he'll reschedule my appointments today so I don't have to come in. He didn't know when he asked her to fill in that we broke up, but since I'm sick I probably won't be coming in anyway. Without texting him back, I throw my phone to the side and get dressed. Since my car is still in the parking lot, I decide to drive it back to my parents' place today. I need to get the fuck away from here. Not only am I losing Quinn and her daughter, but now I'm probably going to lose my job. I spend the day working at the distillery, bugging the hell out of Salazar.

When my mom sees I'm here, she asks me to dinner, and when she invites Quinn and Kinsley, I lose it. It's probably the liquor talking—since I drank more today than I actually helped—but I end up telling her everything about Quinn and her ex. The emotional and mental abuse she's endured that have caused her insecurities.

"What if loving her isn't enough?"

"Oh, Lachlan," she says. "You can't possibly believe that. The thing about loving someone, being in a relationship, is finding the yin to your yang. When she feels weak, you be her strength. When you're lost, she'll be your beacon. When she feels insecure, you lift her up. Love is always enough, but you have to be willing to love even harder during those tough moments. Fight for the both of you when she's given up."

She's right. Whatever is going on with Quinn, she needs me. Even if things don't work out, I love her. She's become my best friend, and I'm not about to let her go through this alone.

"Thank you, Mom, that's exactly what I needed to hear."

After we eat dinner, I call a cab to go home.

On Saturday I wake up with renewed confidence. I text Jax I'm coming to work before he can text me shit, and then I head out to go to Kinsley's soccer game. Aware that her game isn't the place to talk to Quinn, I hang back and watch from a distance. Quinn is sitting on a blanket, surrounded by her family, and even from where I'm standing I can see she's sad. Her eyes aren't sparkling, and she has black circles under her lids. Tonight we're going to talk.

Needing Kinsley to know I was here, I snap a photo of her kicking the ball into the net and send it to her iPad with a message: **Good game!**

Twenty-Six

QUINN

It's been five days since we've been back, since I slipped the engagement ring into Lachlan's pocket and kissed him goodbye. Five days since I told him I needed some space. Since I've felt his warm touch, smelled his delicious cologne, listened to his smooth voice. I don't even feel like I'm living at this point, just merely surviving. Kinsley, of course, doesn't understand what's happened. She thought him giving me the ring would mean he would move in and become her daddy. I didn't have the heart to explain it all to her yet, so when she asked where he was, I omitted the truth and said I wanted to spend some time with her. Thankfully, she accepted that answer.

I did call a therapist on Tuesday morning, and due to a cancellation, I was able to meet with her the same day. Her name is Fran, and she's very sweet but also straight forward. I spent the hour explaining my past, and she said she feels it would be best if we meet twice a week at first. I agreed. Honestly, with as many problems as I have, I'm surprised she didn't suggest we meet five times a week.

I met with her on Thursday, and we dove right in, head first. We talked about the person I used to be and the person I am now. She asked me to make a T-chart and list all of my qualities. On one side are the qualities before I was with Rick, and on the other side are the qualities after Rick. I noticed as I made the list, many of the qualities from before Rick were close to being added to the list after Rick, but only because they came back *after* Lachlan. So I added another column: after Lachlan. But then I deleted it…because it's time I'm responsible for my own qualities. I'm aware I'm not going to change overnight, but I'd like to think this is a good start.

I'm lost in thought as Kinsley and I walk down Delancey Street toward the Japanese restaurant we agreed to meet everyone at—after Jax assured me that Lachlan wouldn't be there. I didn't want to go out, but Celeste mentioned going out for hibachi in front of Kinsley at her soccer game—the first game Lachlan has missed—and I had no valid reason to say no, especially since I've been sucking lately at the whole parenting thing and she could use a good meal.

So when someone calls out my name, I don't question it, simply turning around to locate the owner of the voice. And that's when I come face-to-face with the last person I ever hoped to see again. I'm in such shock over who I'm staring at, I completely forget whose hand I'm holding. That is until she asks, "Who's this?" and I glance down at the *who* in question. My heart pounds against my ribcage as my past and present collide. I try to think of a way to turn back time, but it's not possible.

"I'm Kinsley," my daughter answers for me, extending her hand to politely shake the woman's hand. I watch in fear as the woman eyes Kinsley. She's doing the math in her head, recognizing her bright blue eyes, her button nose, and her lips, the top one slighter fuller than the bottom. Her chocolate brown hair that's about five shades lighter than my black. She's putting it all together. I want to run, but I know it will only make matters worse.

I can tell when it all finally clicks. Her sharp gaze meets mine, and her lips—the top one slighter fuller than the bottom—form into a thin line. Her nostrils flare in anger as she says, "You had my son's child and never told me."

I flinch at her words, but don't deny it. Jacquelyn Thompson isn't a dumb woman. She knows that standing right in front of her, is in fact, Rick's biological daughter.

"There you guys are!" I hear from behind, breaking me out of my shocked state. Kinsley, having no clue what has just happened, releases my hand and runs over to Jax. Only when I turn around, it's not Jax she's running over to. It's Lachlan.

"Daddy! You're here!" she squeals. "I missed you so, so much." My eyes flit from Jaquelyn to Lachlan and Kinsley. I had no idea she was going to say such a thing, but I should've known. She flat out said Lachlan marrying me meant he would be her new daddy, and she's only six. She doesn't understand being engaged isn't the same as actually getting married.

Lachlan takes her in his arms and kisses her cheek, not correcting her. I knew he wouldn't. He would never say something to upset her. As I watch everyone talking and laughing, I feel like I'm on the outside, watching a train plowing forward without any working brakes, and I'm the only one who can see the collision that's about to occur. But I can't speak. I can't warn anyone. Who would I warn anyway? I'm the one on the train that's about to wreck. Just as I finish that thought, Jacquelyn makes her presence known, right in front of everyone.

"Why is my granddaughter calling that hoodlum Daddy?" She never was one to mince words. "All this time, you've had Rick's baby, and you've been hiding her from us, allowing another man to stake his claim on her. How dare you!" Her hand comes up, and I should block her, but I don't. Instead I stand in my place as her palm strikes my cheek, and my face whips to the side from the force.

"Mommy!" Kinsley cries out. Damn it! She saw. "Don't hurt my mommy!" she screams.

"What the hell!" Jax yells, stomping over to Jacquelyn. "You better walk away right now before I call the cops on you for attacking my sister."

Jacquelyn doesn't even flinch, her eyes staying locked on me. "You will be hearing from my attorney," she hisses.

"For fucking what?" Jase asks. I didn't even realize he was standing on the other side of me.

"For keeping my granddaughter away from me," she says, and I don't have to hear what she says next to know where she's going with this. The entire reason why I never told her about Kinsley. "She's my blood, and I have the right to see her. Six years lost. I will see you in court." And with those words, my nightmare has come true. She's going to sue me for visitation, maybe even custody.

She turns on her heel and walks over to the town car waiting for her, taking one last look at me—or maybe Kinsley—before she slides into the backseat and disappears.

My chest rises and falls, my breaths quickening. My hand reaches up to my throat. It's hard to catch my breath. I feel dizzy, lightheaded. The world around me is blurry. I try to speak, but my vocal cords are cut off by the huge lump in my throat. I'm going to pass out. I can feel it. I can't catch my breath. I turn to my brother, trying to tell him something is wrong, but then everything goes black.

I wake up in my own bed with Lachlan's arms wrapped around me, and for a brief moment, before I have time to think about everything that is wrong, I feel complete again. Whole. Put together. His head dips down, and he presses a kiss to my forehead. An involuntary whimper escapes my lips, and the tears spill over the sides of my eyes.

"No, no, no, shhh," he coos. "Don't cry, baby," he soothes.

"How is it I push you away, give you back your ring, and end things with you in the worst way, the cowardly way, and yet you're right here once again putting me back together?"

"Because I love you," he says simply. His words, for some reason, anger me, and I jump out of bed, needing space.

"You shouldn't be here," I tell him, standing at the end of my bed. I might be seeing a therapist now, but I'm far from fixed, and nothing between Lachlan and I has changed.

"There's nowhere else I should be," he says, his pierced brow rising in defiance. I take him in for a second, sitting on my bed, in his standard white T-shirt and jeans. He's sporting his sexy grey beany that I love, and his shoes are off, his sock-covered feet stretched out. His arms are now crossed over his chest.

"We broke up," I tell him, fully aware I'm choosing to focus on us instead of dealing with the much bigger issue of my ex-mother-in-law.

"We're not breaking up," he says matter-of-factly. "I don't know what happened when we were in Ireland, but whatever it is, we'll deal with it."

"There's nothing to deal with," I snap. "I'm about to turn forty and you're twenty-fucking-seven. We were being delusional thinking we would ever work."

"So, we're back to our age difference again?" he says dryly. "Love knows no age." He shrugs like he's already bored of this conversation, and it fuels my fire.

"You're wrong!" I shout. "Love does know age, and it knows that you have your entire life ahead of you. A chance to fall in love and create a family for yourself. And I love you enough to let you go." At my words, Lachlan stands and stalks over to me.

"You're not fucking letting me go," he growls.

"Yes, I am," I argue. "And what happened earlier is a perfect example of why. You deserve a fresh start. To meet a woman who will give you your own babies and create a loving home with you. You deserve more than a damaged single mom with a vicious ex-mother-in-law and a husband who continues to fuck her over from the grave. You deserve a woman who can give you her entire heart."

I slump against the front of my dresser, my vision blurry from the grief dripping down my face. "You deserve more than me." I shake my head. "And I would be selfish to hold onto you simply because you're everything I've ever wished for. You picked up the pieces of my heart, and when you saw it couldn't be fixed, you gave me parts of your own to make me whole." I look up at Lachlan. He's such a beautiful man on the inside and out. "You give me all of you, and I have nothing to give you in return," I admit defeatedly.

I close my eyes to release the built-up fresh tears, and when I open them, Lachlan is standing directly in front of me. His arms cage me in, and his face is only a hairbreadth away from mine. "You give me everything," he says, his voice low and serious.

"Shea said you wanted to have your own kids, and she made it seem like that's why you guys broke up."

"Shea and I broke up for a myriad of reasons, but, yes, our last fight *was* because I said I wanted kids, and she said she didn't want any," he admits.

"You told me you didn't want any kids."

"No." He shakes his head. "You asked me if I wanted my own, and when I said no, you wouldn't let me explain."

I open up my mouth to speak, but Lachlan places two fingers against my lips. "No, now you're going to listen. I gave you a few days of space like you asked, but I'm done. Family isn't blood. Family is heart, and you and Kinsley own mine. When I said I wanted a family to Shea, because neither of us had kids, yes, it meant having our own, but it's different with us. You have Kinsley, and even though she isn't my blood, she's still mine. Many couples can't conceive. They foster or adopt, and if they can't do that, they get a goddamned dog. With Shea, I couldn't imagine having a family with her, but with you, I can see it all. Even if it were only you and me, we would still be a family."

"Your mom said she can't wait to be a grandmother," I say weakly.

"Damn right, she can't wait. She's already sent me twenty pictures of the gifts she's bought for Kinsley for Christmas. She's chomping at the bit to meet her granddaughter, but I told her she has to wait because you need some time."

I gasp at his words, warm liquid gushing from my tear ducts. "But…" I don't even have anything to argue about anymore, but my insecurities can't stop me from trying. Why is it so damn hard just to let him in? Damn it!

"But nothing, Quinn. I love you, and you love me, and we're going to get married, and I'm going to adopt Mini-Q, and maybe we'll even get a dog. End of story." He grins. "No, not the end of the story. It's just the fucking beginning." And then he lifts me off my feet, and proceeds to show me exactly how the story continues—over and over again.

Twenty-Seven

LACHLAN

It's been three weeks since Quinn and I got back together and she put my ring back on her finger. She's seeing her therapist twice a week, and yesterday I joined her for a session. It was hard as fuck listening to her talk about her insecurities, but her therapist seems to have her on the right track. I know it's going to take time for Quinn to finally be able to put her past behind her, but luckily, we have plenty of time.

With Kinsley calling me Dad, and the fact that we're planning a wedding, we decided to move in together. I'm still keeping the condo for Declan, but I'm now one hundred percent living in the townhouse with my girls. *My girls.* Just the thought has me grinning like a damn fool. We've hired an attorney to handle the adoption papers for me to adopt Kinsley, and once we're married, he'll submit them to the courthouse to make everything legal. We're aware of

Jacquelyn's threat to seek visitation-slash-custody of Kinsley, but we haven't discussed it. However, just because we haven't discussed it, doesn't mean I'm not handling shit. I have no doubt that woman won't try to take Quinn to court, but I'm going to make sure it doesn't come to that.

It's Christmas morning, and my birthday, and I'm lying in bed alone. I can hear the girls downstairs, though. Quinn is telling Kinsley that she can pour the chocolate chips into the batter, and Kinsley is questioning why she can't eat the batter if she can eat cookie dough.

Laughing at how adorable she is, I get out of bed so I can join them. There's a massive Christmas tree in the living room. Santa came last night. As Quinn and I put together several gifts so Kinsley would have them ready to go this morning, she kept apologizing for keeping me up until the crack of dawn, especially since it's my birthday. By the third time, I told her it was enough. What we're doing here means everything to me.

When Kinsley sees me approaching, she yells, "Merry Christmas! Santa came!"

"I see that! So when do we open presents?"

Kinsley pouts. "Mommy said after we eat breakfast." Then she perks up. "Oh! Happy Birthday!" She jumps off the stool and gives me a hug.

"Thank you," I tell her. Then I walk over to Quinn, who's standing in front of the stove, waiting to flip the pancakes. Pressing the front of my body against her back, I lean down and give her a kiss to her neck. "Merry Christmas, beautiful."

"Merry Christmas," she says through a smile. "And

Happy Birthday."

After we eat and do the dishes, we spend the rest of the morning opening gifts. Kinsley squeals and shrieks in excitement over every gift. Quinn and I exchange gifts as well. I bought her a necklace with a mini camera on it, and she got me a new tattoo kit I'd mentioned wanting.

"I also got you something for your birthday," she says nonchalantly, but when her cheeks and neck turn pink, I wonder what it is she got me.

"Where is it?" I look around at all the ripped up paper and abandoned boxes. Kinsley is currently running each of her toys up to her room.

"In our room." She smiles sheepishly. What's she up to?

An hour later, Kinsley has conked out for a nap, and I've texted my mom to let them know we'll be coming over once she wakes up. We're doing lunch at my parents' place and dinner at Jase and Celeste's.

"Can I get my birthday gift now?" I ask Quinn, curious. She laughs and nods, pulling a square box out of the closet.

Setting it on the bed, I open the top to find what looks like a photo album. I take it out of the box and flip to the first page. It's a professionally photographed picture of Quinn. She's lying on her stomach, and her sexy ass is slightly in the air. She's wearing lingerie I've never seen before. And she looks fucking stunning. Slowly, I flip through page after page. Different poses, some in the same lingerie, some different, all fucking gorgeous. And not just because every image shows off her perfect tits or curvy hips. But because in every single picture she looks so damn confident and secure about herself.

"Quinn, these are perfect. You're so damn beautiful." I flip through the final pages, each one a tad more risqué than the last, but all tastefully done.

"It's because of you I was able to have this done," she admits.

"No, baby, it's because of you." I close the book and pull her into my arms. "Nobody can make you feel any way but yourself." I'm using the words her therapist has said to her several times.

"I know, but it was through your eyes, I was able to finally see that I'm enough. That's the tattoo I want to get. On my collarbone. I want you to tattoo it on me."

And without even meaning to, she just made this the best birthday ever. Because from those words alone, I know Quinn finally trusts me.

Epilogue

LACHLAN

Three Months Later

I read over the papers Salazar has given to me. While he runs my family's distillery, in another life, he was in the Irish mafia and his connections reach far.

"Got you, bitch." I nod my head a few times, then thank Salazar. "I owe you. Whatever you need…"

"Your family took a chance on an ex-mafia fresh out of jail. You don't owe me anything." He shakes my hand. "The papers have already been submitted, so she will most likely be served any day."

I noticed that. I'm hoping I'll either get to them before they have her served, or we'll be out of the country. Either way, nothing will come of them, but I'd rather Quinn not be stressed unnecessarily.

Once Salazar leaves, I seek out Jase and Jax. Knowing I might need their backup, I've kept them informed of my plan.

"I got what we need." I hold up the papers, explaining to them what Salazar was able to find out.

"So why would they seek visitation or custody then?" Jase asks.

"My guess is they have no clue, but they're about to find out." I smirk. "I'm heading over there now."

"Let's go," Jax says, just as my cell phone begins to ring in my pocket. It's Quinn.

"Hey baby."

"Lach," she whispers, "I need you to come to the hospital." The hair on the back of my neck rises. Why the fuck is she in the hospital? Is Kinsley okay? When I left this morning, Quinn was packing and Kinsley was getting ready for her last day of school before spring break.

"What's wrong?" I'm already heading to the front door when I remember I need to let her brothers know.

"I'm okay… Rick's parents served me this morning, and I-I kind of broke down and Kinsley called nine-one-one." She sobs into the phone. "Sky has Kinsley." Damn it! We were so close.

"I'll be right there." I hang up and tell her brothers what's happened.

"You go to my sister. She needs you. We'll give those pieces-of-shit a visit," Jax hisses, taking the folder from me.

Fuck! I wanted to see the look on their faces when they realized they were fucked, but Jax is right, Quinn needs me more.

QUINN

Two hours ago

I'm rushing around my room trying to finish packing. We leave in two days to Ireland for our wedding! After falling in love with the country, and getting engaged there, we decided to get married there. My brothers and their families will be coming, as well as Lachlan's family. We'll be there for a week since the kids are all on spring break, and my brothers can leave Evan and Gage to run the shop while we're gone. The latest receptionist is still going strong.

The doorbell chimes, and Kinsley yells up the stairs to let me know someone is here since she's not allowed to open the door. I check the clock. It's ten to eight. It's probably Skyla. She offered to take Kinsley to school for me this morning so I can get everything done.

I jog down the stairs and swing the door open without checking to see who it is, and standing there on my doorstep is a police officer.

"Quinn Crawford?"

"Yes."

"You've been served."

With shaky hands, I sign my name and take the envelope from the officer. I barely remember closing my door or opening the document. And everything after I open the flap and read "Notice to seek custody" is all a blur. I vaguely remember feeling like I was having a heart attack, and Kinsley yelling for me. My ears begin to ring and my vision goes blurry. My first thought is that I'm going to die, and my second is that Rick's parents will get Kinsley because Lachlan hasn't officially adopted her yet. Once again, from the goddamned grave, my ex-husband is destroying another piece of me.

I come to in the ambulance, where the EMT tells me my daughter called for help. When I ask where she is, he says her aunt showed up and showed proper identification, so they let her take her. Once I arrive at the hospital, I'm checked-in. Without my cell phone, I can't call Lachlan. Thankfully, Skyla shows up a little while later, while the nurse is drawing blood, and gives it to me, letting me know she dropped off Kinsley with Celeste on her way here. She was too upset to go to school. I call Lachlan, and he tells me he's on his way.

Once he shows up, I tell Skyla she can go. I'll be here for a while, waiting for the test results to come back, but I'm almost positive I just had an anxiety attack.

"Kenneth and Jacquelyn petitioned for joint custody of Kinsley," I tell Lachlan once he's sitting next to me by my bed.

"They will be recanting that petition," he states matter-of-factly. His fingers glide over my newest tattoo. The one he inked on me the day after Christmas. *You are enough.*

"How do you know?"

"Because after she threatened you, I had Salazar start digging for dirt on them." He smiles apologetically. I'm assuming for hiding it, not for actually doing it. "I didn't want you to stress over all this, Quinn." He brushes his knuckles down my cheek.

"Did he find anything?"

"He did, and your brothers are delivering the information to the Thompsons as we speak."

"What did you—"

"Good morning, Miss Crawford." A young gentleman, maybe in his late twenties, strides in. "I'm Dr. Fields." He extends his hand to shake mine, and I take it.

Then he extends his hand to Lachlan, who eyes him up and down like he's some sort of competition. I snort in amusement. "This is my fiancé, Lachlan," I tell the doctor.

"Are you old enough to be a doctor?" Lachlan asks.

"Lach!" I exclaim.

"I am," Dr. Fields says with a grin. Luckily, he doesn't seem offended. "We got your results back, and everything appears to be good. When you were brought in, your heartrate and blood pressure were both elevated, so we ran an EKG, and it came back negative, which leads us to believe your passing out was stress related.

"I did notice, though, that you marked not pregnant on the nurse's questionnaire, but your HCG levels are significantly peaked, indicating you are pregnant. We would like to do an ultrasound just to confirm and make sure everything is okay. I've put the order in and a tech will be by to take you to do the ultrasound. Once we get the results, and if everything looks good, we can let you go."

There is so much he just said. I'm pregnant...holy shit! I. Am. Pregnant. How is that even possible? Well, of course it's possible. I never got on birth control. But I didn't really believe I would get pregnant. But was I hoping to? My hand goes to my stomach, already feeling protective of the possible baby growing inside me. My gaze goes to Lachlan, who thanks the doctor, since I'm not able to speak, and closes the curtain behind him. My lips curl into a smile, and Lachlan's shoulders visibly slump.

"We...we might be having a baby," I breathe.

He leans over the rail of the bed and kisses my belly, then comes up to my face and kisses my lips. "I heard."

The tech wheels me in for the ultrasound and confirms I am ten weeks pregnant. I had no idea. I haven't felt sick or anything. When I convey my concern, she simply says that every pregnancy is different, but everything looks good. She lets us listen to the heartbeat for a minute and then prints out a grey image of what looks like a tiny bean, but is actually our baby.

Our baby. Lachlan's and mine. We're having a baby!

When we get back to the room, Jax and Jase are both waiting for us with small smiles splayed upon their faces. I'm not sure what they're about to tell me, but I take a few calming breaths. I'm pregnant and I'm not going to allow myself to stress out. I've passed out twice recently from the stress, and I need to make sure to put this baby first.

"I'm pregnant," I tell them both before they can speak. "So, if it's something bad, can we talk about it later? I can't let Rick or his family ruin this moment." Tears prick my eyes. "I'll deal with it, whatever it is, but not yet." I feel Lachlan entwine his fingers with mine, and I'm grateful for it. I know with Lachlan by my side, we'll get through anything that comes our way.

"You're pregnant?" Jase grins, then pulls me to him for a hug. "Congratulations, sis."

"Congratulations," Jax says. "And we have good news. Jacquelyn has already called her attorney to remove her petition for custody. She and her husband will also be signing an agreement that they will never petition again, nor will they contact you or Kinsley."

"Wow," I murmur. "Whatever you found must be bad."

"There's only one thing those people love," Lachlan says with disgust. "Money."

"You paid them off?" But they're worth millions.

"No." Lachlan scoffs. "When I had Salazar dig, I wasn't sure what we were looking for. I was hoping to find something to blackmail them with." When I give him a disapproving look, he just shrugs. "I'm not even sure why Salazar thought to read your ex's will, but he did, and in it, it states that if he has an heir, he, or she, will receive his percentage of the company along with all of his assets.

Holy shit! That would mean Kinsley would own fifty percent of the company, and all of the business accounts...She would be a millionaire...which would mean

Rick's parents would have less.

"We didn't even have to threaten them," Jax says. "Apparently because there weren't any known heirs at the time the will was read, the attorney didn't mention it, and your parents never thought to ask. The second we brought it to their attention, they agreed to do whatever we wanted."

"They chose the company over their granddaughter," I say softly.

"They don't deserve to call her their granddaughter," Lachlan says. "Remember what I told you before. Blood doesn't make a family. Love does. Now let's get you the hell out of here and go get our daughter, so we can finally make us a family, legally."

Extended Epilogue

LACLAN

Sixteen Years Later

"Dad won't know if you tattoo me. It's not as if he looks at my back," I hear my fifteen year old daughter, Kaylee, murmur from my office at Forbidden Ink. With Jase retired and traveling the world with his wife, and Jax and Willow retired and enjoying the quiet life, naturally it meant I would take over the family business. I wasn't supposed to come in this morning, since Barrett, my fourteen year old son, has a soccer game this afternoon, but I needed to place a quick order, since I forgot to do it last night before I left. And now I'm damn glad I did...

"It's not happening, Kay," Kinsley chides. I can't help the grin that forms. "Dad would kill me. You know his rule. No tattoos until you're eighteen."

"You're such a downer," Kaylee whines.

"Trust me, you'll thank me later for not doing it."

"Doubtful," Kaylee grumbles.

"Look at the bright side, I just saved a unicorn from being killed." Kinsley cackles.

"Whatever."

I should probably make my presence known, but I don't. It's obvious Kinsley has this under control. She's been officially apprenticing with me for the last three years since she graduated from high school, and this weekend is her first time taking clients on her own. I'm so damn proud of her.

A memory surfaces from the past, when Kinsley was six years old and decided she wanted to become a tattoo artist.

"Dad! Look what I drew." I'll never get tired of hearing that three letter word come out of her mouth. She hands me a drawing of two stick figures with the words Dad and Kinsley over them. They're holding hands.

"Where's your mom and Kaylee?" I ask.

"At home. This is me and you." She points to the square behind us. "And that's Forbidden Ink. My teacher told us to draw what we want to be when we get bigger. I want to tattoo people like you." Kinsley beams up at me with pride, and my heart expands. "When I'm bigger, will you show me how?"

Her eyes are wide with hope, as if there's even a small chance I won't give her anything she wants.

"How about I show you now?"

She gasps. "Really?"

"Sure."

Kinsley's spending the day with me at the shop because there's no school and her mom is home with Kaylee. She's only four weeks old and sleeps a lot, and Kinsley gets bored hanging out at home, so occasionally she comes in with me while I tattoo. She's a great little assistant.

I grab my gun and hand her gloves to put on. Grabbing the black ink, I open the cap. I place my arm on the counter and Kinsley climbs onto the chair.

"You're going to let me tattoo you?" she squeals.

"Yep! But you can't tattoo anyone else until you're licensed."

"Okay!"

I walk her through how to hold the gun, turn it on and off a few times so she can see how it feels, then let her try it for herself. When she tells me she's ready, I point to a small spot on my arm. "Go ahead and give it a go."

"What should I tattoo?" she asks, her voice full of excitement. "A skull or a soccer ball?"

"How about we start small," I suggest. Anything too big will probably leave a hole in my arm.

"Okay," she says softly, "I'll draw a heart because I love you."

She presses the button to start the gun and dips the tip into the black ink. Slowly, she draws a heart on my skin. Tiny beads of red surface. When she's done, she jumps down and grabs a paper towel, wetting it with water and soap, like she's seen us do a million times. She drags the paper towel across my skin, exposing the new black heart tattoo.

"I did it!" she squeals.

"You did. One day you're going to make a great tattooist."

Sneaking out the back, I head over to the high school. I spot my gorgeous wife snapping pictures of Barrett from the stands. Next to her is Skyla and her husband, Sean, who are also here to watch their son, Victor, play since he's on the same team as Barrett.

"Hey you," Quinn says with a smile. "They just started." She leans over with the intention of giving me a quick kiss, but I grab her face with my hands and deepen it further, needing to taste her and feel her. I don't think there will ever come a time when I've had enough of her.

"What was that for?" She giggles, tilting her head to the side slightly.

"Thank you."

"For what?" Her brows knit together in confusion.

"For realizing we were meant to be together. For spending your life with me. For finally seeing yourself through my eyes."

THE END!

Other Books by Nikki Ash

All books can be read as standalones

The Fighting Series
Fighting for a Second Chance (Secret baby)
Fighting with Faith (Secret baby)
Fighting for Your Touch
Fighting for Your Love (Single mom)
Fighting 'round the Christmas Tree: A Fighting Series
Novel

Fighting Love Series
Tapping Out (Secret baby)
Clinched (Single dad)
Takedown (Single mom)

Stand-alone Novels
Bordello (Mob romance)
Knocked Down (Single dad)
Unbroken Promises (Friends to lovers)
Heath (Modern telling)
Through His Eyes (Single mom, age gap)

Imperfect Love Series
The Pickup (Secret baby)
Going Deep (Enemies to Lovers)
On the Surface (Second chance, single dad)

Acknowledgements

First and foremost, I need to thank my children. For being my biggest fans. For supporting my love and need to write. For talking plot with me and helping to approve every cover. I wouldn't be able to do this without you two. To everyone involved in making this book the amazing story that it is, thank you for taking this journey with me! Ashley, Stacy, Juliana, Brittany, Andrea, Lisa, Krysten, and Tabitha, thank you! Ena and Amanda, with Enticing Journey. Thank you for keeping my life together. To Kristi, for listening to me every single day. For showing me what true friendship means. Thank you! To the bloggers, who continue to take a chance on me. Thank you! There are thousands of authors, and it means the world to me that you choose to read and review and share my work. To my Fight Club peeps! You are my safe place. Thank you for riding along on this journey with me. To my readers, you are the reason I get to continue to write books. Thank you!

About the Author

Nikki Ash resides in South Florida where she is an English teacher and writer by day and a writer by night. When she's not writing, you can find her with a book in her hand. From the Boxcar Children to Wuthering Heights to latest single parent romance, she has lived and breathed every type of book.

While reading and writing are her passions, her two children are her entire world. You can probably find them at a Disney park before you would find them at home on the weekends!

Reading is like breathing in, writing is like breathing out.–
Pam Allyn

.

Printed in Great Britain
by Amazon

81300987R00163